PRAISE FOR EVELYN ROGERS' PREVIOUS BESTSELLERS!

TEXAS EMPIRES: CROWN OF GLORY

"Ms. Rogers' clever cast of characters will give the readers some chuckles and some moments of clenching tension!"
—*Romantic Times*

"Ms. Rogers brings to life the struggles to create a new life in a new, rugged land, as well as a realistic love story that brings two strong-willed people together. I loved Crown of Glory. It's the beginning of an excellent series you won't want to miss." —*Rendezvous*

"*Crown of Glory* is an exciting adventure with an unusual approach to romance. Rogers' characters make this story unforgettable!" —*Affaire de Coeur*

"*Crown of Glory* sizzles with history: rowdy Indian fights, anti-slavery issues, the pioneering days of the beef industry, all peppered with the Spanish flavor of Texas."
—*Calico Trails*

WICKED

1997 Holt Medallion Finalist for Paranormal Romance!
"Evelyn Rogers brings this charming story of a man too wicked to be good and a woman too good to be good to life."
—*Romantic Times*

"Evelyn Rogers breathes fresh life into the western romance." —*Affaire de Coeur*

"Humorous, sentimental, and thoroughly satisfying."
—*Rawhide & Lace*

"Temptation at its very best!" —*The Literary Times*

DOWN AND DIRTY

"You taste good, Ginny. Pure and sweet."

"I don't feel pure."

"How about down and dirty?"

She shivered from her hair roots to the tips of her toes.

"Oh, yeah. I feel like that."

"Then let's get down."

One very authoritative hand moved down her side, his skin hot against the slippery fabric of her blouse as he paused to give special attention to the side of her breast. His hand came to rest at the edge of her skirt.

"I love your legs."

"They're nothing special."

"Quit putting yourself down."

She thought about his hand on her thigh and everything it was close to. "There's that *down* word again."

"I've been thinking of that, too."

Down he went, feeling his way to her knees and around to the backs of them, which had never been a special sensory spot for her but was definitely sensitive tonight.

"Keep going," she whispered.

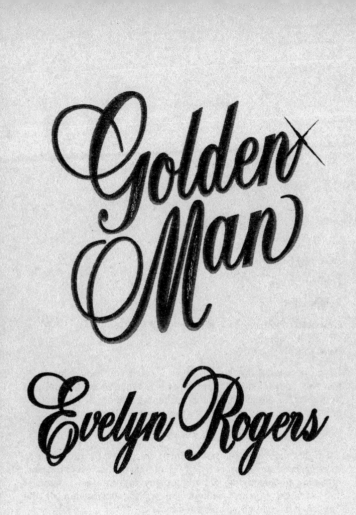

Golden Man

Evelyn Rogers

LOVE SPELL BOOKS   NEW YORK CITY

LOVE SPELL®

February 1999

Published by

Dorchester Publishing Co., Inc.
276 Fifth Avenue
New York, NY 10001

ISBN 0-505-52295-0

The name "Love Spell" and its logo are trademarks of Dorchester Publishing Co., Inc.

Printed in the United States of America.

This book is gratefully dedicated to the men who have taken on the role of President of the United States and therefore served in varying degrees as inspiration:

Michael Douglas
Henry Fonda
Harrison Ford
James Garner
Kevin Kline
Jack Lemmon
Bill Pullman
Roy Scheider
Peter Sellers

ACKNOWLEDGMENTS

My heartfelt thanks to the many people who have helped in the writing of this book, which required far more research than anticipated and, I discovered as the news events of the past year played on, a far closer lookout for potential pitfalls. If I have avoided the hazards, it is because of the following people: Gary R. Martin, chief of the *San Antonio Express* Washington Bureau; former San Antonian Shirl Thomas, who now works for the federal government in Washington; Gary Rucker, American Legion baseball coach in Arlington, Virginia; aerobics buddy Helen Von Der Bruegge and her wonderful husband, John, knowledgeable in the highways and byways of Washington; the tour guides at the White House and the Department of State; the taxi driver who drove me around Ballston; writing compatriots Laura Bradley, Martha Hix, Constance O'Banyon, Jo-Ann Power, and Bobbi Smith, fonts of information and support; the staff at the San Antonio Public Library; my agent, Evan Marshall, the world's best at listening to whines and complaints; and my editor, Alicia Condon, who let the writing muse take me where it wanted, even if it was 1600 Pennsylvania Avenue.

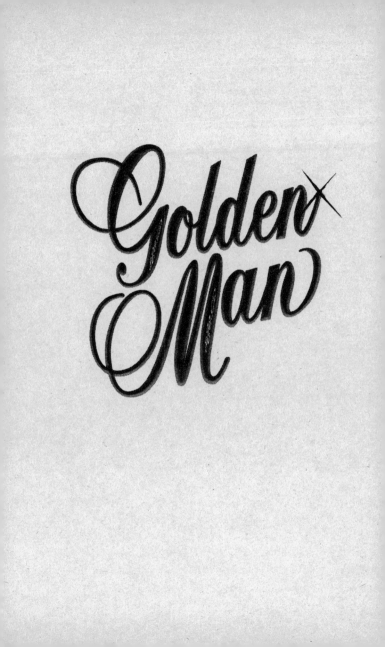

Chapter One

Stephen Marshall was the kind of guy that made a woman think of satin sheets and steamy nights, of wild sex involving handcuffs and whipped cream—and then brass bands, waving flags, and Fourth of July parades.

All-American terrific, that's what he was, tall and bronzed, with hair the color of the sun, thick-lashed blue eyes, and a killer grin slanted against a square jaw—a true Golden Man with a body that made other men look like Don Knotts.

Unfortunately, he was also the thirty-nine-year-old bachelor President of the United States. Considering the scandals of recent years, lusting after him was not only hopeless, it was unpatriotic.

Studying the President's picture on the cover of *Newspeak* magazine, Ginny Baxter was glad lusting wasn't her style. Anyway, what did she know about wild sex? She had never in her life seen a pair of real handcuffs, and the closest she got to whipped cream was the frozen glop she used to dress up store-bought pies.

Giving herself a mental shake, she glanced up and down the long line of tourists waiting to get into the White House. Love of country was all she should be thinking about today, that and the ever-present concerns of motherhood.

Besides, President Marshall was reputed to live practically like a monk. She'd read it in one of the tabloids. Not that she ordinarily read the scandal sheets, or even political news, but that was a comment no red-blooded American woman could ignore.

Ginny sighed. She ought to be honest with herself. Monk or no monk, when she thought of the man, there was definitely lust curling in parts of her that had no business curling. Lust had never gotten her anything other than a rat of a husband, may he rest in an uneasy grave, and a son who seemed determined to destroy what was left of her sanity.

That was it. She was insane. Otherwise why obsess over a man who could have any woman in the world?

Worse, she was babbling again, if only to herself, as if she was nervous or something. What did she have to be nervous about? Upset, of course, over Jake, but that wasn't anything new. She was in line for the regulation White House tour, not scheduled for a private audience in the Oval Office. Did she really think she would be seeing President Marshall today?

"Do you think we'll see him today?"

Ginny started.

The woman behind her giggled over her shoulder, her eyes directed to the magazine. "I hope so," she continued. "It's why I'm here."

"I don't think he comes out for the tours," Ginny answered in her most practical but gentle voice, the one she used at work when a customer's car wasn't ready on time.

"Have you seen the pictures of him in jeans? He's a real Oklahoma cowboy. I read he has a stable over in Maryland with a horse and everything, for when he can't get back home. They say he could ride well enough to take up rodeoing, if he wanted."

He was a real Oklahoma cowboy, all right, Ginny thought, plus a Yale Law School graduate who'd inherited his father's oil and cattle millions.

"Those jeans'll win my vote any day," the woman went on. "Tight in the butt, faded in the crotch. You ever wonder why jeans get faded there?"

Ginny caught herself speculating on a response. Good grief. Women weren't any better than men in the ogling department. Including Regina Ferguson Baxter, single mother from Ohio who had moved to D.C. for the noblest of purposes, the welfare of her child. For purposes of survival, no matter where she lived, she had foresworn having anything to do with men, romantically speaking.

It didn't matter that she got lonely sometimes. She hadn't the talent for romance, nor the judgment.

With a flush, she offered the magazine to the woman. "Here. There's an article inside with more pictures."

The magazine was snatched from her hand so fast she got a paper cut. Sucking on her finger, she glanced once again down the line. There was no sign of Jake. So what if he didn't show up? He hadn't actually promised, just said he would try.

The problem was, he seldom came through on those *tries*. No wonder her blood pressure had been inching into the stratosphere.

A distinct and easily recognized discomfort hit her in the abdomen, an urge that was hard to ignore. She definitely should not have started in on the pills the doctor ordered, not today of all days. Should she leave? She hesitated. Jake wasn't the only reason she was in the line. They had been living in the area two months and this was the closest she had gotten to the White House. Hers was the only country in the world that allowed free and regular access to the home of its head of state. Every citizen should take advantage.

It was her turn to glance over the woman's shoulder. She looked down at the President's thick-lashed eyes. *Come on*, they said.

"Whatever you want," she whispered in answer, like she was some kind of love machine and he knew how to turn on her switch.

Ignoring the discomfort, she followed in line past security police through the East Wing door, opening her purse for inspection, then filing down the corridor past the Library, the Vermeil Room, the China Room. It was the Vermeil Room that got her attention. As she peered inside, admiring the elegance and the displays of gilded silver, portraits of Jacqueline Kennedy and Nancy Reagan stared back.

These were beautiful women, sophisticated, sure of themselves, women who belonged in the home of the most powerful man on earth. Ginny flushed once again. There they were, eternally thinking lofty thoughts, and here she was considering the cut of her President's jeans.

What a pitiful creature she was, in every way. The former First Ladies were dressed in beautiful gowns. Ginny had entered the White House wearing her work khakis and white shirt. She even had her name embroidered on the pocket.

And her hair. Nothing like Nancy's and Jackie's. Hers was mousy brown, shoulder-length and straight as a board. Ordinary brown hair, ordinary brown eyes, ordinary features. And she'd been contemplating Stephen Marshall as an object of lust.

Pitiful indeed was the way she had given in to her feelings, even momentarily. Forget the handcuffs. Forget the whipped cream. For all that the President was accessible to her, he might as well live on the moon.

"Mr. President, you need a woman."

It was not the usual advice from a chief of staff, but then, Redford Davidson, more familiarly called

Ford, had been a friend since long before the election. And it was advice he had offered more than once, though he usually put it in a more subtle way.

Davidson ran a hand through his graying hair and stood straightbacked. At five-two, he was a full foot shorter than his President and was frequently pulling himself up straight.

"If you don't find her," Davidson continued, "you're liable to lose the next election."

Steve Marshall leaned back in his chair, his long legs stretched full length beneath his Oval Office desk, and fought back a rising irritation. He was barely past year one in his first term of office, with much of his agenda still to be accomplished; he wasn't ready to start worrying about the possibility of a second term.

"All I need is a cold shower every now and then. I wouldn't want to embarrass the electorate."

"Stephen."

His eyes cut to the woman standing beside Davidson. Not much taller than the chief of staff, with her white hair cut into short waves and her pale blue eyes wide, Doris Tanner looked soft and bosomy and innocent, everyone's idea of the perfect maiden aunt. Beneath all that soft, bosomy innocence beat the heart of a field general.

"You know what Ford means," she said, unimpressed by her nephew's lowering glance. "You need one woman, not the flock of bimbos you've been squiring around lately."

"I didn't realize bimbos came in flocks."

18

Aunt Doris rolled her eyes.

"Besides," Steve said, "I would hardly call Ambassador Lawrence's Radcliffe-educated daughter a bimbo. Nor the widow of the late Governor Patterson of the Commonwealth of Virginia. And then, of course, there's Senator Gray's lovely daughter Veronica. You can call Roni many things, but 'bimbo' isn't one of them."

Which wasn't exactly the truth, but that was something Aunt Doris didn't need to know.

Doris's eyes narrowed. "You can't fool me. I can tell you're not entirely in disagreement."

"How?" he asked, momentarily mystified, knowing Aunt Doris would not let him remain so for long.

"You answered me in your state-of-the-union voice. You always do when you're not totally sure of yourself."

Ford Davidson snorted, then covered his mouth and coughed.

"Besides," Doris went on, "have you been listening to yourself? You've identified each of these women by her relationship to someone in government. Not one has an identity of her own."

It was unfortunate that Aunt Doris knew him better than anyone. His only blood kin, his official hostess, with White House quarters of her own, she was supposed to see to the running of the place, offer help when requested, serve tea as needed. She kept expanding her duties. He loved her as much as he had ever loved anyone, but all too frequently she could drive him up a White House wall.

Her major saving grace was that she continued to call him by name. To even his oldest friends, he was now "Mr. President."

Steve glanced at his watch. "Okay, I have fifteen minutes until my next appointment. Tell me how I'm supposed to find this woman with an identity of her own. They don't run around throwing themselves at my feet."

"They would if the Secret Service let them," Aunt Doris said.

She nodded at Davidson, who pulled a piece of paper from the inside pocket of his pinstripe suit. "I've made a list," he said.

"I'm not surprised," Steve said dryly.

"The three you mention are on it, plus some others. You ought to be able to choose one as a regular companion," Davidson said. "There's a reception at State for the new British ambassador. To begin with, you could escort her there."

Steve's two principal advisers settled themselves into the chairs facing his desk. At their feet lay the presidential coat of arms woven into the royal blue carpet; the presidential seal decorated the ceiling over their heads. All around were the accoutrements of his office—the artwork, the crystal, the U.S. and presidential flags, and at his back, between yellow damask draperies, windows overlooking the stately columns of a colonnade and on beyond, lay the Rose Garden.

Stroking the oak desk, a gift from Queen Victoria

to Rutherford B. Hayes that his predecessor had rescued from storage, Steve felt a thrill and the usual surprise at finding himself in this setting. Within these walls, more than anywhere else, he felt the burden of office, and the responsibility.

And all his chief of staff could worry about this morning was getting him a steady date. Steady dates had not mattered to Steve since his hell-raising days of adolescence. Public service was his passion; it had been for a long time, and he didn't care to analyze why.

All he knew for sure—and all that mattered—was that the passion had well served a country kid whose wheeler-dealer father had been known across Oklahoma as Black Bart.

"Anyone sound possible to you yet?"

Vaguely, he was aware of Ford putting the question to him.

"I prefer Minnie Mouse," Aunt Doris said. "She would appeal to the rodent vote."

"Not a bad idea," the chief of staff responded. "The next convention is a natural for Walt Disney World. We could have a Magic Kingdom theme, sort of our answer to Kennedy's Camelot."

Aunt Doris nodded enthusiastically. "Think of what we could do with mouse ears instead of political buttons. It would be a whole new campaign. None of those tin badges with MARSHALL written on them, the way we did last time. I always thought they were a little hokey."

21

"I can see the slogan now. I'M LISTENING TO YOU, AMERICA."

Steve held up his hands in surrender.

"All right, give me a break. I admit I wasn't paying attention. Do either of you object to my reading the list?"

Neither did. He knew they wouldn't. It was one of the perks of being President. He read fast. He saw Lawrence, Patterson, and Gray, plus others he didn't recognize.

He pointed to the first woman on the list. "Who's she?"

"A volunteer at party headquarters," Davidson said. "A lawyer by trade. Smart, attractive, knowledgeable. You could do worse."

Steve grunted and asked about others. Most were associated with politics, either inside the Beltway or in their home states. Two were Washington hostesses, another a prominent fund-raiser from New York who could, Ford assured him, be in Washington at a moment's notice, piloting her own private plane.

He glanced at his aunt. "Didn't you once tell me I needed a simple girl? A homebody, as I recall, someone to fill our house with kids."

He hadn't told her at the time that he agreed with her, at least in theory, and he wasn't going to tell her now. His life was packed with accomplishments, pretty much exclusively on a public rather than a private level; he'd be a fool to think he could have it all.

Doris shrugged. "That was before we moved here. Simple girls do not survive in Washington. If they do, they don't stay simple for long."

"You really need to pick one," Davidson said. "Otherwise you could easily get a reputation as a womanizer, which could prove disastrous. Don't look so skeptical. There's already been speculation in *The Inside Scoop*. Not much, a few hints, but the stories will grow. No telling who in the media will pick them up next. I'm trying—*we're* trying—to keep you above the sleaze that's haunted the presidency lately."

Steve shook his head. Womanizer, was he? The monk stories, started in tabloids like the *Scoop* right after the New Hampshire primary, had him dead on, even where Veronica was concerned. Dear, hot Veronica, who was certainly luscious and willing enough. If she couldn't get his blood pumping, he doubted anyone could.

He looked at the list again. Each entry seemed innocuous. These women came with credentials. Maybe that was the problem. They had papers, like pedigreed pups.

"Am I supposed to fall in love?"

"Don't be absurd," Doris snapped.

Davidson cleared his throat. "Let's not be hasty. I hadn't given it thought before, but we all know Americans have a weakness for love stories. The President could give the appearance of being smitten. Isn't that the purpose of his settling on one woman?"

Ever the opportunist, that was Ford. It was why he was so good in his job.

Aunt Doris's features softened, and her pale eyes took on a distant look. "A White House wedding would be nice. In the East Room, like Lynda Bird's."

"It's only April," Steve said. "If I hurry with the courting, we could have a June ceremony in the Rose Garden." The whole scenario got to him. "Provided, of course, that the sex is good."

"Stephen . . ." Doris said, but he was too wound up to stop.

"You didn't do all your homework, Ford. There's nothing on this paper that indicates whether these women are good in bed."

He crumpled the list of names and threw it on the desk. "I'll tell you what. You want me to settle on a single woman? I've decided who she is."

"Who?" Davidson and his aunt asked in unison.

"The next eligible female who walks through the door."

"He's joking," Doris said.

"Of course he is," Davidson said.

"Why do you say that?" Steve asked. "I mean it. I'll escort the first woman I see, provided I haven't met her before. If it's fresh meat you want, it's fresh meat you'll get."

"He means it," Doris said. "He tries to deny it, but there's a lot of his father in him. He can be as devilish and stubborn as Hobart Marshall ever was."

A rap at the door caused them all to jump. Steve's

personal secretary entered. Marilyn Conklin was widowed and more knowledgeable about Washington than half the senators and most of the congressman. That made her definitely eligible, except that he knew her well, she was sixty, a doting grandmother, and as far as Steve could tell, totally without a sense of humor. He really preferred a woman who could laugh honestly, especially at his corny jokes, and not be sucking up.

"General Cartwright is here, Mr. President," Mrs. Conklin announced. She looked around the room at the intense faces turned to her. "I'm sorry to interrupt, but you told me to let you know when he arrived."

Steve looked beyond her into the anteroom, where stood the imposing uniformed figure of General of the Army Patton Cartright, chief of staff of the Army and an all-around pain in the butt. Cartright stood military stiff, his chest resplendent with ribbons and medals. He had every right to wear those medals, but Steve had an enlisted man's aversion to them. Totally irrational, he knew. He'd won a medal himself when he served as a corporal in the Persian Gulf.

"Don't worry, Mrs. Conklin," Steve began, but the rest of his message was lost as the outside door leading to the Rose Garden slammed open and a body hurtled into the office, landing on the floor beside Steve's chair.

Both his aunt and his chief of staff yelled out. Steve, of a calmer nature and with a better view, looked down into a pair of terrified brown eyes. They had every right to be terrified, considering the half-dozen Secret Service agents who were thundering into the room on the heels of the intruder and the half-dozen Secret Service guns they had trained at her head.

The agents covered the woman like a blanket, crowding the space behind the desk.

"Don't panic, Mr. President," one of them growled. "We've got her."

Another positioned himself between the fallen figure and Steve, who felt his chair being dragged away from danger.

General Cartright loomed in the doorway. "Be careful, men. She could be wearing a bomb."

Jerking her to her feet, two of the agents ran their hands over her body, while a third searched through her purse.

"She's clean," one of them said.

"Don't be too sure," the general said. "She could have the explosive stuck up her—"

"General Cartright," admonished Aunt Doris, who was peering on tiptoe around the wall of men for a better view.

By now the agents were handcuffing the woman's hand behind her. She kept staring at Steve with the biggest, brownest, most frightened eyes he had ever seen.

"Do you?" he asked.

A half-dozen voices started in, but he waved them to silence. "She can answer. I assume she can." He found himself smiling at her. He recognized her terror. He had felt it the first time he faced enemy fire.

He looked her over. There wasn't much to her: medium height, medium weight, maybe a little on the thin side. Still, those were definitely a woman's breast straining against the shirt. He wasn't so monkish that he failed to notice such details.

Early thirties at most, he estimated, and so pale she looked carved out of chalk. If she really was a would-be assassin, she wore a good disguise. She had even gone so far as to embroider her name on her pocket.

"Ginny," he said, "do you have a bomb stuck somewhere?"

She shook her head and blinked.

The general took a step closer. "Let me take over, Mr. President. I'll find out the truth."

Steve waved him back. "The agents have her subdued." He glanced at his chief of staff. "Ford, do you think you could see that the general is escorted outside?" He assumed his Okie voice, the one that showed him calm and in control, even if he was a little bit country. "I'm sure Mrs. Conklin can find him a cup of coffee while we straighten this out."

He looked at Cartright. "I'm sorry, but it's possible we'll have to reschedule our meeting. My secretary can let you know when."

The general's razor-thin features twisted in disapproval, but Steve knew from experience that when the commander-in-chief spoke, a well-trained military man listened, no matter how high his rank. It was one of the perks the former corporal enjoyed the most.

"And General, it would be unfortunate if news of this were to get out. I'm certain there's an innocent explanation. We wouldn't want to cause panic, would we?"

Panic was just what the man would welcome. The world was far too peaceful at the moment, and Washington much too quiet. During such times it was tough acquiring the appropriations the Pentagon called essential.

"No, Mr. President," Cartright said, "we wouldn't."

The general made a snappy about-face and left the office, Mrs. Conklin in his wake. She closed the door behind her, leaving the office strangely quiet, considering the number of people crowded inside, all of them standing and all of them staring at one slender woman whose eyes had not once left the President.

"Mr. President." It was William Alcorn, chief of security, who spoke. "We need to get her out of here and find out what the hell's going on."

"I was looking for a bathroom."

The words came out so softly, Steve wasn't certain he'd heard them correctly.

All eyes turned to the woman labeled Ginny. A blush put color in her cheeks.

"I was on the tour, but I took some new medicine this morning. My blood pressure's been a little high lately, what with the move and all, and with Jake still not settled in, and the doctor thought I could use a diuretic, so you see I really had to go."

She ran the words together, as if once she started talking, she couldn't stop. It took a moment for Steve to sort them out. When he was done, he still wasn't sure he understood all she'd said. *Diuretic* and *had to go* seemed to be the salient points.

"Preposterous," Ford said. "There's no way she could get from the East Wing over here without being intercepted."

Steve looked from her to his chief of security. "Is it possible?"

"Of course not, Mr. President," Alcorn snapped, but Steve saw the doubt in the man's eyes. "We'll get the truth out of her, rest assured."

"I imagine we already have," Steve said. "Minus a few details."

"My nephew's right," Doris said. "Look at the child. She's frightened out of her wits, and I imagine unless she's had an accident, she still needs to find a ladies' room."

"Good grief," the captive said, studying the carpet. "This is so embarrassing."

Her hair fell straight on either side of her face, effectively blocking her expression. But Steve could hear the distress in her voice.

"Embarrassment is the least of your worries," Alcorn said. "Trust us, Mr. President. We'll conduct a thorough investigation."

Again she glanced at Steve. This time, instead of

panic, he saw vulnerability in her eyes and, deeper, a determination not to let her emotions push her into hysteria. Whatever else she was, Ginny was brave.

"Could you remove the handcuffs?" Steve asked.

Her face softened in gratitude, but only until Alcorn responded.

"No, sir," the chief of security said. "Begging your pardon, Mr. President, but not until we've made sure you're safe."

Steve nodded and shrugged at her. The Secret Service was the only branch of White House workers he couldn't order around.

With a nod, Alcorn and his fellow agents hustled her out of the room, back through the door leading to the colonnade, and on to the floral splendor that marked the Rose Garden in April. Steve doubted she was appreciating the tulips; she must feel she was on her way to the guillotine.

"Goddamn," Davidson said as he lowered himself back into his chair. "She had to go to the bathroom. That's hard to believe."

Aunt Doris sat. "I took a diuretic once," she said. "It does make its demands."

Steve looked down at them, but he was thinking of those wide, deep eyes and the slender face and body, and the courage it must have taken for Ginny Whoever to speak up with all those guns pointed at her.

The political animal in him said that here was a prime example of solid, everyday American womanhood, even if she was a little light in the judgment department. The man in him said she was cute, too.

An idea came to him fast, the way ideas sometimes did; he knew this was one he had to act on. There would be hell to pay, or at least a thousand protests to endure, beginning with his present company. But the devil in him asked, "So what?"

The devil didn't speak up very often, but when it did Steve knew not to ignore it. No matter how he tried to forget his heritage, he was still Black Bart's son.

He sat behind the Victorian desk and thought very un-Victorian thoughts. First he buzzed Mrs. Conklin to let her know that the intruder had been carted away and all was well, and that he would be available for his appointments shortly.

And then he flashed the devilish Marshall smile that graced the cover of so many magazines.

"There you have her," he said, looking mostly at his old friend Ford.

"Have who?" Davidson asked.

Doris was quicker. She blanched. "You can't mean it."

"You know I do."

"But you said *walk through the door*. She didn't walk. And it's the wrong door."

"You're quibbling, Aunt. I imagine that by sundown we'll know everything there is to know about our visitor. If she's eligible—and there was no ring on her finger to indicate otherwise—she's the woman I'll be taking to receive our new ambassador. Remind me to ask her to let up on the pills that one night."

Both Doris and Davidson spoke at once, but Steve's mind was made up. He waved away their protests.

Davidson's eyes narrowed. "You know, this could be good." He thought a moment. "Hell, it could be great. No society woman for you." His eyes widened as the thoughts churned. "She's not even a beauty. There's nothing about her to make the women of America jealous. She's someone they can identify with, an ordinary woman like themselves. Mr. President, I've got to hand it to you. You've got an instinct for politics that would make your predecessors proud."

Having already reached the same conclusions as Ford, with the possible exception of the instinct remark, Steve was thinking of other matters. One of his strengths was the ability to compartmentalize. Already Ginny was tucked into her own cubbyhole, where she could be reexamined if the need arose.

"Ford, do me a favor as you leave. If the general is still around, please ask him to come in."

He lifted a heavy volume from a side desk—*An Analysis of the President's Budgetary Purposes; Prepared at the Request of the Senate Commission on Appropriations*—and opened it in front of him. The analysis came through the office of Senator Roger Gray, Veronica's estimable father. Father and daughter were as unalike as two such close blood relatives could be. Even more different than Black Bart and his son had been.

"I'm suddenly in a mood to go over facts and figures," he added. "And see if you can get me the secretary of defense on the phone. There are a few items in this report that need clarifying."

Davidson left, but Aunt Doris lingered.

"We have to talk," she said.

"No, my dearest, we don't."

His aunt was not so easily put off.

"Allow me one word of warning, Stephen. Ford seems to think this could be a political bonus for you. I'm worried it might backfire. We don't know anything about this woman."

"But we will. Trust the FBI. And trust me."

Steve came around the desk and gave her a peck on the cheek. "Stop worrying. You and Ford are both making too much of this. Nothing is going to go wrong. I promise."

Reluctantly she departed, and he returned to his work. As far as he was concerned, he had settled one problem and was ready to go on to the thousand others that arose daily for the President of the United States.

If he faced them this morning with more enthusiasm than usual, he didn't bother to ask himself why.

Chapter Two

When Ginny finally got home, Jake was pitching his fast ball into the net he'd hung across the back fence. A dozen balls lay scattered around his feet; his habit was to choose one, wind up, and let loose with an eighty-mile-an-hour zinger, and then another and another until his shirt clung damply to his back and his light brown hair had darkened with sweat.

Each ball landed with a muted thud against the fence, one after the other. Changing his pace, changing his grip, he could go on for hours at a time, and usually he did.

Normally, she would watch him for a while; this late afternoon she had energy left for only a quick glance. Still, it gave time for something to squeeze around her heart. Her sixteen-year-old torment and joy was almost six feet tall, taller than his father had ever been, and he was mostly arms and legs and so tight with resentment and needs he wouldn't acknowledge that sometimes she thought he would explode.

Another ball thudded against the net, and she knew it hit exactly where he had been aiming. Someday he would be the best pitcher baseball had ever seen, better than Nolan Ryan or Sandy Koufax or even Roger Clemens.

This evening she had no room for pride. This evening she wanted to crawl into her bed, pull up the covers, and die. Unfortunately, dying wasn't an immediate option, and neither was going to bed, at least not right away. She slept on a sofabed near the dining table, a few feet from the alcove kitchen, and she needed to cook supper before she did anything else.

Besides, every time she let herself relax, visions of summer eyes and forever legs thrust her close to hysteria. The bruises on her wrists were reminder enough.

With the rhythmic thud of the balls providing a background dirge, she entered the small apartment. A converted garage, it sat at the end of a long drive behind a two-story colonial that was the home of her landlord. The place wasn't fancy, it wasn't even big enough, but Professor Carl Morris, who taught economics at George Mason University, had taken pity on her and rented it cheap when she came looking two months earlier.

Ginny wasn't so proud that she would shun pity, especially if it helped with Jake. Located in Ballston, a section of Arlington across the river from the capital, it was near the high school, near a Metro stop, and a long-but-possible walk from the auto shop when the weather was good enough and on a bus line when it wasn't. En route she even passed a kickboxing studio, where she could continue the exercise/defense classes she had started in Cincinnati.

The screen door creaked as she went inside. Vaguely she was aware that her son had straightened up the place, washed the breakfast dishes, made up the sofabed. He was the neat one. Besides, he was compensating for not showing up at the White House.

She stopped herself. Never would she think of that place again, which was going to be difficult since she lived in a D.C. suburb where the television screens and newspapers made it seem to be the center of the universe. She should start packing up for a return trip to Ohio, but she'd put down two months' rent on the apartment and hadn't enough money left to run.

The evening was warm and, with her hair pinned away from her neck in a careless twist, she slipped into a pair of cut-off jeans and one of Jake's old Cincinnati Reds' T-shirts before putting on water for the macaroni. Tonight she would vary the menu. Instead of cheese, she would cover the pasta with canned tomato sauce and chunks of the meatloaf left over from last night. She'd even sprinkle some dried oregano over it all, which was as close to gourmet cooking as she could get.

Jake wasn't picky about food. It was one of his most endearing traits.

Someone knocked at the screen door. One sniff told her who was coming, even before she made out the professor's broad figure in the outside twilight.

She walked over to let him in. Glancing at the plate of warm cookies in his hand, she said, "You shouldn't have." She spoke from her heart.

Carl Morris was a big man, bearded, the plate dwarfed in his huge hand. A neighbor had told her he was brilliant, a leader in his field, but something in all that brilliance must have short-circuited his sense of taste. His cookies tasted like sawdust and grease.

How could they smell so good and taste so bad?

But then, how could she desperately need to be so smart and do so many stupid things? Ginny sighed. There she went, regressing to the morning fiasco. She concentrated on her guest.

He was wearing his after-school attire: striped wool trousers, a plaid shirt, and a paisley vest. There had been some unseasonably warm evenings lately, but every time she saw him he still wore the same clothes, or an equally mismatched, overheated outfit. She had never seen him sweat. With his white hair and beard and smiling, deepset eyes, he reminded her of Santa Claus.

But he was a Santa with a sharp glint that backed up the smile in those eyes. As he walked inside, she saw the glint right away.

"Let me take those," she said, reaching for the plate and wincing involuntarily.

"Something wrong?" he asked.

"Nothing," she said. Nothing but a few bruises and strained muscles she'd picked up on the Oval Office floor. She'd never realized how uncomfortable it was to have one's hands bound the way hers had been. She couldn't imagine how handcuffs could ever be useful in sex.

She set the cookies aside on the linoleum countertop. "We'll have them later for dessert."

"How did the tour go?" he asked.

She turned to add the macaroni to the boiling water. "Fine."

She closed her eyes for a moment. Babbler though she was, important stuff she kept to herself, especially her personal humiliations. But all afternoon she had been at work, pretending today was like any other day, and the need to tell someone the truth had her close to exploding.

The water bubbled over the pot, and she lowered the gas heat. "Jake couldn't make it, but I went on."

Professor Carl grunted. She didn't know how he felt about Jake, which was a surprise—most people let her know right away what a know-it-all he was—but she thought maybe he was sympathetic to the boy.

Ginny's knuckles turned white against the edge of the counter. Professor Carl came as close to being a confidant as she had in all the world. And she had to talk, her babble cup being fuller than she had thought.

Pushing a loose strand of hair back into the twist, she gestured for him to sit at the table. Taking a facing chair, she listened for the comforting *thud* sounds coming from the backyard, cleared her throat, and plunged ahead.

"It wasn't exactly an ordinary tour. Nothing will come of it, of course, and the agents assured me I wouldn't be arrested, so there's nothing to worry about. Still, I'd just as soon Jake didn't find out."

No response, no reaction except for a brief nod and one raised bushy white brow. But she had his attention. Boy, did she ever.

"You see, I took this pill," she heard herself say, as if someone else were talking, and then the rest spilled out, how she'd walked down the East Wing entrance hall stairs to the ground floor in search of a rest room, had gone through what she later found out was the Palm Room, out onto the West Colonnade and somehow ended up in the Rose Garden.

"And then there were these shouts and men running, and I thought if I went through one of the doors, I could just circle back and rejoin the tour. The problem was, the room I entered turned out to be the worst possible place I could have invaded." She attempted a small smile. "Want to guess where I was?"

"The Rose Garden, you say?" Professor Carl thought for a moment. "That sounds like the Oval Office, but that couldn't—"

Her nod gave him pause. He stroked his beard. For once he didn't look as if he had known all along what she had been about to say.

"No one stopped you in all that time?" he asked.

"I had to walk through my route a dozen times, later, after the agents unlocked the handcuffs. Mr. Alcorn said it was a series of blunders and unusual circumstances, little emergencies in different offices that didn't amount to much but still distracted people. I must have looked as if I knew what I was doing. Who would wander so openly through the place bent on mischief with her name written on her chest?"

"This Mr. Alcorn is a Secret Service agent, I take it."

She nodded. "Chief of security."

"You were fortunate the President wasn't around. You could have been shot."

Ginny shuddered. If she lived to be a hundred, she would never forget Stephen Marshall's incredible blue eyes staring down at her as she landed at his feet. Fool that she was, her first thought had been that Golden Man was better-looking in person than in any of his pictures. And his legs certainly were long.

But then she had been jerked away from him and rough hands had gone over just about every part of her, and she'd been handcuffed and everyone seemed to be yelling at once. When she was forced to confess she needed to go to the bathroom, her humiliation had been complete.

She summarized the scene simply. "He was there."

"That's when you were handcuffed."

"Yes," she said, remembering the guns trained on her more clearly than the steel bands around her wrists.

Silence descended. The professor certainly was taking all this calmly. She heard only the boiling water on the stove.

The macaroni! She'd always overcooked it. Grabbing a hot pad, she took the pot from the stove and dumped its contents into a colander in the sink. It landed with a thud, like one of Jake's baseballs, in a solid, sticky mess. Oh, well, Jake was used to it. The tomato sauce would loosen it up some. Anyway, he would sneak out later for a hamburger, thinking she didn't know.

She heard a rumble behind her. She turned in alarm. Professor Carl's face was dangerously red, and it took her a long minute to realize what was happening. He was laughing. The laughter erupted like a bark, and the sound echoed from wall to wall in the small apartment.

At first Ginny wanted to hit him with the pot, and then she found herself smiling, and then giggling, and finally laughing right along with him, collapsing back in her chair and letting go until the tears ran down her cheeks. She'd never in all her life laughed so hard or so long. The release was wonderful.

It was probably a little closer to hysteria than

simple laughter, but that was all right, too.

Jake appeared in the doorway, and she sobered. If he knew the truth, he wouldn't be laughing. He would be asking about what the Nazi agents had done to her and declaring that he knew she should never have gone to that center of corruption known as the White House, especially by herself.

But then she would have countered with a reminder that he was supposed to be there, too, and he would say—

Ginny sighed. He would have a lot to say, none of it anything she wanted to hear right now. Much as she loved him and understood his anger, she couldn't cope tonight, and so she waved him away with a mutter about supper not turning out right. It was a story he could believe.

As she returned to the macaroni and its disguise-of-the-night, she wondered what the President and his agents would think if they knew their intruder harbored an anarchist under her roof.

Ginny had to wait only until the next day to learn the repercussions of her adventure. To begin with, her boss called her away from the auto shop front desk, where she had been attempting to mollify a customer whose '86 Ford clutch needed replacing at a cost exceeding what the car was worth.

Ted Waclawski was usually back in the garage overseeing the repairs. Today he led her into his seldom-used, bare office. Like her, he wore a white shirt and khakis; everyone at Sam's Auto Repair did. The shop was one of a chain. Who Sam was, she didn't know, and neither did anyone she had asked.

"What's going on?" he asked without ceremony. "Are you in some kind of trouble?"

Ginny's heart sank. "Not that I know of. Why?"

"I got a call this morning, someone wanting to know your work record, and I told him—well, never mind, I just didn't think it was anybody's business how long you'd been here and if you were working out. And then my boss calls from company headquarters in Baltimore, wanting to know why the hell I didn't cooperate with the FBI."

Ginny's face burned. The news couldn't be doing her blood pressure any good.

Ted had been good to her, accepting the credentials she'd brought from the shop in Cincinnati, giving her a job alone right up front with the customers after only a day's trial run. Her application had come at a good time, right after the woman she was replacing announced she was leaving to get married.

Ginny had been able to swear she would never make a similar announcement. She'd been married before; once was enough.

All she'd had to do was get back to Cincinnati, load up her son and their few possessions, and head back for her grand experiment at finding a life away from memories of the past.

And, of course, work on relieving Jake of his

hangups about government. Everything she did was basically for him.

And now this. The FBI definitely had not been part of her plans.

"You know I asked off yesterday morning so I could go into Washington for the White House tour." She took a deep breath. "I wandered off a little bit and some men hustled me back with the others, and I guess they thought I was a suspicious character."

Ted chewed on the inside of his cheek. He was a big man with leathery skin and permanent grease stains under his nails. While he had seemed appreciative of her work, she didn't really know much about him.

"You've been working out real fine, Ginny, but I don't much care for calls from the big guys. Are you in the habit of wandering off like that?"

Real fear hit her. She couldn't lose her job.

"No, sir. Never. I promise you, I'm never going near a government office again. Not in Washington."

"That might be kinda hard. They're damned near everywhere."

"Okay, the White House then. I've seen all of that place I ever want to see."

She would have thrown herself at his feet and begged his forgiveness, but she'd landed in a similar prone position yesterday, and the results had been a living nightmare. Besides, she was still stiff and sore, so she just stared at him with her big brown eyes and willed him to understand.

He dismissed her with a nod. When she went back out to the front of the shop, she felt his eyes on her. For a moment she felt panic and a little of Jake's resentment because her government had put her in such a shaky position.

And then she gave herself a sharp lecture. Of course she was being investigated. She had been close enough to the President to do him real harm. So what if a series of flukes and mistakes had gotten her there? That loudmouth general could have been right; she could have been wired with a bomb.

The rest of the day she grew more and more understanding about the whole mess. When she arrived home, her understanding was tested by the person who usually tested everything: her son.

"They're after me," Jake said when she walked inside the apartment.

"Who?"

"The feds."

Guilt crashed in on her.

"What are you talking about?"

"Someone's been asking the neighbors about us."

She set her purse on the table, along with the bag of groceries she had bought at the Giant on the way home. "How do you know it was a federal agent?"

"I just know. I told you we never should have moved here."

Where Jake had gotten this paranoia about the government, she didn't know. His father had moved out when he was twelve, and then moved back in when the cancer was diagnosed. Maybe she shouldn't have let him return. Maybe she should have said her replacement could nurse him, but Wife Number Two had moved on by then and he was dying, and she thought Jake might learn to forgive him, if not love him again.

But things hadn't worked out, and she'd had to deal with two men who had malignancies eating at them. The pancreatic cancer had finally taken Jonas. His son's hatred and distrust lingered on.

Ginny set about preparing supper. Tuna casserole, she decided. It had been her mother's standby, and it had become hers.

"What makes you think the agent was asking about you?" she asked as she got out a can of mushroom soup.

Jake stretched out on the sofa, his feet dangling off one arm. "I just know."

"What did he say?"

"He asked how long we'd lived here, if we ever had visitors, that kind of thing."

She tried to smile. "Maybe it was someone interested in me. You know, a potential male friend."

It was the wrong tack to take if she wanted to cheer him up. She had gone out with a couple of men after the split with Jonas. She'd never thought about divorcées having a racy reputation until she became one. She found out right away.

So had Jake. He walked in on a date who'd been reluctant to take no for an answer. Actually, the bastard had stuck a hand up her skirt while she was squirming and kicking and fighting to get away. Until then, she hadn't known how much muscle pitching a ball could build, even in an adolescent. The last she saw of her would-be lover, he was hurtling through the front door. Soon afterwards she took up kickboxing. Jake shouldn't be protecting her. He needed to preserve himself for his professional career.

And what was she preserving herself for? A healthy, if not exactly ecstatic, old age.

"That was a joke," she said. "I don't intend to date again."

"You're only thirty-four."

"Yes, but it's an old thirty-four."

In that, she wasn't joking. At the moment she felt about eighty. The thought of having a social conversation with a man was about as appealing as that of mopping the Pentagon.

She had even less interest in sex. She couldn't believe how eager she had been as a teenager, ready to explore all of life's possibilities. Thank goodness all that was behind her.

For some reason, with Jake watching, she thought about Stephen Marshall and the way he had looked down at her. What if he were lying on top of her, looking down exactly the same way, and she was pressed down into a soft mattress, and they were both naked—

She jerked herself back to the present, grateful that Jake and the FBI couldn't read minds.

"Has something happened at school?" she asked as she opened the can of soup.

"Same boring stuff."

"No trouble?"

"I don't cause trouble."

He spoke defensively. He also spoke truthfully. Jake was not only taller and more honest than his father, he was also smarter. He gave the teachers back what they gave him, he remembered everything he heard and read, and he made good grades. She knew he didn't care; she figured he went along with the system, as he called it, because of her.

She kept expecting him to start puncturing various body parts with jewelry, an ear or maybe even a nostril—heaven forbid it should be his tongue—but he said that was going along with a group, participating in a fad, being dictated to. He preferred to keep to himself. Except where baseball was concerned, he was a loner, and that was fine with him.

Ginny knew better. Her brilliant, talented, injured son was the loneliest person she had ever known.

And also, like every other adolescent she'd ever met, he thought the world was centered on himself. If strangers were asking about the Baxters, they were really asking about the son.

Matters weren't much better the next evening, when she got a call from a friend in Cincinnati, who said someone was making inquiries about her there. She put her off by lying about having applied for a loan. The friend didn't believe her. Ginny didn't lie very well.

When the professor showed up to say he'd been subjected to similar inquiries, earlier in the day before he'd left for the university, she threw up her hands. This invasion was too much, all because the White House had inadequate plumbing facilities for its visitors. If she could afford a lawyer, she would get one. Maybe she would go to FBI headquarters the next day and lodge a complaint.

Not a good idea, she decided as soon as the thought hit her, and so she simply shrugged as if to say she was sorry, but there was nothing she could do about it.

The screen door squeaked, and Jake entered.

"Something's going on."

Ginny collapsed in a chair. "What now?"

He glared from her to the professor, then back out the door. "There's a black sedan at the end of the drive. I think the Gestapo's come to arrest me."

If Ginny hadn't been looking at Professor Carl, she might have missed the flare of emotion that flashed in his Santa Claus eyes, so dark and deep it startled her. Before she could ask him what was wrong, she heard footsteps on the path outside her door, and then a knock. Through the screen she could make out a man poised in the twilight. She felt vulnerable standing in the lighted room. Instinctively she moved between the door and her son.

"Mrs. Baxter?" the man asked.

"Yes. Who are you?"

"I've come from the President."

"President who?"

Dumb response. As soon as she uttered the words, she felt like a fool. She could imagine the man's smirk.

"The President of the United States," he said matter-of-factly.

She had no choice but to open the door for him, shooting Jake a warning glance to please, please, please be quiet. Professor Carl sat in his chair, quiet, watchful. Her son had her in such a jumpy mood, Ginny could feel the handcuffs encircling her wrists again.

The man entered and introduced himself, but she didn't catch the name, so intent was she on the envelope in his hand. He passed it to her. "I'm to wait for an answer," he said.

The envelope was addressed to Mrs. Regina Baxter. Inside was a lone card, the writing carefully scripted by a calligrapher's expert hand. She read the card twice before the words registered. She was holding an invitation to a reception at the Department of State.

In her cut-offs and T-shirt, she wasn't dressed properly to receive such an elegant thing.

She looked up at her visitor. He was dressed in a dark suit with a white shirt and conservative black-and-red striped tie, and a red handkerchief peeked out from the edge of his coat pocket. His features were tight, sharply hewn, and without expression.

He reminded her of William Alcorn. She was beginning to think all agents of the President looked alike.

"The President is sorry he could not deliver the invitation himself," he said, "but an emergency arose that required his attention. I am to tell you he very much regrets any inconvenience you suffered because of him."

Whoever this guy was, did he actually think she believed the President wanted to be here himself? She really must look like an idiot.

He cleared his throat. "And—" the man actually appeared to blush—"I'm to assure you that the Martha Washington Ladies' Room will be available all evening."

Either the President was a smart aleck or he was genuinely apologizing for what had happened. She leaned toward the former. But that didn't keep her from being totally nonplussed.

She passed the invitation to her son, who passed it to the professor, who passed it back to her.

Both Jake and Carl were staring at her. The whole world seemed to be staring at her, and she said the first thing that came into her mind. "I don't know where the Department of State is."

"The President will send a car for you. Since you are his special guest. I assume your answer is yes."

She could tell he couldn't imagine anyone turning down such an invitation. For a moment she lost all sanity. Neither could she.

She nodded once, and the emissary from the

most powerful man on earth made a quick departure. But not before he'd given a quick glance at her bare legs.

"Well, well, my dear," Professor Carl said, "you must have made quite an impression on our President."

"You met Stephen Marshall?" Jake asked.

She nodded dumbly. She needed to say more, certainly to Jake, and she would. For the moment, the only thing she could think of was that she didn't have a thing to wear.

Chapter Three

Ginny's big evening came the following Saturday. She was standing in the bathroom, debating whether or not to put on another layer of mascara, when the telephone rang.

This had to be the call she was expecting, the one in which a White House spokesman informed her that the invitation had been a mistake. Clutching the tube of mascara, she hurried into the living room, unsure whether to be sorry or glad.

"Mrs. Baxter?" a woman's voice asked. "Please hold for the President."

Ginny collapsed onto the sofa.

"Mrs. Baxter? Regina Baxter?"

The speaker gave a nice, rolling cadence to her name.

The best response she could come up with was a nod. When the silence on the phone lengthened, she managed, "Yes."

"This is Steve Marshall."

She juggled the phone, then held it in a deathlike grip, picturing the man at the other end. The image came right off the cover of *Newspeak*.

"Mr. Marshall . . . Mr. President . . ." Brilliant. "I'm sorry, but I don't know what to call you."

"Steve would be good."

I'll bet Steve would be very good. She almost said it. Even the man's voice could turn her into a love machine.

"All right, Steve." Much too breathy. Good grief.

"And may I call you Regina? Or Ginny. It's a nice name."

He sounded very smooth, very sure of himself, the way a President should. And maybe a little too familiar. Ginny gave herself a mental slap. There was something otherworldly about all of this. Too much so.

She frowned into the phone. It was time for a reality check. So the President of the United States was personally calling her humble home, was he? Ha! Someone must think her a complete fool.

She wasn't talking to Golden Man. No way. The President had a thousand imitators, more than Richard Nixon and George Bush combined. One of them was trying out his act on her.

Thank goodness she'd come to her senses. A woman in her position couldn't be too careful, what with all the crazies in the world. A woman had to look out for herself.

"Ginny's fine with me, Steve." Or whoever you are. "What's on your mind?"

Hesitation. "Tonight."

"Oh, yes, it almost slipped my mind." She was back in control, as much as she ever was. Instead of Golden Man with the killer smile, her mind saw a short, squat, balding guy with a smirk. He'd be an acquaintance of someone in the neighborhood, or, more likely, someone at work, a married guy with six kids to support.

"We're supposed to have a date tonight, right?" she said.

Yeah, sure. A date with the President. An evening at the State Department was unbelievable enough.

"It was my understanding the invitation was delivered to you." A little less drawl, a little more clip to the words, implying that they really had a date. Sure they did.

"It got here, all right. I'm just used to my men friends setting things up themselves, that's all. Things are more personal that way, if you know what I mean." She wished she chewed gum so she could pop it in his ear. "What's the point in having a man-type friend if he's not the kind that's up close and personal, that's what I always say."

When necessary, Ginny could be a smart mouth as brassy as the best of them. She'd heard enough examples in her day.

A long hesitation. "Do you have a lot of men friends?"

"Dozens." She waved the tube of mascara, getting into the role. "Of course, most of them are back in

Ohio. I haven't really gotten started here in the East."

She could have sworn she heard paper rustling in the background.

"Strange, there's nothing in the reports about them."

Whoever he was, he was good.

"We had to be careful, what with the wives, you know. Some of 'em could get real ugly."

"I'm sure they could."

Ginny was feeling good. No way was she going to be intimidated by this prankster. He'd find out she could give as good as she got.

"I'm glad you called, Steve. Since this is our first date and all. I don't know what someone in your position expects from a woman, but I don't go all the way, not right away, if you know what I mean. Maybe later, if we hit it off, but we definitely don't do the nasty first time round the track."

That shut him up for a minute.

"Look," he said at last, "you may be expecting other calls, so I'll get to the point." He'd completely lost the drawl. "I won't be able to ride out to get you myself. But a car will be there at a quarter to seven. Please accept my apologies."

He hung up without waiting for a reply. The guy fairly dripped with dignity. Whoever he was, he was really, really good. He had her almost believing he was the President. As if a man like the real Stephen Marshall would hop in a limousine and tool across the Potomac to pick up a nobody like her.

Good grief. She'd had to put up with talk at work all week, and now she had a practical joker on the phone. She shouldn't have told anyone about the invitation, but she'd wanted to show it to Ted, to prove that she really wasn't in trouble with the FBI, and somehow the word had spread.

Some had believed her, some thought she was putting them on. That was who the joker had to be, one of the doubters, someone from work, one of the guys from back in the garage putting her to the test. He'd known someone who could imitate Marshall—there were a lot of them around—and couldn't resist placing the call. She could picture him and his buddies gathered around a phone while she blathered on.

But that didn't speak for them all. The ones who took the invitation seriously were treating it like a big deal, which she supposed it was. She was their delegate to the big time. Monday they were expecting a report.

People around here certainly were obsessed with anything to do with the federal government. Back in Cincinnati it was mostly the Reds and the Bengals that got attention.

Returning to the bathroom, she voted against the mascara. Instead, she gave herself another shot of hair spray.

When she heard a car pulling into the driveway, she peeked out the door. Naturally enough, it wasn't the President who got out. The same man who'd who delivered the invitation was striding toward her. Common sense told her that she ought to panic, but life had already thrown so much at her, she didn't get panicky easily. Even her blood pressure had settled down over the past few days, which didn't make a lot of sense. The details of her existence seldom did.

The head and shoulders of her next-door neighbor appeared above the wooden fence that separated the two residences, and then another head, husband to the first. She got the feeling the nosy couple wouldn't have been there if the President were in the car. William Alcorn and his posse would have seen to that.

Ginny waved at them, just to show that their presence was fine as far as she was concerned. She would have taken them along with her if she could.

She didn't feel so bad about how she looked. She was wearing her best dress, a sleeveless, scoop-necked, thigh-high black silk she had splurged on three years ago just before Jonas moved back in. Her wrap was a fringe-and-lace mantilla she'd picked up in a used-clothing store. She had pulled one side of her hair away from her face and fastened it with a rhinestone barrette. She wore no other jewelry. Best to keep things simple, which wasn't hard, given her spare wardrobe.

Tonight she was as simple as a President's guest was liable to get. Besides, she would be hanging in the background, gawking most of the evening, trying to remember everything she saw for tomorrow's reports. Typical tourist, she wanted to take her camera, but she figured that might be a little too much.

If her substitute escort disapproved of her appearance, he gave no sign. But then, neither did he break out in a big grin of appreciation when she said hello. Come to think of it, she hadn't seen anyone around the President smile. Maybe it was against protocol.

Or maybe it was because she was considered such a potentially dangerous character, no one dared.

When her escort reintroduced himself, this time she caught his name and title: Edward Seale, special assistant to the President. He was wearing a tuxedo and a black tie, and she realized what a formal occasion this was. As she walked past him into the cool evening, she could have sworn he gave a quick glance at her legs. She was probably showing too much of them, but they were her best feature and this was the best dress she owned.

The last thing she wanted was to flaunt herself.

The one encouraging detail about the whole scene was Jake's absence. He was at an organizational meeting of the local American Legion baseball team. She had much for which to thank the game of baseball. Tonight's meeting came high on the list.

At first, talk in the limo was desultory, mostly about the weather and the Washington sights she had taken in since she arrived in town. She would have preferred talking to the driver, who seemed a mile away. The two of them could have discussed the car.

The limo had been moving along at a fast clip, but now it began slowing down, at last coming to a complete halt high over the Potomac. The driver's voice boomed back, announcing that there had been an accident on the bridge ahead.

"I hope the delay isn't long," Seale said. "You'll miss the receiving line."

Ginny pulled her gaze from the acre of car in front of her, giving full attention to the President's special assistant, sitting at a right angle to her on a side seat.

"Receiving line?"

Even in the dim light she could see the look of pity in his eyes. Sometimes she accepted pity, when it could help her with Jake. Tonight, no.

"You really don't know what to expect, do you?" he said.

"People standing around talking, drinking, eating chips and dip. I've been to cocktail parties before."

"There's more to it than that."

"So tell me," she said, and the anxiety she'd expected to feel all week began building in the pit of her stomach.

"The guests will be gathered in the John Quincy Adams Room, and then the President and the ambassador will be announced." His voice turned public. "His Excellency Albert Brookings, Her Majesty's ambassador for the United Kingdom." And then in a more normal tone he added, "Since neither man is married, there are no wives to introduce."

"The wives usually do get included, then."

"Oh, yes. They're very important adjuncts to their husbands. The President and His Excellency will stand to the side as the guests file by and introduce themselves."

A frightening thought struck.

"I'm not supposed to curtsy, am I?"

"Oh, no, that's only for royalty. All you do is say your name and shake hands."

"And then go to a neutral corner and watch."

He studied her for a moment. "It's possible you won't be allowed."

"What do you mean?"

He hesitated. "It's hard to say. Evenings with the President don't follow any particular pattern, especially with this President. What should happen is that everyone will drift through the columns into the Thomas Jefferson Room for wine and hors d'oeuvres. At eight o'clock it's on to the Benjamin Franklin State Dining Room for dinner. Normally the secretary of state would be there, helping to lead the way, but he's in the Middle East right now."

He droned on with names of others who had been invited to the reception, but she barely heard him. She was too busy fighting her long-delayed case of nerves. Wine, hors d'oeuvres, dinner. A corner would be hard to find.

The nervousness edged toward panic. Forget the Monday morning reports at work. She would give a week's salary to be able to bail out of the car and hike back to Ballston.

She could claim illness. It wouldn't be a lie. Her symptoms were fast taking on the characteristics of projectile vomiting.

At last the car began to creep forward, and she realized her fate was sealed. Traffic had built up during the delay, and it took a quarter of an hour to complete the short journey. She was surprised when the limo stopped beside a large, plain block of a building and Seale hopped out. The Department of State didn't look elegant in the least. Despite its paneled walls, neither did the elevator that whisked them to the eighth-floor reception rooms.

But oh the difference when she stepped into the entrance hall. Marble busts, paintings, and antique furniture lined the walls. She walked past them on Oriental rugs; crystal chandeliers sparkled above. She could hear the sounds of talk and laughter ahead as Seale took her by the arm and led her down the way, turning left into another wide corridor he called the Gallery.

He nodded toward an open double door to the right at the far end. "That's the Martha Washington Room. The President wanted me to let you know where it was."

Ginny's cheeks reddened. She hadn't taken a diuretic in days.

When he guided her to the left into still another room, wider and longer than anything yet encountered, she saw where the talk and laughter were originating. Men in black tie and women in glitter filled the place, everyone chatting, all the guests seeming to know the people around them. If appearances meant anything, there wasn't one lost soul in the bunch.

Some had drifted through a row of marble columns on the far side into the adjoining room, where they had already been served wine.

"We're too late for the receiving line," he said. "Sorry."

She wasn't.

As Seale led her inside, the crowd parted to let her pass. Could it really be that all eyes were on her? Surely not.

The jewels she saw looked genuine, and she saw a lot of them, resting on ivory throats, dangling from shell-like ears, adorning long-fingered hands. She wanted to tear the rhinestones from her hair. She also wanted to wrap her mantilla around the hem of her skirt. No wonder they noticed her. She was the only one showing legs.

Instead she laced the ends of the shawl through her fingers, clasped her shoulder-strap purse against her stomach, and looked straight ahead. She was turning into another Jake, thinking everything in the universe revolved around her. She wasn't important enough to warrant attention. Whatever she received had to be temporary and only because it was obvious she didn't belong.

Good grief, she had already spied two movie stars in the crowd.

Evelyn Rogers

She became aware of background music coming from somewhere in the room, strings and what sounded like a harp. Live music. Class.

"This is the John Quincy Adams State Drawing Room I told you about," Seale whispered near her ear.

And this was Regina Ferguson Baxter's moment of truth. It wasn't too late to duck out and run for the nearest Metro station. From old habit and a sense of caution, she had tucked mad money inside her purse. But back in Ballston the professor waited for a report, and by Monday so would half the neighborhood and everyone at work, including the mechanics and a couple of customers she had gotten to know. And then there were the doubters. There was no way she could tell them she had turned tail and run.

It would give her mystery caller too much satisfaction.

She sucked in her gut, then let out a rush of air when she saw the President. One glance and the urge to run died a quick death.

He stood at the right side of the room in front of a pair of yellow wing chairs. Like every other man around, he was dressed in a tuxedo, but he didn't look like every other man. He looked better, golden and glowing, more masculine, a man in control, every inch of him Golden Man, every inch inspiring thoughts of satin sheets. The last thing he resembled was a monk.

As she stared at him, the background music

swelled. She was certain of it. Her imagination wasn't fertile enough to dream it up. She could also have sworn the lights shone solely on him.

His wheat-in-the-sun hair was carefully combed, yet it looked ready for a woman's fingers to mess it up. He stood straight and square-jawed, and from twenty feet away she could see the startling blue of his eyes.

"That's the British ambassador beside him," Seale said. "His Excellency Albert Brookings. When you address him, call him Your Excellency."

Standing next to President Marshall, the ambassador, a thin, pale, gray-haired gentleman of obviously aristocratic breeding, didn't stand a chance at getting attention.

Seale's strong hand guided her toward the two men. Behind the wing chairs the American and British flags hung on separate posts, making everything look very official. In front of them stood a tall blonde who had poured herself into a shimmering white floor-length gown that caught the light a little like fish scales. Ginny took an immediate dislike to her. She was probably hiding skinny legs.

Both men directed their attention to the woman, who seemed to be charming them with an animated anecdote. At one point the ambassador threw back his head and laughed. Marshall flashed his magazine-cover smile.

The blonde shifted, and Ginny saw that her gown was split to the thigh. The exposed leg, visible for only an instant, didn't appear skinny in the least.

"The woman is Veronica Gray," Seale said. "Her father is chairman of the Senate Budget Committee. He's one of the most powerful men in Washington."

Ginny nodded. Apparently it was important to know who was who in this town to get the power structure right. She wondered how she would be described. The only person in all the world she could call a relative was Jake. She was subbasement material at best.

Another man appeared at her side. Short and dapper, he looked vaguely familiar. Maybe he was in one of the newspaper pictures she had been poring over this past week.

"Good evening, Mrs. Baxter," he said. "I'm Redford Davidson. How nice to see you again."

He didn't sound sincere.

"Again?" she asked, feeling stupid.

Then she remembered. He'd been witness to the debacle in the Oval Office.

She glanced in panic at Seale, who mouthed, "Chief of staff."

"The President's aunt wanted to be here to greet you," Davidson said, "but she had a prior engagement this evening."

"She was there, too, wasn't she?"

He nodded.

"Sorry we were delayed," Seale said. "Traffic."

"The driver called." Davidson looked at Ginny. "The President has been looking forward to your presence this evening. Come, let me take you over to him."

Seale dropped away, and Davidson took over. His hand wasn't nearly so supportive as the younger man's.

They were only a few feet away when the President saw her. For a moment his eyes didn't leave hers, and then they traveled down the length of her and back again. He made her feel naked. And very, very warm.

In that moment he didn't look in the least presidential. He looked like a man who could drive a love machine.

As suddenly as it had appeared the look was gone, and he simply stared at her, closer to cool than friendly as Davidson guided her to him. Then the ambassador was looking at her, and so, too, was the blonde. It seemed to Ginny that the room quieted, but she couldn't tell for sure, what with the roaring in her ears.

Woodenly, she moved forward and stuck out her hand. "Mrs. Regina Baxter," she said, then added as an afterthought, "Your Excellency."

"Good evening, Mrs. Baxter," the ambassador said, taking her hand for a brief, exactly-the-right-pressure squeeze. One battle done.

She dared glance at Marshall. "Mr. President."

"Ginny," the President said, "don't be so formal. I'm Steve, remember?"

His voice had a decisive edge. The roar became deafening. What was going on here?

"Shall we go in for wine?" he asked.

At least that's what she thought he said, and she found herself beside the President, with the senator's daughter and the British ambassador leading the way.

"I'm sorry you were delayed." He nodded to someone in passing, but he kept his low words just for her. "Surely you and Eddie found a way to pass the time."

"Yes, sir," she mumbled, minding her manners, and then the words struck.

"What's that supposed to mean?" she asked, forgetting to whom she spoke.

The smile he flashed her was definitely not the magazine-cover variety. This one had a hint of wickedness in it. As they swept into the crowd, it was the only response she got.

Something was wrong. Very, very wrong.

Inside the Thomas Jefferson Room she concentrated on the huge statue of the third President set into an alcove in the wall to her left. She was fighting a great clawing panic that was doing terrible things to her insides.

All men are created equal, Jefferson had written. But there were some women who were definitely subpar. One in particular: Regina Ferguson Baxter. Where men were concerned, she did nothing but make mistakes. If what she feared was really true, this was the dooziest mistake of them all.

The only thing to keep her from being sure was that it was too horrible to have actually occurred.

I don't go all the way, not right away.

She hadn't bothered to add that she hadn't been all the way in almost four years. It was probably too late to mention the details, should anyone be interested. Her fervent prayer was that nobody cared.

Whether or not people had been staring at her before, they definitely were now. She was the woman the President had escorted in for drinks. That pretty much made her his date. If she had any doubts about her evening's role, the looks Veronica Gray shot her way removed them.

"Wine?" Steve asked. Might as well think of him as Steve. It was what he wanted.

She shook her head.

He leaned close. She was vaguely aware of a lemony aftershave scent. "You don't drink on a first date, either?" he whispered.

Fears confirmed.

Ginny's knees gave way, and she grabbed his arm for support. His very hard arm. She let go right away, half expecting the Secret Service to handcuff her again. She dared one quick glance at his face, the square jaw and the firm mouth and the sky-blue eyes.

Big mistake. All men were definitely not created equal. Jefferson had got it wrong.

Steve moved in even closer and her breast brushed against his biceps. Was everything about him hard?

"Maybe alcohol makes you want to do the nasty."

It took a moment for the words to penetrate. It was if she were remembering them in her mind. But they were on her President's very sexy lips, and they mocked her.

Suddenly Ginny found her sense of self. If he had let the first comment stand alone, she might have continued in her humiliation. But he was rubbing it in, reminding her of everything she had said.

She'd made a mistake, that was all. A huge, mother-of-them-all mistake, for sure, but nothing really harmful. A gentleman wouldn't have brought it up.

Which told her something about the President. He was not only gorgeous and powerful, he was a man with the usual flaws that accompanied his sex.

She matched him stare for stare; she tried to match the taunt in his smile, but what she got for her effort was more taunting. For all his vaunted goodness, there was a great deal of devil in the President. A lot more devil than monk.

The devil in him was dangerously attractive. Despite her anger, she felt herself growing flushed. She wasn't the only one. That definitely was a bead of perspiration on his brow. Monk, was he? Ha!

Not that she felt flattered by his heat. He probably liked to talk dirty, especially in a crowd.

She was spared further conversation when his chief of staff called him away. For a moment she was left staring at the senator's beautiful daughter. They shared a long stare, as cool as the one with Steve had been hot. Veronica obviously considered her an unworthy opponent, for she turned away to one of the movie stars, an aging British actor who last March had won an Academy Award.

Ginny found herself standing beside the ambassador. He smiled at her as if he actually expected her to speak. She said the first thing that popped into her head—the first thing, that is, that didn't involve *all the way* and *nasty* and a very roguish male.

"What do you think of the Rolls Royce?"

Dumb. Really dumb. Silence would have been better.

"I'm definitely for them," he responded, not in the least taken aback. "I sincerely wish the rest of the world shared my sentiments, even though they're not actually a British product anymore."

The man was smooth. And she found him strangely unintimidating.

"You've got the Jaguar," she said, "And the Aston Martin. They're very popular."

"You know cars, Mrs. Baxter?"

"I work in an auto shop."

"How interesting." He seemed genuinely sincere, not like someone else she could name. "Please tell me how that is."

"I don't do the actual repairs, of course. I man the front desk."

"I shouldn't think you could man anything very well," he said in such a gentlemanly way, she couldn't take offense.

"You are a diplomat."

71

"As you Americans say, it's my stock in trade."

She found herself liking the man. After Stephen Marshall, he seemed refreshingly uncomplicated. She wondered where the President was right then, but she was too cowardly to look around.

The topic turned to antique cars.

"I had a '57 Chevy once," she said.

"Had? Please do not tell me something happened to it."

"My father bought it when it was new, long before I was born. He taught me to baby it. When he died, it was my main legacy. Later"—no need to go into details—"I had to sell it."

"I understand. More than one Rolls Royce has gone to auction in recent years."

Several men joined them, including the Academy Award winner, and the talk veered to the car clubs that had sprung up on both sides of the Atlantic. Ginny was more than relieved to let the guys take over the conversation, leaving her simply to nod.

From the corner of her eye she saw a phalanx of women watching. Somehow she didn't think the onlookers were her friends. Suddenly she felt foolish and very much out of place in her too-short skirt and her rhinestone barrette.

When she spotted Steve Marshall heading her way, she figured it was time for dinner. She looked beyond him into the Benjamin Franklin State Dining Room, to the dozen round tables crowded with glasses and china and lighted candles. Very possibly she would be seated beside the President, where

72

she would be given countless opportunities to do something wrong. She could handle the forks and the food—she wasn't a complete nincompoop—but she doubted anyone at the table would be fascinated by her knowledge of automobiles.

Or baseball. Or the trials of single parenthood.

Her conversational skills definitely needed work, but not tonight. Muttering an excuse that didn't make much sense, she retreated, hurrying through the John Quincy Adams Room, seeking refuge in the facilities named after the first First Lady. The Martha Washington Ladies' Room was the fanciest one she had ever seen. On an antique desk in the large sitting room—if that was what it was called—she found what she was after: a stack of stationery and a pen.

Scribbling a note, she went out to the Gallery and found her second objective, a Secret Service agent standing guard. She thought she recognized him from the White House, but she couldn't be sure.

Without ceremony, she thrust the folded paper in his hand. "Please see that the President gets this." Then she hurried out to the elevator and went down to the real world.

Okay, she was being a rabbit, running the way she was. But it was the only way rabbits knew to survive.

Outside, the wind had picked up. Despite the layers of spray she had used, her hair blew wildly. She pulled her mantilla tight and started waving for a cab on the almost deserted street. For once luck was going her way. One pulled up to the curb practically right away.

As she was climbing into the back seat, she heard a noise behind her. Pulling back, she turned at the precise moment a flashbulb went off from somewhere close to the Department of State. Tourists, she thought.

She started to ask to go to the nearest Metro station, but then decided, what the heck. She'd just passed up dinner with the President. She deserved a ride all the way home.

"Ballston," she said, and with less than steady hands she began to count her change.

Chapter Four

Doris dropped the newspaper on the table beside Steve's breakfast plate and took her place at the table across from him.

He went on chewing his dry toast. He hated dry toast, but his aunt had decided he should go on a diet. He'd tried to tell her that the most powerful man in the world could choose his own food, but he'd ended up with dry toast anyway.

Lest he try to ignore her this morning, she tapped at the paper.

"You need to take a look at this. Edward Seale just sent it up."

"Ah."

Noncommittal. Seale reminded him of last night. Last night was not a happy memory. For the first time since sixth grade a female had dumped him. *I have to leave*, she had written. *I apologize*.

Apology not accepted. It was a childish reaction,

maybe, but every now and then a man felt like being a child.

Aunt Doris shook the paper. He saw it was *The Inside Scoop*.

"I don't read tabloids," he said.

"You should. They get the juicy stuff first."

The two of them were having their usual Sunday morning meal in the family dining room on the White House second floor. Steve had been going through the *Washington Post*, the capital's prestigious and usually reliable newspaper, when his aunt had decided to change his reading matter.

He liked the rare, leisurely perusal of the *Post*, which he followed with the *New York Times*. Every day staff members summarized a dozen newspapers and magazines for him, but these two Sunday publications he liked going over personally.

This was the one morning of the week when he didn't have to be up and dressed and downstairs and ready to deal with the world before eight. On Sunday morning his aides fielded his calls. Only emergencies warranted his attention.

Last night did not fall under the category of emergencies. Extreme agitation, yes, but nothing he had to deal with again. Ford had even promised not to push him into any more social explorations.

Regina Baxter had not worked out. He couldn't fault the FBI for the inadequate report. She had fooled them into thinking she was a modest, hardworking single mother with high values and a sense of decorum.

She had fooled him, too. He could take being fooled. He just didn't like being dumped.

The cook Florence sidled up. "Here's your poached egg, Mr. President."

Steve glanced up at her, none too cheerfully. Florence McKelvey was a tall, big-boned woman, with high cheekbones that showed the Indian blood in her. She had worked for him in Oklahoma; he'd brought her with him to Washington, primarily because of her pancakes. And here she was, poaching eggs.

"Would you like some more toast?" she asked.

He shook his head, and she went off grumbling about how there wasn't much challenge in cooking anymore.

On most days she was aided by a butler, but not on Sundays, when with Florence's blessing he gave the man the day off. Steve was a throw-back to Harry Truman. He had a hard time accepting a bunch of servants at his beck and call.

Aunt Doris tapped the tabloid. "Give it a look."

He glanced at the front page. Mostly it was one large picture; the picture was mostly of a woman's legs.

It was typical *Scoop* garbage. The tabloid was printed in D.C. late Saturday night, distributed locally the next morning, and on Monday it went nationwide. Of all the tabloids, the *Scoop* was the most openly irritated by his monkishness. That was why the trash-writers there had started the womanizer speculations.

Much of the capital spent Sunday pouring over this prime example of journalistic junk food. Steve so far had resisted.

He started to look away, then stopped. He knew those legs. In the photo they belonged to a woman who was getting into the back seat of a taxi, her skirt hiked up to show most of one thigh. One very shapely thigh.

He dragged his eyes away from the thigh, up to the rounded bottom, the fringed shawl, and on to the wide, dark eyes of Regina Baxter. She looked startled, taken by surprise.

So was he.

Damn. Here she was again, except that she looked different with her skirt riding high and her hair caught by the wind, giving her a wanton look, as if she was just crawling out of a man's bed—or was ready to crawl in. Where had she gone in that taxi? Did she have a late date?

I have to leave. She hadn't bothered to say why.

He spared another look at the legs. He'd liked them last night, and he liked them today.

The headline was big and black and bold:

THE MONK'S MYSTERY WOMAN

and in much smaller letters

SEE STORY PAGE 2.

Of course he did what every other Washington reader was doing this Sunday morning: he turned to page two and scanned the story.

"Varying from his usual list of beautiful Washington socialites, President Stephen Marshall caused a sensation Saturday evening with a new companion on his arm, a sexy mystery woman identified by our in-house correspondent as Jennifer."

Correspondent, my ass, the President thought very unpresidentially. The unnamed ratfink was a spy. And a dumb one. He or she hadn't been smart enough to catch Ginny's right name.

Under his aunt's watchful eye, he read on:

The scene was a reception for the recently appointed British ambassador, Albert Brookings, at the Department of State. The mysterious Jennifer, batting her baby browns, wowed the ambassador and most of the men by talking cars. That's right, readers, cars. Seems she is something of a mechanic, adding to the mystery surrounding her.

One enthralled gentleman commented, "She can check under my hood any time she wants."

Steve would bet his morning toast the quote was a fake.

"Most mysterious of all, she ran out of the dinner before the salad was served. She's seen in this exclusive *Inside Scoop* photo ducking into a cab outside the State Department, leaving the President to eat his endives alone.

"Could our fair-haired leader have found the woman of his dreams? Could she have pushed the right Presidential button? Could it be that all along he's wanted a woman who plays hard to get?"

The story went on to enlist help in identifying her. Below the story were pictures of Veronica Gray and the other "beautiful Washington socialites who are frequently on the President's arm."

"Garbage," he said, tossing the paper aside.

He reached for a piece of toast and shredded it into crumbs.

"But interesting garbage," Aunt Doris said. "Edward saw it at a newsstand in front of McDonald's. He had to wrestle two men for the last copy."

"He shouldn't have bothered."

"You want to tell me about last night?"

"I told you. Mrs. Baxter came, she saw, she left early. Formal receptions aren't her cup of tea."

Doris shifted the paper to her side of the table.

"You're not telling me everything."

"The ambassador enjoyed her company. He wondered if he were the reason she left."

"I don't imagine he was. You probably frightened her off. She looks positively terrified in this picture."

"Startled, not terrified." And wanton, too. "She just had a flashbulb go off in her face. Deal with the facts, Aunt."

"I'm trying to learn them. You know, I'm not one to say I told you so, but I did. I warned you this whole idea of yours would backfire. She obviously didn't belong in such a setting. Look at that dress. It looks like a blouse with pretensions."

One of the thousand aides who always seemed to hover just out of sight materialized and set a telephone beside him.

"It's Redford Davidson, Mr. President. Will you take the call?"

Steve nodded and picked up the receiver.

"Have you seen it?" Ford asked.

"You shouldn't be reading the *Scoop*."

"Ah, you have. I warned you—"

"That's my aunt's line. You told me it could be good. She was an ordinary woman, someone the American public could accept without jealousy. You forgot to check out her legs."

"I didn't know she would show so much of them. And now everyone's checking them out."

Steve spent a few minutes assuring Ford that there was nothing to worry about.

"The story will make me look more human," he said.

"You didn't get elected for being human," Ford countered and hung up.

The telephone was taken away, then returned within the minute.

"Alan Skinner, Mr. President."

Steve took a guess at why his press secretary was calling. Without preamble, he said, "You've seen the *Scoop*."

"I've been talking to Davidson and Seale," Skinner said. "We've got some ideas about the spin we can put on this."

Steve's principal advisers were nothing if not thorough. The three had been with him since before the New Hampshire primary, Ford going back to his first election as an Oklahoma congressman. Usually he considered everything they had to say, but not this morning, not when the topic was as inconsequential a matter as Regina Baxter.

"Did anyone else pick up on this? Anyone from TV?" he asked.

"No, sir."

"Then we ignore it."

"I don't think that's a good idea."

"I do." Steve tried to be charitable. "Anything we say will only bring Mrs. Baxter more embarrassment. Let's leave the woman alone."

Across the table, Aunt Doris's eyebrows notched upward.

"What makes you think she would be embarrassed?" Skinner said. "It could be she set up the whole thing. After all, considering the way she called herself to your attention, anything's possible."

At last Skinner had got to him. Sharp as ever, the press secretary put into words the one real concern that could get to Steve. Too well he remembered every minute of that phone call. With Ginny Baxter, anything was truly possible. Nobody really knew her—nobody inside the Beltway, that is. The only thing for sure was that after one evening she was bringing the presidency bad press. Steve had been elected because he was honorable, because he was scandal-free. Hell, celibacy had practically been in the party platform.

But honor—at least the perception of honor— was a fragile thing. He stared at the picture and considered snatches of that telephone conversation. Maybe she'd left last night because, after having been so blunt with him, she had felt uncomfortable, just as he'd told his aunt. Although Ambassador Brookings had been surprised by her unexplained departure, and he had been the one who talked to her the most.

The woman who had talked with him on the phone did not seem like the woman who'd charmed the ambassador. She was, it would seem, a mystery woman far more than the *Scoop* understood.

What if she wasn't through with her President yet? There had been something in the FBI report about a troubled son. Maybe she was one of those twisted people who blamed the government for everything.

Mrs. Sexy-Legs Baxter was either more or less than she seemed; he didn't know which.

He shoved aside the cold poached egg. Damned if the woman wasn't turning into more than a temporary distraction. Was she the wide-eyed innocent who had stared up at him from the Oval Office floor, the one he had taken a liking to? Or was she the fast-talking hussy who didn't do the *nasty* on a first date?

That particular quip, he had to admit, had started him thinking of things he hadn't considered in years. Well, he'd considered them, but not quite so seriously as he had last night. Damn, she had good legs.

Never once had he run from a problem. He'd learned in his early days in politics, when he'd first been a candidate for Congress and faced charges of being Black Bart's lackey, that running was no way to win. Regina Baxter was a problem. Not running meant he had to see her again.

Once he understood her, and his reactions to her, he could deal with her, and then he could thrust her into an appropriate compartment and get back to the important issues of his work. He was a big boy. Besides, damn it, he was the President. He could take care of himself.

Hanging up the phone, he made the mistake of saying he would be seeing Ginny again, only because he wanted to understand her, leaving out the part about understanding himself.

"Stephen, enough with this woman. She'll only bring you more embarrassment. I feel it in my soul."

When she wanted to make a point, Aunt Doris could veer toward the dramatic.

"I'm a big boy, dearest. I can take care of myself."

"Of course you can," she said, but she didn't sound sure.

He needed a plan. It was cogitation time, and for him that meant only one thing.

He had a lot of reading to catch up on and some reports to edit, plus a speech he was giving tomorrow to a group of Girl Scouts. Nothing, thank God, was of an emergency nature. All of it could wait until later in the day.

Work at the White House never stopped, whether he was there or not. He viewed the executive mansion as something like the *Titanic*, all those powerful engines grinding below, unseen, while the showy stuff went on above. He wasn't sure he liked the *Titanic* comparison, but in all ways but one it was apt. And it told him to watch out for icebergs in the dark.

He shoved away from the table and stood. He was already wearing jeans and boots. They were his best thinking clothes.

He would get out to the stables right after the agents made their usual sweep, maybe ride awhile, then muck out the barn. When it came to working through a worry, especially the kind that came with being President, there was nothing better for clearing the mind than shoveling piles of manure.

Ginny didn't get to sleep until dawn on Sunday. Far too early she woke to the ringing of the telephone. It was her next-door neighbor, muttering something that didn't make much sense, something about a picture. Ginny figured she was asking if there had been photographers at the reception last night.

The reception.

She groaned into the receiver about not being awake. She'd no sooner hung up when the phone rang again. This time it was someone she didn't know, asking if her name was Jennifer. She slammed down the phone without an answer. What were salesmen doing calling so early on a Sunday morning?

She cracked one eye open. Eight o'clock, according to the clock beside the sofa bed. Barbaric.

The phone rang.

"No one home," she mumbled, then turned off the ringer.

With a heavy heart, she rolled off the lumpy mattress and tiptoed to the bedroom. Jake was fast asleep in a tangle of covers. He would be until noon. It was the only normal teenage habit he had.

Why was she feeling so bad, so alone, as if she had lost something very important to her? Jake was okay, and he was all that really mattered in her world.

In the bathroom she stared into the mirror and groaned. Her hair stood up in spikes, and mascara was streaked beneath her eyes. She looked like a ghoul. She felt like a corpse.

A splash of cold water woke her up just enough for images of last night to assault her. Images of beautiful people—acres of them—and the best of them all, Apollo in black tie, mocking her with wintry blue eyes.

It was the pair of mocking eyes that caused her heavy heart.

Pulling on a T-shirt and cut-offs, she tugged a brush through her hair and stumbled into the kitchen, her stomach growling. She couldn't remember eating supper, but she didn't try to remember too hard. There was no telling what else she would recall.

The crunch of cereal was too cruel to contemplate. It might wake her up all the way. Maybe Professor Carl had found a decent recipe. With mixed emotions, she peeked outside the screen door. A box of doughnuts rested at her feet. Ginny had never seen anything more beautiful in all her life.

The doughnuts came with a written apology because they weren't fresh-baked muffins. The professor had needed to be at the university early to meet with a student. He would be gone all day, but she was free to use the washer and dryer on his back porch, Sunday being her usual wash day.

It must have been divine intervention that brought those doughnuts at her hour of greatest need. Along with a glass of orange juice, she scarfed down three of them, leaving the rest to Jake. Both of them needed to get to church, if for no other reason than to express gratitude for the breakfast, but Jake always refused to go with her and she couldn't face a crowd today. Someone in the congregation would ask how the reception had gone.

She never wanted to think about last night again.

To that end, she pretty much managed to keep busy all of Sunday. She spent the morning washing and ironing, the afternoon at the kickboxing studio sweating instead of thinking, and the evening watching a televised movie with Jake.

It was on one of the high-number channels, the apartment having already been wired for cable, which was something she had never enjoyed in Ohio. The movie had been made in India and the English dubbed in. The plot needed more concentration than she could give it, but Jake seemed interested. He watched only foreign films. Hollywood produced nothing but propaganda, he said.

It didn't matter to him that the telephone ringer was turned off. After her disastrous call from the man she refused to name, she never wanted to use the thing again. In her possession it became a lethal weapon, the primary victim being herself.

Neither did Jake mind her questions about yesterday's baseball meeting. After the movie was finally over, with most everybody in the cast dead or dying, he talked about the coaches and the dates of the games and when the tryouts would be. Whatever resentments he harbored had never been turned against her.

Or against baseball.

When she finally crawled into bed, sleep didn't come any easier than it had the previous night. Phrases like *going all the way* and *doing the nasty* kept assaulting her. What a fake she was. All talk.

Jonas hadn't wanted her a long time before he finally left. Work frequently took him out of town. She should have known he was seeing other women. With men she wasn't too smart.

Nor, apparently, was she especially desirable. The few guys she had dated after he left made it clear they sought her company only because as a divorcée she was obviously easy, even though she said flatly she wasn't interested, at least not until she decided if she even liked them.

Good grief, she could pick losers. Their idea of foreplay was, "Is the kid around?"

And, of course, one night Jake had been, the night her escort had gotten a little frisky and been tossed out the door.

Why on earth would Stephen Marshall want to have anything to do with her? It was definitely not because she was divorced.

That was the part of all this that didn't make sense. Why had he invited her to the reception? Ginny knew her shortcomings as well as anyone. She could crawl into his bed buck naked and he would probably turn over and go to sleep.

Which was what she should do—go to sleep, that is—except that she couldn't, not until it was almost time to get up. Bleary-eyed, she arrived at Sam's Auto Repair early Monday morning and found a crowd waiting inside.

Sam's must be having a sale on oil changes.

One or two of the customers would be wanting to know about Saturday night. She had her story ready, having practiced it on the long walk to the shop. Most of it was the truth. She had been picked up in a limousine and whisked to the beautiful reception rooms of the Department of State. She would describe each room in detail, along with the beautiful people who were there, especially the movie stars. She would talk about the ambassador and how nice he had been, and how he had been interested in cars. She would say the President looked even better in person than he did in pictures.

She would *not* say his manners needed work, although she sincerely believed they did.

Then she would say she'd caught a taxi and come home.

End of story.

End of the most bizarre, luckily brief, chapter in her life. No need to go into all of her regrets. No need to go into the *might have beens*, if only she had behaved differently and so had the President.

The only realistic *might have been* was that they would have sat beside one another at dinner, she would have noted all that was served, and she would have listened to the conversation of the rich and powerful.

And then she would have gone home, probably much the way she had.

She was no sooner inside the shop door when someone yelled, "Looked under any hoods lately?" and someone else waved a newspaper in her face. It took her a minute to focus.

Were those her legs? Was that her rear sticking up as she bent over to climb into the taxi? Was she really the frightened creature whose photo was splashed across the front page?

THE MONK'S MYSTERY WOMAN, the headline read.

"Good grief" didn't seem nearly strong enough.

She remembered the flash of a camera. The tourist had been no tourist at all, but a news photographer. As if she was news.

Apparently *The Inside Scoop* thought so. Along with everyone at Sam's Auto Repair.

Hurriedly she scanned the story. *Sexy mystery woman* leaped out at her. She wasn't in the least sexy. Shameless, maybe, but not sexy. Her mother would have called the woman in the picture a tramp. Her father wouldn't have paid attention. He had always seen her as his son.

With more courage than it would take to rock climb the Washington Monument, she looked beyond the crowd to her boss, Ted Waclawski, standing behind the counter.

"Morning, Mystery Woman," he drawled, doing a pretty fair imitation of the President. "Looks like you've picked up a few fans."

If Ginny thought her day had been bad, what with the thousand questions that bombarded her without end and the skeptical looks that met her almost-true description of Saturday night's events, that was nothing compared to the feeling that hit her when she got off the bus and saw two Secret Service agents standing on the sidewalk in front of the professor's house.

A long black limousine sat in the driveway. The agents watched in silence as she made her way back to her apartment. She couldn't see if anyone was in the limo; the windows were too dark.

Another agent waited by the screen door. Without a word, he opened it for her and she entered, expecting to see Edward Seale waiting inside. Instead, she saw a white-haired woman in a pearl gray silk dress seated on the sofa. Professor Carl rose to his feet beside the dining table. He was wearing his casual attire, the striped trousers, plaid shirt, and paisley vest. He looked beautiful, friendly and protective at the same time.

"I hope you don't mind, Ginny. Miss Tanner asked to wait until you arrived home. I'll ask her to leave if you prefer."

It was a curiously strong thing for him to say.

The woman stood, shooting the professor a look that said *you'll have to toss me out*, then smiled coolly at Ginny. "Doris Tanner," she said. "I'm the President's aunt."

The screen door slammed behind Ginny, like a rock sealing a tomb. The President's aunt. Why was she surprised?

The woman wasn't very tall, and she had a soft, bosomy look to her, but her eyes were a paler version of her nephew's. Ginny could see the same steely determination in their depths.

They shook hands. Miss Tanner's grip was stronger than the ambassador's. Ginny nodded at the professor, to tell him everything was all right.

Which, of course, it wasn't.

Ginny glanced around the room. Once again Jake

had straightened the mess she left, and she vaguely wondered where he was. She loved the boy so much her heart ached. Her hardest chore in life was to keep from being overprotective at the same time she tried to raise him right.

At least it had been her hardest chore until she got herself involved with the First Family.

Miss Tanner sat back down on the sofa. Ginny took a chair across from the professor. She kept calm, as if she received such exalted visitors every day in the week. She had a fatalistic attitude toward everything that was happening to her. The nightmare would never end.

"You must be wondering why I'm here."

The President's aunt didn't bother with small talk.

Ginny glanced at the professor. His Santa Claus face gave no clue as to what was going on.

"I tried telephoning," the aunt continued, "but no one answered."

"The ringer was turned off." She ran a thumb down the crease in her khakis. "Besides, no one's here during the day."

It was a fact Miss Tanner should have realized, if she knew anything about the real world. Women worked, whether they wanted to or not.

"The ringer's back on now," the professor said.

Miss Tanner shot him another hostile glance. "Is the gentleman's presence necessary?"

"Yes," Ginny said, proud of her courage. "I told

93

him about how the President and I met. But only him. Our secret's safe."

Miss Tanner's expression remained cool. "I'm sure you realize as much as I how unfortunate that meeting was. I don't imagine anything like that has happened before."

"I regret it as much as anyone," Ginny said, her fatalism giving way to impatience. Must she apologize forever for taking that pill?

"As a boy, my nephew liked to take in stray animals."

Ginny couldn't see how that had anything to do with anything, but she kept quiet.

"My sister, his mother, died when he was young, and his father devoted himself to accumulating his fortune."

"Black Bart's methods are studied in some economics classes," the professor said.

Miss Tanner frowned. "I'm sure they are. University classes aren't what they were in my day."

Ginny looked questioningly at the two of them. "Black Bart?"

"Hobart Marshall's unfortunate nickname," Miss Tanner said. "Of course, it referred to the oil discovered on his land, but there were those who insisted it was the color of his heart. He could be quite ruthless, you know. He was proud of the epithet, enough to have it engraved on his tombstone."

Ginny got the picture, and a feeling of sadness settled on her, directed toward, of all people, the President.

"So Steve gathered strays," she said.

"Steve?"

"The President. He asked me to call him Steve."

"I'm sure he did."

And then Ginny understood what the President's aunt was getting at.

"You think I'm one of those strays."

"I think he still has a soft heart for misfits and malcontents."

"See here, Miss Tanner," the professor interjected, "that hardly describes Ginny."

The professor and the aunt stared at one another. This would not develop into a friendship, Ginny knew for sure.

"And he also hates it when a stray turns on him and bites," the woman continued.

Professor Carl started to speak, but Ginny shook her head. She had to handle this on her own.

"Is that what your nephew thinks I did?" she asked.

"It's my opinion that he does. All I know for sure—and with Stephen that's always a risky thing to say—is that he's not done with you." She pursed her lips a moment. "I can't imagine why not. He's already honored you far more than you had any right to expect."

The aunt had enough sense to look embarrassed. "I'm sorry, my dear, for being blunt. That dreadful newspaper article has me upset. Stephen came into office on a platform of honor and high morals. He is my life. I will do anything necessary to see that nothing about his reputation is tarnished."

It seemed to matter little that Ginny's reputation had also gone through a little discoloration since the *Scoop* hit the stands. Of course, to such high-placed critics as Doris Tanner, she didn't matter.

Except to herself and to Jake, and just maybe, if the unusual fire in his eye was any clue, to Professor Carl. He had obviously seen *The Inside Scoop*. Somehow she knew he believed she had done no harm.

Miss Tanner's manner softened. "I sound harsh, but only because I love my nephew very much, and I know he is good for this country. He needs stability in his life, a good woman and a family. He does not need a divorcée with a troubled son."

"Balderdash," Professor Carl barked. "Mrs. Baxter is a fine woman and an exemplary mother." His white beard quivered with indignation. "The last thing she would harbor is a design on the President of the United States."

At this most inopportune of moments, Ginny remembered the lust she had harbored for that very same man. She hadn't considered it a "design" on him, exactly, but then she had never considered the possibility that the two of them would ever get close.

"I have not accused Mrs. Baxter of any such thing," Miss Tanner said with equal indignation.

The two were staring at one another ready to do battle, as if no one else was in the room.

"Please," Ginny said, determined to settle the issue amicably, although she wasn't quite sure what the issue could be. Somehow she had upset the First Aunt. How? What did she and Jake have to do with the presidency?

Her first and only child took that moment to arrive on the scene. The door squeaked and banged to announce him, and the Secret Service agent watched alertly through the screen.

"Mom," he said with all the assurance of his youth and the courage of his convictions, "our government is power mad. They have no right to harass you this way."

She rubbed at her forehead. "I'm not being harassed," she said, but Jake was in no mood to listen. He stood beside her, towering over her as a pillar of strength, launching into one of his harangues about the abuses of authority. He didn't get started very often, but when he did, he was impossible to stop.

"See here, young man," Miss Tanner said, but whatever she added was lost in Jake's diatribe. The professor joined the chorus. The only quiet one in the room was Ginny.

And then the telephone rang. Loud. The professor must have turned the ringer to high.

Everyone jumped.

"It's probably a reporter," Ginny said, as she went to answer. "I'll get rid of him." In truth, she welcomed the interruption. Dealing with *The Inside Scoop* would be a breeze compared to what she was facing now.

"What do you want?" she snapped into the receiver.

"Ah, another persona. The angry one. I kinda liked the tentative, nervous woman who first answered on Saturday."

Ginny sank onto the arm of the sofa, her back to the others. She recognized the voice, the slight drawl, the persuasive tone. A sense of dread, of doom, gripped her heart, at the same time that she felt an anticipatory tingle at a few points lower in her anatomy, her body not knowing how to react any better that did her mind.

He—the big *he*—was calling again.

This couldn't be happening to her, ordinary-looking, usually timid, typical-single-mom Regina Baxter. But it was.

Chapter Five

"Ginny, without saying anything revealing, could you tell me if my aunt's there?"

The President came on serious and confidential and a little cowardly, as if his aunt intimidated him, which Ginny could understand. He also sounded incredibly casual, as if he called her every day of the week.

What he *didn't* sound was taunting or teasing or sexy-insulting, which she told herself was all to the good.

"Oh, yes," she answered with a pinch more fervor than she'd planned, wondering at the same time if she were caught in the middle of a First Family feud.

"That's what I figured. I'm truly sorry. She's my mother hen."

"She's good at it," Ginny said, figuring it was too late in her bizarre relationship with power to start being mealymouthed. If she had to play another role in this had-to-be-a-fantasy drama, it would be the strong, dignified woman who had been wronged.

After one or two experiences with Stephen Marshall, she was finding that speaking as an equal to him was really not so hard. It helped that she didn't have to look at him while she talked.

"She was that bad, was she?" he asked.

"Oh, yes." Several pinches of fervor.

"Did she say anything about my deserving a good woman?"

"It might have been mentioned."

"Then I owe you big time, both for her and for my rudeness at the reception."

Was he actually apologizing for the way he had behaved? She started to tell him he had been justified, to thank him for his concern, hang up, and get back to the real world. But he wasn't done.

"How about dinner tomorrow night?" he asked.

"Definitely not." She practically yelped the response. He couldn't possibly be serious.

"Nothing public. Neither of us would be on view." A slight pause. "We could talk and get to know one another better."

His voice had changed since the beginning of the call; now it was the most soft and wheedling it had ever been and, she had to admit, despite her distress, very, very sexy. She wondered when he used it other than with her, doubting it did him much good with his adversaries on Capitol Hill.

Unless he directed it toward congresswomen and

female senators . . . but that was a sexist thought and Ginny always tried not to be sexist.

"It'll be in the White House," he added. "Upstairs."

Too well she remembered her last visit to the executive mansion.

"That's even worse."

"You don't trust me."

I don't trust myself.

She rubbed her forehead. This couldn't be happening. What could the President possibly want with her? What could she truthfully, realistically, morally want from him?

Truthful and realistic she could be. Besides being rich and famous and powerful and gorgeous, the man had stirred up yearnings she hadn't felt in years.

It was the *moral* that gave her trouble, both his morality and hers. She remembered the tabloid picture that had everyone in her corner of the world gossiping. Could he really think she was the sexpot the *Scoop* had portrayed?

He should have seen her Sunday morning, when she first got up. That would change his mind.

She took a deep breath. She'd thought Steve Marshall's first telephone call had been otherworldly, but it was nothing compared to this. The one improvement was that this evening she knew it really was he.

Memories of past White House scandals, both alleged and real, intruded.

"Do you remember what I told you when you called me the first time?" she asked.

"You said several things. I assume you mean how you don't go all the way on the first date."

She winced. On his lips the words sounded worse than ever. "Yes," she said.

"And this would be the second date, more or less."

It was more less than more, but she wasn't in the mood to quibble.

"The same rule applies," she said.

If that wasn't the stupidest thing she had ever said, it came close, but under the circumstances, which were by no means clear, she had no choice. After all, he had said they could get to know each other better, but he hadn't said in what way. She doubted he was referring to their separate politics.

"You think I want you to fool around," he said.

"I . . . I don't know. I mean, I know it sounds ridiculous now that I think of it . . . well, maybe, I guess you could say that was what I was thinking, although I know it's crazy, you being who you are and me being me."

The more she babbled, the more she realized how crazy she must sound, delusional, downright insane. So she'd worn a short skirt. This was the President of the United States she was talking to. Her legs weren't *that* good.

"You have nothing to fear but fear itself," he said.

"Fear can be a healthy thing."

And it can lead you to make a jackass of yourself.

Later, when she went over this conversation in her mind, she would probably die a thousand deaths, but right now she didn't know how to shut up.

"I promise that the monk will leave his mystery woman alone. Besides, my aunt will be there."

His announcement worked where her will to shut up had failed. She could think of nothing to say.

Ginny pictured the grim-faced woman sitting behind her taking in every word. Doris Tanner's promised presence wasn't much of a selling point. Her silence must have given him a hint.

"It'll be informal. I'll be wearing jeans."

Considering the way he looked in them, that *really* wasn't a selling point, not one that put her mind at ease, anyway.

Again, silence was the best response she could come up with.

From the way he breathed, she could feel the change in his attitude. No more wheedling. It was time to be President.

"A car will pick you up tomorrow at seven. Don't worry; it won't be a limousine. I'll send a pickup if I can find one."

He hung up. Ginny didn't recall accepting the invitation, but apparently the President assumed she had.

She held on to the phone, listening to the dial tone as if it might tell her something she didn't already know. Stephen Marshall wanted her upstairs in the White House, for dinner, he claimed, as a payback for what she wasn't quite sure, although he'd given her a couple of choices.

His aunt's interference? A private dinner at the executive mansion seemed like overkill. Doris Tanner wasn't that bad. In a way, to a mother with a problem child, her concern, misplaced though it was, touched a sympathetic chord.

Other motives occurred to her, some of them unspeakably dark. Was the man a sex-crazed phony whom she alone among the populace had found out? Was he hot for her body, seeing the error of his monkish ways?

Or was he the great American everyone assumed him to be, reaching out to an ordinary citizen who had been both publicly and privately humiliated because of him? After two telephone conversations and one brief, brutally memorable evening, she genuinely didn't know.

Hot for her body seemed the more absurd conjecture, but he *had* called her twice; her, ordinary Ginny Baxter, who possessed not an ounce of political clout.

He'd been downright rude the other night, asking if she and Eddie had found a way to pass the time. This evening he had been courteous and even friendly—right up until the end, when he assumed she would do what he asked. The President had her very much confused.

He also had her thinking of the insistent way his voice had wrapped around her, the way it continued to do so even in memory. In a cloud of confusion, the lust came galloping in again, like one of his Oklahoma studs.

Ginny turned back to the room and realized, both incongruously and belatedly, that the professor's beard and Doris Tanner's hair were the same shade of white, as if that linked them in some way. She concentrated on the woman. Along with Professor Carl and Jake, the First Aunt knew who had been on the phone. She had both exasperation and resignation in her eyes.

No offense taken. Miss Tanner wanted nothing more than to protect her nephew from scandal. Ginny understood.

She spared a glance at the professor, who stared at her with warm concern, and at her son, whose warmth more nearly approached righteous indignation. His was the emotion she should have shared, if she had any sense.

Which she didn't. Worried, puzzled, frightened by the prospect of dinner with Stephen Marshall, she also felt more excited than she had in years.

She stared haplessly at the agent outside the screen door.

Golden Man meets the love machine.

Here she went again.

The next evening, while waiting for the pickup, Ginny made another in what was becoming a series of needless mistakes. She watched the network news.

She vaguely recognized the setting that flashed

onto the screen—the Rose Garden—recognized it not from her initial dash through the flowers but from the repeated treks with the Secret Service over her misbegotten route.

She recognized the man behind the microphones far more quickly, recognized him all too well, from his sandy hair to his square jaw to the casual, in-charge air he wore as easily as he did his expensive suit. The President was addressing a gathering of Girl Scouts; naturally, they were charmed.

"The strength of America depends upon the strength of its women." He flashed the killer smile. "And of its girls."

The camera flashed over the eager, nervous faces of the youngsters in their uniforms. He had them enthralled. The camera moved on to a bank of Girl Scout leaders standing at the side. He had them panting.

The President went on to urge the girls to study, to volunteer, to be the best they could be. In every-thing he said, he was kind and funny and encour-aging, and he spoke in a down-home voice that was at once reassuring and provocative.

It certainly was provoking her.

She closed her eyes for a minute and pictured all that provocation eased into tight jeans and an open-throated shirt, and every bit of it waiting for her. Hurrying into the kitchen, she poured a glass of cold water from the pitcher in the refrigerator. Half she drank, the other half she dribbled over the inside of her wrists.

Tonight she would be dignified, polite, interested in her surroundings as any patriotic citizen should be. But demure in her interest. Very, very demure. How he must be laughing because she'd voiced the possibility of being anything else.

Somewhere in the conversation she had considered the possibility of trying to explain her behavior the first time he called.

I thought you were someone else, she'd say.

Didn't I identify myself? he'd say.

I thought you were someone imitating you, she'd say. *So I made up some stuff.*

Does this mean you really do go all the way on a first date?

And the talk would go downhill from there. Forget it. Some things were best left alone.

Directing her attention to the TV, she decided that she and Stephen Marshall were as different as two people could possibly be. He was smooth and in control, master of the world. Ginny had never been in control of any facet of her life.

And that included tonight. A private dinner in the White House with the President of the United States. Incredible. Even more incredible, she was going not only because he had insisted, but because she wanted to know what kind of man he was.

She rubbed at her forehead, a habit she had formed the past few days. Though she wanted to know about him, she was learning far too much about herself. Pitiful creature that she was, her hormones were not dead.

107

And, of course, there was the glamour and the hint of danger that went with edging near the fires of power. Tonight her task would include not only assessing the character of the President, but also protecting herself from getting burned.

Jake, normally her source of strength, wasn't helping her any. He didn't want her to go anywhere near Stephen Marshall. Before he'd left for ball practice, they'd come as close to an argument over the issue as they had over anything since she'd allowed Jonas to return home.

She had assured him that she could take care of herself, that Doris Tanner would be there, that the President was simply apologizing because of the *Inside Scoop* embarrassment.

Jake had not been impressed.

The news was just ending when she heard the car in the drive. She was wearing linen-blend, natural-colored slacks, a taupe blouse, and a cocoa jacket, all bought at an Ohio discount mall. And, of course, sensible shoes. She wore little makeup and her hair was brushed loose.

There would be no rhinestone barrette tonight, no hair spray, no display of legs. When her limbs were covered, there really wasn't much for a man to look at. Ginny suffered no delusions about her physical charms. If Stephen Marshall was a leg man, he would have to rip the slacks from her body to glimpse so much as a knee.

Golden Man, the catch of the western world, was as likely to do that, and she to let him, as the marble

Thomas Jefferson was to skip down the steps of his lofty memorial monument and take a dip in the Tidal Basin.

Her new/old buddy Edward Seale met her at the door. He was clad in his usual suit. The usual driver was waiting outside, wearing his chauffeur's uniform but without the cap. Instead of the limo, he sat behind the wheel of a cinnamon red Ford Taurus Sho. Nice wheels, she thought as Seale opened the back door.

"I was on the lookout for a pickup," she said as she slid inside across the leather seat. She liked the Taurus better than the limo. It had more human proportions, although it was almost as far from her world as the block-long Lincoln.

"The President wasn't able to find one on short notice," said Seale, holding the door. "I believe he's decided to have one of his own brought from the ranch in Oklahoma within the week."

When he got into the car beside her, she suddenly saw the evening as he must see it. She needed to set him straight.

"This isn't what you think it is," she said as the car wound its way through the crowded streets of Arlington, headed for the George Washington Parkway and the Theodore Roosevelt Bridge.

"I'm not thinking anything," he said, looking straight ahead.

He couldn't be much older than she, thirty-six, thirty-eight at the most. He was also a liar. As special assistant to the President, he had to be thinking something, and it couldn't be very nice.

"I'm having dinner with Steve—with the President and his aunt."

She got no response.

She stared at the bald spot on the crown of the driver's head. The driver must be thinking things, too.

"Do you do this often, Mr. Seale?"

He looked at her. "Do what?"

"Bring in women for your boss."

The driver coughed loudly. Seale's face turned red.

At least she was getting a reaction.

"That's like the old question, are you still beating your wife?" Seale said. "There's no way I can answer that yes or no. Besides, even if I could, I wouldn't."

She could see she had shaken him.

"Because of loyalty, I imagine."

"The President is an honorable man."

"So you don't bring in women often."

"Mrs. Baxter, I know you're not his woman, and I'm not bringing you in."

He was right on one count, the *his woman* part.

"The President doesn't have women—"

He stopped himself. He must realize how that sounded. He needn't have worried. If there was one thing Ginny knew about Stephen Marshall, it was that he was not interested in men.

No one spoke for the next few minutes, and Ginny figured conversation with the President's special adviser was pretty much dead. The resultant silence created a tension she couldn't endure, and she leaned forward as far as the seat restraint would allow her. Car talk had worked with the ambassador; it ought to work with a chauffeur.

"Does this have a V-8 engine?" she asked the driver.

He took a moment to answer. "Yes, miss, it does."

"I thought so. It rides smoothly."

"Thank you, miss." He spoke proudly, as if he had built the car himself.

"I noticed the spoiler on the rear. Does it help with the gas mileage? I've heard comments pro and con."

"I really wouldn't know, miss. We have a service that maintains the fleet of cars."

"Who?"

"I'm not at liberty to say." His voice had turned considerably cooler.

She sank back in the seat. "You could do worse than Sam's Auto Repair."

"I'm sure we could, miss."

He spoke with finality. So much for car talk. Maybe her version was interesting only to British aristocracy.

They were across the Potomac now, and Ginny experienced the same impulse she had felt before—to jump out the door and hike back home. In lieu of a purse, she'd tucked mad money in her pocket. She could hire a taxi if she had to.

She felt Seale's watchful eyes on her. "I guess

who takes care of the cars is pretty much classified information, isn't it?"

He nodded, and she could imagine this conversation being reported to another of her new/old buddies, William Alcorn, chief of White House security. This dinner was a bad idea. She was playing way out of her league.

No one spoke for the remainder of the ride. The Taurus wound around the White House, which was gloriously lit against the night sky, a sight to stir every American's heart. Hers would probably be stirred like anyone else's, if she could only get it to beat.

Her escort led her through a back door, into a West Wing hallway, to a waiting elevator, his hand firm on her arm, as if he thought she might bolt. Smart man. She saw several agents scattered about, a few in uniform, none she recognized.

Ginny hadn't completely forgotten her manners, even though she'd abandoned common sense.

"I wanted to thank you for your coaching Saturday night," she said as the elevator doors closed. "You helped me get through the evening, at least the first part."

She felt his accusing eyes on her and heard the unspoken question about why she had run.

"I didn't belong," she said. She felt butterflies in her stomach that had nothing to do with the fast-rising elevator. "And I don't now."

She barely whispered the latter, but he heard her.

"Don't underestimate yourself, Mrs. Baxter," he said.

She looked at him in surprise, but before she could ask him what he meant, the doors opened and he led her through another hallway with another agent guard, and at last into what could have been a living room on an Oklahoma ranch.

A very wealthy ranch. Seale stood back and let her look around. The brown leather eight-foot sofa backed up to a fan window that took up most of the far wall. A dark, carved double door occupied much of another, and scattered over the Indian wool rug were overstuffed chairs in prints and stripes, the color of sand with splashes of red and dark blue.

Distressed oak tables, cabinets, book shelves held pottery of all kinds—bowls, vases, mugs—as well as books: leatherbound, cloth, paperback.

On one cabinet a bronze sculpture of a cowboy on a bucking horse reminded her of the Frederic Remington she had seen in the ground floor corridor early in her East Wing tour. Above the sculpture hung an oil painting, a panoramic western scene of soaring mountains backed by thunderclouds on the horizon. At the base of the mountains a small stream cascaded over boulders and fallen dead trees.

What kind of man would live in such a room, so different from the grandeur of the West Wing? Everything here was expensive, certainly, but in a comfortable, lived-in sort of way, without in the least looking worn.

It would take a down-to-earth man to like these very American things, but not one who was necessarily uncomplicated. No, the man who could relax here and then go down to the Blue Room with its James Madison chairs and priceless art work for a reception with kings and queens was not simple in the least.

She moved closer to get a better look at the painting. Its grandeur took her breath away. There was something savage in it, too, the same agony and ecstasy that were etched on the face of Remington's high-riding cowboy.

"Thomas Moran's the painter," a familiar voice said. "Do you like it?"

Ginny's knees almost buckled beneath her. The evening had officially begun.

Light-headed, she nodded, not trusting herself to say anything. The most art talk she'd ever attempted had been over Jake's elementary school efforts at the PTA. What could she say? *I don't know art, but I know what I like.*

Definitely not. Around Stephen Marshall, silent beat stupid every day of the week.

"My father bought it after he made his first million. He liked to show off his money. There's another Moran downstairs, but this one's mine."

He sounded possessive, proud.

Ginny remembered the things Doris Tanner had said about Hobart Marshall. Black Bart, the self-made billionaire and absentee father, had left his son and heir more than just lonely memories. There

114

were some things money really could buy.

Sucking in her gut, Ginny turned to face her President. He'd come in through the dark carved double doors and closed them and she hadn't even heard. Despite his promise of an informal evening, the dominant image of him in her mind came from the last time she had seen him in person, a sophisticated man in a tuxedo and with a mocking glint in his eye.

The guy she saw in front of her wore jeans and an open-throated white shirt, black boots, and a black belt with a big silver buckle centered just above an abdomen so flat it was practically concave, drawing attention to his lean hips and long, long legs.

The man was in his late thirties, for crying out loud. He had no business being built that way.

His skin was leather-tan against the white shirt, the jeans tight, faded, discolored in the crotch. Not that she let herself study any particular part of him, especially his crotch, not for long. There were so many places to look. She wished he would turn around, like a runway model, so she could get a glimpse of them all.

In her loose-fitting trousers and boxy jacket, she felt like Frump of the Month.

He nodded to Seale, who backed out of the room, closing the door behind him. She wanted to follow him as fast as her sensible shoes would take her.

And then Steve gave her the full power of his attention. It was like being struck by gale-force winds, and she forgot the urge to leave.

"Hello, Ginny," he said. "It's good to see you."

"Hello, Steve. It's good to see you."

They sounded like an animated Barbie and Ken, both saying the nice, polite things that were expected of them.

He started toward her. He walked differently in jeans and boots, his gait rolling, sort of like John Wayne moving in on Maureen O'Hara.

"I'm afraid I have to disappoint you," he said.

Not in any way she could figure.

"My aunt's indisposed," he added.

"Who?"

"Aunt Doris."

The significance of what he had said hit her, and the magic of the moment was gone. Well, sort of. Nothing could take away from how he looked. But her reaction to him did a sharp about-face. John Wayne had always played honorable men, no matter how much his leading women provoked him. She wasn't sure about his Presidential counterpart.

But then, investigating his honor was exactly why she was here. That and the fact that he had asked her.

"What's wrong with her?" she asked. "I hope it's nothing serious."

"A chest cold. It came on suddenly."

Yeah, sure.

"Sorry I wasn't here when you arrived, but she's not a very good patient. I was making certain she got her chest rub."

Now that was an image Ginny didn't pursue.

"I don't think you believe me." He moved in close. "Take a whiff. I probably smell like Baume Ben Gay."

Lemony aftershave was probably closer to the truth. He halted not much more than a foot away and she took a whiff. He smelled musky, a scent that went with the clothes; lemony was more for black tie. She caught no hint of Baume Ben Gay.

"You smell fine." Dumb. He smelled great.

"So do you," he said.

She knew that she did; she'd used the last of a sample of Red she had picked up at a Cincinnati department store months ago, enough for a dab behind each ear and a touch between her breasts.

Not that anyone would be sniffing around down there, but the scent made her feel better in her frumpy clothes and utilitarian underwear.

"Aunt Doris said you could peek in on her if you like, although I have to warn you that there's a vaporizer pumping away. Her bed looks like it's in the steam room at the Washington Athletic Club."

"I believe you when you say she's ill. Why would you lie?"

"Why, indeed?"

He was much too close. Ginny backed up against the oak cabinet, wondering whether to grab the Remington bronze as a weapon, drop into her kick-boxing stance, or throw herself into his arms.

He gave her his killer smile and she saw the crinkles at the outer edges of his eyes and the depth of the blue irises, and the too-casual-for-who-he-was way his sand-colored hair fell across his forehead, almost meeting his thick, sand-colored brows.

With all that sand color, how could his lashes be so black, and so thick and long? Maybe she should have put some mascara on her stubs after all.

Easing around him, putting distance between them, she stared through the window onto the sparkling lights of the capital. He must have hit a switch somewhere because the lights in the room lowered to the power of a half dozen candles, giving her a better view. If she really concentrated, she could probably pick out a monument or two, but she felt him draw close and forgot the outside sights.

"It's a little warm in here," he said. "Would you like to take off your jacket?"

"I'm fine," she said, a little too fast.

In truth, she felt like the antique gas oven back at her apartment; regardless of where she set the gauge, it went from cold to five-hundred degrees with no stops in between. She had abandoned her cold setting the instant she heard his voice.

"I'm fine," she repeated for both of them.

"What about your blood pressure? That can be a hard thing to regulate."

"It's fine, too. No problems," she said, and then couldn't keep from adding, "No pills," as if he would be interested in her bladder problems.

"Good. Would you like a drink? Wine? A soda?"

"Nothing, thank you. I don't want to spoil my appetite."

"Neither do I."

She glanced at him over her shoulder. He was the picture of innocence, even in the semidark. That didn't mean she trusted him. Just because he hadn't jumped her the minute he walked into the room didn't mean he wasn't going to. It could be he had a fetish for frumps.

"Do you mind if I sit?"

Without waiting for an answer, she made her way to the sofa and sank into a mound of leather-wrapped down. She didn't know if she would ever be able to get up.

Much to her regret, he sat beside her, one leg bent and propped on the other, the way ordinary guys sat. His boots looked polished but worn, like ordinary boots, and his jeans looked . . . well, they looked the way they did in the magazines, only more . . . three dimensional was the cleanest way she could put it.

"Nice room," she said with a wave of her hand.

"It's home," he said modestly, as if his address wasn't 1600 Pennsylvania Avenue, Washington, D.C.

Steve Marshall was about as deceptively simple as the room and, more exactly, the Moran painting. For all his western-style grandeur, she suspected he was also capable of both savagery and ecstasy.

He leaned close, but not so close that he actually touched her, not so close that she could justifiably take offense. But he was close enough for her heart to go crazy and her breathing to cease, and her brain to die a sudden, inconvenient death.

Demure, she reminded herself. *Demure*. But she wasn't sure all her parts got the message.

"You've made it clear what you don't do on a first date," he said. "Would you mind telling me what it is you do?"

Chapter Six

Steve wasn't handling this very well. He was practically leering at the woman. What had happened to his legendary finesse?

Still, he wanted to hear her answer. What *did* she do on dates?

She looked at her hands, looked at the floor, looked at the door to the West Wing corridor—rather longingly, he thought—but she did not look at him.

Her lips were moving. He picked up something that sounded like *demure*. Or maybe *manure*, although he doubted it. She didn't look like a country girl who mucked out barns.

With a very noticeable sigh, she tucked her hair behind her ears and at last looked at him. What fine eyes she had, he was base enough to notice. The ears weren't bad, either.

"I don't have first dates," she said. "Or second. I don't date. Ever. All that talk on the phone was just that. Talk. You're the President. If you were to touch me right now, I'd probably faint."

Ginny was definitely not a politician. Once she started talking, she clearly if not immediately got to the point. And she held nothing back.

Would she be like that in bed?

Steve couldn't believe he'd thought such a thing, and about a fellow American.

But who was he supposed to ogle? A Byelorussian?

Not that he had anything against Byelorussians, the politician in him was quick to point out. He simply didn't see many of them day-to-day.

He tried smiling at her, but she wouldn't look his way, having obviously decided she'd seen about as much of him as she wanted. Steve felt a little like a cad. The poor woman looked as lost as she had when the Secret Service guns were pointed at her head.

Unless she was acting. Wasn't that what he wanted to find out?

He got up to pour her a glass of water from the crystal pitcher that was always kept chilled in case his presidential throat went dry. When he thrust it into her hand, she managed a weak "Thanks," and he settled back down beside her, an inch or two closer than he had been before.

He watched her drink, paying particular attention to the play of her throat as she swallowed. She had fine lips to go with the fine eyes and ears. She was either the most skillfully predatory female he had ever met or she was worse—a cute and sexy woman with the kind of wholesome appeal that could trap an Oklahoma boy.

"I'm not going to touch you," he said, not sure he spoke the truth.

She grimaced, as if embarrassed. Great; now he'd driven her from terror to humiliation. He should have asked for a script from Edward Seale.

"I didn't mean to imply I thought you were going to do anything like that," she said. "Good grief, look at me and then look at you."

Which was exactly what she did, from the corner of her eye and then straight on, as if to prove she could hold her own with the leader of her country. Just once he wished she would look at him as if he were nothing but a man.

"It's just that we are here alone," she said, "and I keep remembering all those stories I've heard about Presidents. Not that I keep up with politics much, but these aren't the usual White House news stories, if you know what I mean—"

She slammed on the verbal brakes and looked away from him, her eyes trained on the door. Studying her profile, the slant of her neck, the slope of her shoulders, Steve credited her with understanding the situation quicker than he. She was right to plan her escape. For all his goody-goody image, he wanted to jump her bones.

He hadn't used the phrase since undergraduate days, mainly because he hadn't felt this way since then. Once he'd taken the path of public works, his energies had been poured into his duties, like negotiating Arab-Israeli peace treaties and balancing the federal budget.

Not that he hadn't shared an occasional bed with a woman—his intemperate zone wasn't completely dead—but that had been before he decided to run for President. For two years he really had been a monk.

But he'd been feeling frisky since she walked into the ambassador's reception flashing legs that could make the male animal do some very foolish things.

Steve wasn't in a position to act foolishly. Thinking foolishly was bad enough.

Ginny Baxter wasn't a beauty, but she was pretty in a wholesome, all-American way, with her wide brown eyes and straight brown hair and lips as expressive as her eyes. Right now she was biting the lower one as if she wanted to recall her last words.

Yep, she was cute and sexy, a woman to take on a picnic and, later, on a long, not-so-leisurely walk in the woods.

If he was going to carp, it would be about the layers of clothing she had wrapped about herself. He wanted to rip the brown armor off her delectable body and do unspeakable things. If he followed through on his urges, it was hard to predict who would be the more surprised, her or him. He hadn't been an Oklahoma boy for a long, long time.

Ford had been right: He needed a woman, although not in the way his chief of staff had meant.

No, he wasn't handling this well at all. He wasn't

supposed to get involved. He was the President, for crying out loud. Above all else, he was honorable.

Tell that to his libido.

Maybe he ought to let Ginny know Seale was on call not far outside the room, in case either one of them needed help. He could also tell her that Ford Davidson had insisted on installing a small video camera, just in case she cried sexual harassment later.

Steve was the only one who was to view the tape, unless it became necessary for others to do so, but its existence made him feel like something he'd shoveled out of the barn Sunday morning.

"Let's eat," he said. "TV trays okay?"

She glanced at him in surprise.

"Plain TV trays," he said. "Nothing early American that James Madison ordered from France. Definitely no antiques."

"Antiques?" Her lips twitched with the hint of a smile. "I don't think they've been around long enough."

Steve was definitely ready to jump. Other outdated phrases came to mind. *Cop a feel. Getting to home base.*

Good God.

At her nod, he picked up the phone on the table in front of them, gave the necessary orders, then moved to one of the chairs, distancing himself not only for her peace of mind but for his. After a day of playing host to a pack—or was it a den—of Girl Scouts, meeting with Patton Cartright and his military brass from the Pentagon, then going over the latest in HMOs with the secretary of Health and Human Services, and in between it all handling a barrage of phone calls and acceping a dozen lengthy reports, he was ready to unwind.

When he looked back at her, he caught an old-fashioned blush on her cheeks. She looked down fast, as if he'd caught her at something.

"What's wrong?" he asked, never one to be shy.

"Nothing." She let out a long, slow breath. "Nothing that I can find."

He got the distinct impression she had been looking him over, just as he had been studying her. But of course he'd been looking at her surface. Shame on him. He was supposed to be trying to figure out the kind of person she really was.

He'd almost forgotten. Say good-bye to thoughts of jumping bones and copping feels and running bases. Now was no time to unwind. The day's tasks were not yet done.

"Tell me about yourself," he said.

"You already know everything. It's in the report."

"So tell me something that isn't. About your father, for instance. I know he was a civil engineer who died when you were twelve. But that doesn't tell me very much."

She thought for a moment. He liked the way the skin wrinkled between her brows when she concentrated.

"Charlie Ferguson wanted a son and he got me. Is that the kind of thing you mean?"

"It doesn't have to be negative. Besides, how could he not want you?"

She looked at him suspiciously, as if she should maybe read something into his words. He parried her suspicion with his western cherub smile.

She crossed one leg over the other and he got a glimpse of ankle. Wow.

"My father loved me. A great deal, considering I was a girl. He taught me all about cars. By the time I was ten I could hotwire any make and model that came out of Detroit."

Steve laughed, genuinely, without an ulterior motive in mind. "I don't think I've ever dated a woman who could hotwire a car."

"This isn't a date. It's an apology dinner."

He snapped his fingers. "I forgot. So tell me something else I don't know."

She looked reluctant to proceed.

"I'm not trying to pry, Ginny," he lied. "And I don't know all that much about your background." Here he spoke the truth. "If the FBI was giving you a high security clearance, I'd know pretty much everything."

"But I'm low security."

"Medium."

"Good. I wouldn't want to be too low."

She had a sense of humor. Double wow.

She stroked her cheek with nails that were short and round and coated with clear polish. Nice.

"I'll tell you some more if you do the same for me," she said. "Fair's fair."

"My past is an open book," he said, retreating to his politician's spiel. "I was born in Bottle, Oklahoma, to a ranching family. My mother died when I was eight, my father during my first term as congressman."

There was a great deal more he could say, and from the look in her eye she must know it, but he wasn't inclined to reveal details he wouldn't discuss even with his aunt.

"That's it?" she asked.

"That's it. You don't really want to hear about the days at Yale, do you? Or my record as a congressman. I served two terms before running for President, but that's all a matter of public record."

"What about your horse?"

"Oh, yes, I ride. I also shovel manure. It prepares me for dealing with the press."

She fidgeted with the buttons on her jacket and almost smiled. He wondered how a full-blown grin would change her face. Nicely, he decided. Very nicely.

She looked from her lap to the door to him, and her chin tilted upwards a bit. "Okay, here's something else personal about me. I can also repair toilets. I'll bet that's a new one for you, too."

"It's a topic that hasn't come up before."

He tried to picture Roni Gray playing with the plumbing, but the image wouldn't form.

The little grin that had been on Ginny's face disappeared. "I had to learn a lot of things after my father died. My mother should have been born to wealth. But she wasn't. She just lived like it."

"Went through the money, did she?"

"Like a rat through cheese." She frowned. "That's unfair. She spent the money on me as well as herself. I was saving for college and she was buying me tons of clothes and cute little Sony TVs and a bunch of stuff I really didn't need."

"So you didn't go to college."

She shook her head. "I had thought about being a teacher. Maybe someday opening my own school. I guess some things are just not meant to be."

He heard no bitterness in her voice; she was simply reporting the facts. Steve liked that about her. Too, he liked her sense of humor and the way she was nervous and nervy at the same time. If he weren't who he was, he'd be out of the chair and putting the make on her.

Putting the make on her? Good God. That had been antiquated in '73. He needed to look up *seduce* in a thesaurus with a current copyright date.

What was going on here? He'd devoted his life to public service. Okay, so the analyst he'd gone to once years ago told him it was a backlash against Black Bart and his wheeler-dealer, me-first ways. That didn't make his dedication any less sincere.

Or less constant. He'd chosen a public life instead of a private one, the ordinary private kind that involved personal relationships. Not once had he questioned his choice.

But now here was Ginny Baxter. She was definitely more dangerous than she appeared. She had him horny, another term he wasn't sure was still used; talk around the White House focused more on public policy and impending legislation than the methods of landing babes.

A knock at the door signaled the arrival of the food. The butler moved silently into the room, set a tray on the coffee table, then took a pair of folding oak tables from behind one of the cabinets and set them up in front of Ginny and Steve. A doily went on each small table, then a plate of food from the tray. Cloth napkins, ornate silverware, and crystal wineglasses joined the plates. He excused himself, returning shortly with a silver wine bucket, from which he served each of them.

All of it was accomplished without a sound.

"Thanks, Daniel," Steve said. "I'll take over from here."

Was that a pinched look of disapproval on his very proper butler's face? Probably. Daniel had been here since the beginning of his administration, but it would take more than two years of serving a master wearing jeans and boots to chip away his formality.

Over the protests of Florence the cook, Aunt Doris had selected the food: quail and wild rice and strips of steamed vegetables carefully arranged on the perimeter of the plate to give a sunburst effect. Fruit compotes awaited on the tray as the final course. There wasn't a french fry or a baby back rib in sight.

"I hope this is all right," Steve said. "I asked for

barbecue, but it's in pretty short supply around these parts."

Ginny eyed the quail with open suspicion. "It's fine," she said and proceeded to fork the fallen bird around on her plate, pretty much decimating the sunburst.

An uneasy silence descended.

"You were telling me about yourself," Steve prompted.

Wrinkles formed between her brows, and it was a full minute before she spoke.

"I guess the report said I'm divorced."

"That's all it said, just divorced."

"My husband ran around on me. I don't have a high opinion of men."

"That's honest of you."

"The only thing he gave me besides a hard time and debts was my son."

"And, of course, your low opinion of men."

"There is that." She took a bite of red pepper and washed it down with a sip of wine. "Your turn. You've never been married, have you? Are you planning on it?"

"Not in the near future."

"What about Veronica Gray?"

She asked the question innocently enough, but he noticed that she was waiting very quietly for his response. She reminded him of Morley Safer on "Sixty Minutes." Steve had answered a similar question on national television; he was ready now.

"She's the daughter of a man I admire very much.

131

As chairman of the Senate Budget Committee, Senator Gray and I cross paths often. Roni and I have naturally developed a friendship, but nothing more."

"She's got a great body."

Now there was something Morley hadn't said.

"I believe she does."

Understatement. The woman was built like Miss Universe. She also had the will and nerve of Richard Petty, except that her goal wasn't to win a NASCAR race. She wanted to get little Stevie in her bed.

He veered fast from the subject. "Tell me about your son."

For a moment the watchful expression in Ginny's eyes gave way to softness. But then the watchfulness was back, sharper than ever. It would appear he'd discovered her private line of demarcation; her one and only child was off bounds.

"Why do you want to know? What was in the report?"

"Nothing except that he plays baseball. And that he's considered pretty much a loner and a rebel."

"He's a good boy."

"I'm sure he is."

"He cleans the apartment. I'm pretty much a slob."

"He's a rebel for sure."

"And I don't cook very well, but he never complains."

"He sounds like a saint."

"And I don't sound like a very good mother."

"I'll bet you always went to his games."

"I still do. When I don't have to work."

"Is he any good?"

"Better than you could ever imagine. Better than Roger Clemens. He'll make it to the majors some day."

She was speaking with passion as well as pride. He liked that in her. There was nothing much about her that he didn't like, and he was a pretty good judge of character. This woman was no predator. This woman was for real.

"Your son's a pitcher, is he?"

"His fast ball has already been clocked at over eighty miles an hour. And he's only sixteen."

"You must have been a child bride."

"You know I wasn't. I was eighteen." She hesitated. "Why the smile on your face?"

"I was picturing you at eighteen, young and very much in love."

"I was in heat." She pressed her fingers against her lips. "There I go again with the big mouth."

"Don't worry about it. Most eighteen-year-olds are in heat."

"Yes, but they don't discuss it with their President."

She dropped her fork, set the table away from her, and stood.

"Look, I don't mean to rush or anything, but it's getting late and I've got to get up early and I guess so do you, so if you'll tell me how to get to the nearest Metro station, I can get myself home safely enough."

She headed for the door. Halfway across the room he stopped her with a hand on her wrist. She looked down at his hold, and he let go.

"Was it something I said?" he asked. "No, it was the quail. I told Aunt Doris you wouldn't like it."

"I didn't know what it was." She shrugged. "Look, you eat quail and I eat macaroni and cheese. And not even real cheese. I use the cheap kind out of a tube."

"Right now that sounds pretty good."

"It's awful. I always overcook pasta. You'd think one night I would get it right."

She looked sweet and vulnerable, as worried over her macaroni as he was over day-care legislation; but then, overcooked pasta was what she dealt with while he dealt with laws. Suddenly he had a revelation, the way he sometimes did when negotiations had come up against a brick wall.

"That phone call, the first one, the one you brushed off as just talk. You didn't think it was me, did you?"

"Do you always change topics so fast?"

"Ah, there is some politician in you. Answering a question with a question is an old ploy. What was all that talk about doing the nasty? And the married boyfriends. You thought someone was imitating me and you were turning the joke back on them."

She blushed. It was something she did very nicely.

"Yeah, well, you see how that worked out."

Silently he cursed his stupidity for not realizing the truth right away. While he was cursing, she was edging backwards toward the door.

"Did it work out good or bad?" he asked, going after her.

She lowered her eyes. He could swear she was looking somewhere in the neighborhood between his belt buckle and knees. If she kept looking, she would see some activity going on.

At what point had she realized that it really had been her President and would-be date on the phone? The reception, of course, when he'd been such a boor. No wonder she had left. He knew a few generals who would have run faster than she.

"I'd like to kiss you," he said. "I'd like it very much."

That got her wide-eyed and staring up at him. "Why?"

"Because that's what I do on a first date. And believe me, Ginny, this is a date."

"That's crazy. I'm a nobody."

"Don't be too humble. I like the smart mouth in you. Nobody else dares. This is in some ways a very lonely job."

He wasn't just throwing a line at her. She didn't know it, but he was telling her something he'd never told anybody else.

"You really want a kiss?"

"More than you can know. But only if you give it willingly."

She lowered her eyes to his throat and his chest and maybe lower still, but she was so fast he wasn't sure. When she looked back up, her expression had warmed a dozen degrees.

"Oh, it would be willing enough. You wouldn't have to worry about that." She sighed. "I guess you're afraid of some kind of lawsuit."

"My advisers said I should be."

"You talked about me with them?"

"It's impossible to keep secrets in this place."

"They'll know about the kiss."

He thought about the video camera. "I'm not going to tell them."

She looked at him for a long while. "It's hard to be human around here, isn't it?" she asked.

His jeans were getting downright uncomfortable. She had no idea how appropriate the word *hard* was.

"With you, Ginny, it's impossible not to be," he said and meant it.

She put her hands on his arms, then lifted them fast, as if she had violated some kind of law.

"It's okay," he said, and her hands went back to his sleeves in a gesture that was both innocent and sexy as hell.

He slipped his hands inside her jacket to hold her by the waist and pull her close. She was slender yet reassuringly solid and warm.

"I'm a public man, Mrs. Baxter, and you're a woman who's been investigated by the FBI. There's not much mystery about us, is there?" He concentrated on her lips. "Except how you'd taste."

A man out of practice, he started slow, a brushing of his mouth against hers. She inspired him to do it again, and again, each touch a little firmer, a little longer, a little sweeter. She didn't flinch or try to pull away, no more than she tried to rush things by throwing her arms around him.

He wouldn't have minded her rushing a little bit.

He slid his hands around her waist to her back, exploring as he went, feeling the hooks of her bra beneath her blouse, and he wondered if they would ever get to the stage where he was fumbling with the cursed thing.

Hearing her sigh, he forgot where things might lead, concentrating instead on the present. He pulled her tight against him. Her hands stroked against his shirt and found their way to the back of his neck to a section of skin that had always been particularly sensitive.

It was the way to make him forget who and where he was. He covered her mouth with his and gave her an old-fashioned French kiss, and she responded as if it was the most natural thing in the world for the two of them to be doing, which it was.

He tasted the wine on her tongue and maybe a little of the pepper, but mostly she was darkly wet and sweet, sucking at his tongue as if she had no intention of letting him get away any time soon. He managed to do some sucking of his own while he was thinking of a number of places they could put this sucking to good effect.

His hands moved lower, down to her waist, and then lower still until he was cupping her round little mounds and holding her tight against his over-taxed jeans, bringing some muscles into play as he ground himself against her, truly forgetting everything but the sensations that were shooting through him. He wanted to drag her down to the rug and ride her until the cows came home.

He didn't know which one of them came back to sanity first, but without his knowing quite how it happened they were breaking the kiss and he was easing his hands back to her waist, putting some space between their hips, and finally stepping back to look down into her eyes.

Except that her eyes were downcast. When he whispered, "Ginny," she kept them down. He wasn't so far gone that he couldn't give her a minute to get composed. He estimated it would take him an hour or so.

In a world that was filled with disappointments and frustrations, she was no disappointment in the least.

But the frustrations she visited upon him were more painful that she could ever guess.

Steve hadn't gotten where he was without being headstrong and persuasive.

"Look at me, Ginny."

She did. Her lips were swollen and her eyes round and she had a just-out-of-bed look even though all they had done was kiss.

"Are you all right?" he asked.

138

She nodded, and then she shook her head.

"So which is it?"

She shrugged. He could see that she was puzzled and heated and frustrated, too. She did body language very well.

Backing up, she managed to open the door, and there was Edward Seale waiting in the corridor. The man had an uncanny knack for knowing when he would be needed. Right now he was irritating the hell out of his President.

The two men looked at one another, and it was Steve's turn to shrug. Let Eddie interpret that anyway he wanted. Ginny set out at an escape pace. The last glimpse he caught was of her godawful jacket and flying hair as she rounded the distant corner of the corridor. Seale had to bound after her to catch up.

And that left Steve to close the door and retreat to the window overlooking the capital. In all of Washington, he thought his was the best view. He stood there for a long time, letting his mind take over his body while he thought about what he was going to do with Ginny. In this case the only adviser he could call on was himself.

At first he thought of several scenarios that weren't in the least presidential, some even more detailed than the ones that had come to mind when she was still with him and they were playing dancing tongues. She'd looked pretty cute in handcuffs. He wondered if he could get her to wear them again.

And then he came to his senses. She was a nice woman, a single mother, a voter, for God's sake, and he had run for office on the honor ticket. The only reason he'd been a candidate in the first place was that his party's first choice, a sixty-year-old former governor from Idaho, a long-time husband and grandfather of three, had been caught in a scandal involving a bevy of politico groupies who were following him on the campaign trail.

The second-term bachelor congressman from Oklahoma had been a quick and, as it turned out, popular second choice. But voters could turn on a President fast. Look at what had happened to George Bush.

It took a long time before he reached a conclusion. Ginny had had him going there for a while. She had made him lose his composure at the ambassador's reception and now tonight. She offered some tempting challenges, the main one being not to act on all those outdated clichés he came up with every time he looked at her.

Steve was not a man to run from challenges. After much cogitation, he decided on the compartment of his life into which she would best fit, offering as she did an opportunity for him to be human and presidential at the same time.

His was the perfect plan, one that would benefit everyone concerned. And maybe it would make him feel not quite so lonely.

When he laid it before Ford Davidson, he knew that his chief of staff would agree.

Aunt Doris would be a harder sell. He would wait until she was on the road to recovery but not yet completely well before he approached her. That way she wouldn't argue more than an hour or two.

And what about Ginny Baxter?

He wasn't Black Bart's son and leader of the most powerful country on earth for nothing. Sooner or later she would definitely come around.

Chapter Seven

On the ride back to Ballston, the interior of the Taurus was silent as a hearse. Ginny had no idea what was going through the minds of the two men with her, but she didn't care, not with the humiliation she felt.

She'd practically thrown herself at the President. Being a man, he had naturally reached out for what she had thrown. Some love machine she was turning into. She was gunning her motor too fast.

She shouldn't have told him about Jonas and how he'd taught her to hate men, as if she were challenging him to make her think differently. She didn't hate men. She just didn't trust them. And asking about Veronica Gray. Dumb. Plus that crack about her having a great body, as if she was jealous or something. Double dumb.

She'd practically begged him to kiss her. Being a healthy male, he had complied, making it seem as if the idea were his. The President, her Golden

Man! She wasn't so lost in self-flagellation she couldn't remember the details of the kiss. And enjoy the memory. The most powerful man in the world certainly knew how to use his lips and tongue. She had no idea how many other women had already found that out. As far as she was concerned, it was a secret she would take to her grave.

Anyway, no one would believe she had come by her knowledge firsthand.

She could still taste him. He'd tasted musky, just the way he had smelled, and he'd felt solid and warm . . . no, make that hot, about as hot as she had been feeling. His hands had done a bit more roaming than they should have, but she had encouraged him, throwing herself against him the way she had.

If he had kept it up, there was no telling where the kiss would have led. Probably right down to the Indian rug on the floor. And in the White House of all places! She would never make a patriot, not in a hundred years.

When they parted, she hadn't slapped his face, either, the way she would have any other man, or told him never to do anything like that again. But then, with any other man, she wouldn't have been opening her mouth wider than she did for the dentist and trying to swallow his tongue.

If she had said anything at all, it would have been to beg for another kiss.

Oh yes, her motor was definitely racing too fast, and not just because he looked and felt and tasted the way he did, but worse, because she really liked him. She not only felt the loneliness of his position, but in her own very ordinary way she shared it.

The timing on her idler arm better be reset right away or else she would be burning out.

When the presidential car rolled up beside Professor Carl's house, she was out the door before it came to a complete stop. Without looking back, she dashed down the driveway, drawn by the comforting sight of lamplight spilling through the screen door of her apartment.

Stephen Marshall could have the White House; her home, small though it was, looked like a castle to her tonight. The thought occurred to her that he didn't own his place of residence anymore than she owned hers. That didn't exactly put them on an equal footing, but it was something.

At least she didn't have to have guards outside her door.

Along with the light, familiar sounds were also spilling into the night. Jake was watching a baseball game on TV, probably a late broadcast from the West Coast. Standing outside, she thought over what she would tell him about how things had gone. Their almost-argument came back. He hadn't wanted her to go, but she didn't think it would help her cause to admit he'd been right.

She would talk about the terrible dinner and the magnificent painting on the wall. He would appreciate the contrast of the bad with the good. She could even mention how she'd remembered his elementary school drawings. He ought to like that.

The door opened without a squeak. He had told her he would pick up some WD-40. He must have done so.

Jake was slumped on the sofa, his long legs stretched out in front of him, the remote control held carelessly in his hand. He was wearing jeans and a plain white T-shirt with the sleeves cut out, and on his extra-large feet was a pair of ratty sneakers. Except for baseball shirts, he never wore clothing that said anything, which she appreciated, since she'd seen some shockingly obscene phrases on kids younger than he.

Neither did he shave his head nor wear his light-brown hair longer than collar-length. Straight down the middle, that was Jake, never calling attention to himself. Never reaching out to touch anything because there was little in which he believed.

Except his mom. He didn't always think she was right, but then, she felt the same about him.

His face was long and lean, just beginning to settle into the strong, straight features he would bear all his life. She tended to think of him as too thin, but she could see the muscles that had formed in his biceps from all that pitching. He'd started to shave, too, three times a week.

And there was the Adam's apple, so prominent in his long neck it looked like he'd swallowed a real piece of fruit.

Her baby was growing up—he'd be seventeen soon—but that didn't mean he would abandon her the way so many children did. They were too close, too dependent on one another.

What a wonderful, loving, thoughtful son she had. What a comfort to a single mom. He was her life. Okay, so she got lonely every now and then, but with him around she would never be alone. So what if they'd had a mild disagreement about tonight? Neither of them bore hard feelings for long.

He glanced up at her, then directed his attention back to the game.

"Did he get in your pants?"

Ginny wasn't certain she had heard right. She glanced at the flickering light across the room to see if maybe the words hadn't come from the television set. It could have been one of those safe-sex public service announcements aimed at teens. Nope, the screen was showing one of those slow times during a game when a new pitcher was warming up and the announcer was rambling on about the stats on the relief man.

At least she thought such times were slow. Jake found them as fascinating as everything else about the game.

Just then he muted the sound. Whatever she'd heard had to have come from him.

She circled around until she could look straight at her son. He didn't blink or look up. He didn't appear to even be breathing.

"Did you say something?" she asked.

Jake's brown eyes flicked up at her. "Did he get into your pants?"

Not *hello, how are you?* not a smile, not a wave. Instead, he came at her with hurt and anger, as if she had betrayed him in some way. She fell back into one of the dining table chairs. She had never seen him like this. He tended to rant sometimes when he watched the news or "Dateline Tuesday" or whatever night it was, but he had never in his life directed his scorn at her.

"I can't believe you asked that."

His lips flattened. "He did."

Jake sounded as if he took satisfaction in having his suspicion confirmed.

"He did not," she said, giving him back the same anger he was throwing at her. She sounded a little more defensive than she would have preferred, but he had taken her by surprise.

"I'll bet he tried."

Ginny remembered a pair of broad, strong hands on her rear. Technically Steve hadn't actually tried to get inside her slacks, but he'd let his fingers find out what they could about how she was built.

"The son of a bitch," Jake muttered. The words slipped out far too naturally for a youth who never used obscenities, at least not around his mom.

Ginny took a deep breath, determined not to show shock, and tried to understand what was going on here. She had a son who thought she was a terrible judge of men—which she was—and who thought anyone in government was a self-serving crook.

In Jake's eyes, Steve would have two strikes

against him . . . no, make that three, because of the high office he held. And maybe because of the way he looked and his appeal to women. Four strikes. He was way past being out.

"Mr. Marshall invited me for dinner, that's all," she said, trying to be reasonable, trying to sound calm, an impossible task since the ground was slipping out from under her.

"His aunt was supposed to be there. Was she?"

Ginny shifted nervously in her chair. "She caught a cold."

Jake looked pleased at the news.

"She did. Steve said she rubbed her chest with Baume Ben Gay. He said I could visit her if I wanted."

"Did you?"

"Well, no, she was in her sickbed and—"

"That's what I thought. He knew you wouldn't. What did you have to eat?"

He threw the question at her the way he delivered his fast ball, not letting up so she could catch her breath.

"Some kind of, I don't know, a little dried-up bird. He told me what it was but I forgot."

"Did you taste it?"

She sat up straight and got back some of her nerve. How dare he reverse the parent-child relationship on her?

"Look, I don't see how that's any of your business," she said, trying to summon some motherly dignity.

"You didn't taste it, did you? I'll bet you didn't take a bite."

She was beginning to wonder whether he had inside information. No, he was just suspicious about everything. When someone was cynical all the time, he had to be right now and then. That was it. He wasn't questioning her. He simply didn't like her going out in a world he refused to recognize.

She forgot to be mad. "Jake, I'm all right." She reached out to touch his arm. "Really."

He jerked away. "Yeah, sure."

He clicked off the television set before the game was over. It was something he never did.

"What makes you think I'm not?"

"You didn't see the way you looked when you walked in."

He threw the words at her as if she had harmed him in some way. She smoothed back her hair and touched her mouth. He caught every movement. She might as well have told him she'd been kissed.

Jake tossed the remote on the table beside the sofa.

"Look," he said, "if he gets fresh with you, I can't throw him out the way I did that other guy. The FBI would shoot me down."

"The Secret Service," she said. "They're the ones—"

Trying as hard as she could to be calm, she couldn't go on.

"Whoever," Jake said. He stood. "I'm going to bed."

"When are your tryouts?" she called after him, but he was gone before she got out all the words, his door shutting firmly behind him.

"Come back here this instant," she shouted through the closed door. "Show your mother some respect."

She'd never done anything like that before, yelling at him and then demanding something that had always been there.

Hugging herself, she tried to make sense of what had just taken place. This couldn't be happening, so many things falling one on top of the other, first Steve and now . . .

Shaking, she fell back on the sofa. The only time she could remember that Jake had been truly upset with her was when she told him they were leaving Cincinnati before the opening of the Reds' season. It was traditional for the first home game of the new year to be held at Riverfront Stadium. The two of them always played hooky from work and school and went to see it.

But she'd found a job and an apartment in the Washington area much faster than expected, she'd gotten a great deal on the Chevy, and she'd felt compelled to sell out and move on. For his sake she had done it; everything was for him.

She'd held great hope that getting away from where he'd been unhappy would bring some changes in his life, soften him and make him strong at the same time. Surely, she'd thought, being surrounded by the evidences of American history would help him understand what his country was all about.

Jake hadn't seen it that way, and they'd had some long discussions over the move. Compared to tonight, those had been mild disagreements. Tonight a real gulf had opened between them, and she had to understand it. Jake was everything to her.

And she was everything to him. She knew it. That knowledge was the source of her strength. He was afraid she was getting into something she couldn't handle. Worse, neither could he. Since Jonas had walked out on them, her son had felt as responsible for her as she had for him, at no time more strongly than he did tonight.

That was it. He was overly concerned.

As much as she wanted to strangle him, she loved him more now than she ever had. But he had to see she could take care of herself. His life was his to live without worrying about taking care of her.

She could handle her life without being a burden to him. Maybe, just maybe, she and her son were too close. It was a thought that she would never have considered a week ago.

And then she thought of Steve Marshall and the way he had kissed her and held her, and the way he had looked at her when he'd pulled away, wanting to keep going and knowing he shouldn't, letting her know that if she gave him the least encouragement, he would forget all about who and where they were and get back to the kissing.

She'd wanted to throw herself right back into his

arms, not caring whether or not they fell to the floor, hoping more than fearing some hot and heavy things would take place once they got there.

Somehow she'd refrained. It must have been some kind of miracle, that or a strong dose of cowardice.

Handle her life?

She could, just maybe, after she had made peace once again with Jake and, more importantly, if the President of the United States never called her again.

She looked toward the bedroom, then turned toward the outside door and thought about the streets and bridges and freeways that separated her from Stephen Marshall. For a few weeks she'd been happy in this little apartment; at least she'd believed she was. The worst thing Steve had brought her was not a breach with her son. That breach was temporary. She could believe nothing else.

No, the worst thing was a terrible new feeling of discontent, a sense that her life was sadly lacking something she could never get from Jake.

"You want to do what?"

Ford never shouted. He was shouting now.

Steve smiled benignly over his Oval Office desk at his chief of staff, who had pulled himself to his full five-foot-two as he glared at the leader of the free world.

"It's not simply what I want. It's what I'm going to do."

Ford was not mollified. "Look what happened at the State Department."

"I overreached. I won't make that mistake again. She'll have to be brought along slowly to attending occasions like that."

"So what good is she if you have to keep her a secret?"

"I'll take her out in public." Steve was beginning to get irritated. "Without a bag over her head."

"How about her legs?"

"You seem more interested in her legs than anything else about her. Is there a problem with you I don't know about?"

It was an unkind shot, but Steve wasn't feeling particularly warm toward his old friend. On this early morning after the night with Ginny, he was not asking his chief adviser for advice. He was telling him the way things were going to be.

"I don't think I'm the problem," Ford said stiffly.

"And neither is she. Look, you're the one who wanted me to settle on one woman as a companion. So I have. Seale probably told you she left here a little upset last night." Ford nodded, and Steve couldn't keep himself from asking, "Did he tell you anything else?"

"What else was there to tell? She's usually a chatterbox, but something shut her up. She didn't say a word the whole ride home. And she jumped out of the car as if it were about to explode."

Steve appreciated what he heard. Ginny was a woman he could like.

"It was a natural reaction. I kissed her."

"You *what?*"

"It's what happens between men and women. It was a simple kiss," he lied. But there had been nothing simple about it; he'd given her his best. "We both enjoyed it and then we stopped. She must have gotten to thinking about who she was kissing—not me, but the office I hold—and gotten nervous."

Ford eyed him suspiciously. "Maybe I ought to look at the videotape. With your lawyers."

"I did a Nixon on it."

"You destroyed it?"

What he'd done was pack it away in his personal belongings. For what purpose he didn't know, but the action was something else he would keep to himself.

He shrugged. "There's nothing on it that anyone needs to see. Besides, I was more affected by the kiss than she was. But not so much I can't keep from doing it again."

At least, he could give it that old Yale try.

He put his considerable persuasive powers to work, explaining how he would escort Ginny Baxter to a few public events, have dinner with her, let the public see she was an ordinary woman, a fine, hard-working single mother who represented the best of American womanhood. He could get insights from her. He would look like a great guy.

And he might find himself able to relax away from his work, get some perspective, maybe once or twice get another kiss. Definitely nothing more, nothing like jumping her bones. But he didn't tell all of this to his chief of staff.

"Do you know that twenty-eight point three percent of working mothers are single?" he asked. "And the number is rising. She'll be representing almost a third of half of working America."

He had no idea whether the statistics were anywhere close to accurate, but Ford loved statistics. Steve used them whenever he could.

It took a little more talking, but Ford usually realized when he was defeated. He did so today, promising to talk to Edward Seale and the press secretary, Alan Skinner, preparing them for what Steve planned.

In the afternoon, after attending conferences with the directors of the Office of Management and Budget and the National Economic Council, and after listening to a report from Vice President Richard Posey on the state funeral he'd attended in Peru, Steve tackled the main challenge of the day: Aunt Doris.

She had shown a remarkable recovery from her cold, swearing it was the chest rub and the vaporizer that had done the trick.

Steve needed her approval as much as her cooperation. He wanted to send Ginny flowers. He'd seen the movie *The American President*, and while he thought it was amusing, he didn't want to go through the problems suffered by the fictitious President when he'd wanted to send a bouquet to a woman. But Michael Douglas had been operating under a handicap: The writers hadn't given him an aunt.

Doris was in the small sitting room next to her bedroom, wrapped in a pink flannel gown and robe and fluffy pink slippers and eyeing him like a . . . well, like a maiden aunt who suspected her nephew was up to no good.

"I thought you would never get around to reporting," she gruffed. "How did things go last night?"

"Fine. Except for the quail."

"You can't eat barbecue all the time."

He hadn't tasted barbecue since a trip to the ranch two months ago, but he didn't think antagonizing her with facts was the best approach now. One of the mysteries of the office was how Lyndon Johnson had gotten away to Texas and Richard Nixon to California so often, when he could rarely get out to the stable for a ride.

The BB Ranch in Bottle, Oklahoma, might as well have been on the moon for all he was able to enjoy it. All his finances had been put in a blind trust, but the land was still there for him to ride.

"Did she behave?" Aunt Doris asked. "Did you?"

"Tsk, tsk, Aunt Doris. What a dirty mind you have."

"That's not an answer."

He gave her his boyish smile. "Yes to both. Except for the time we were grappling around on the floor tearing each other's clothes off, of course, but otherwise, she was a lady and I was the perfect gentleman."

"Humph."

Steve wondered what he would have told her if they really had done a little grappling. And then he wondered what the grappling would have been like, and he enjoyed some decidedly inappropriate images, considering where he was and whom he was with.

"I need a favor," he said. "Could you order some flowers for me and have them sent to her?"

"What would you like? Hothouse roses? Should the card read *Thanks for last night*?"

Aunt Doris could have a smart mouth on her. If she and Ginny ever really got to know one another, it would be either instant affection or abiding dislike.

"You pick the flowers. I don't know anything about them. That's why I'm asking for your help. And sign the card *Steve*."

"You figure she'll know which Steve they're from?"

"More than likely."

"I guess this will put an end to this fascination you have with the woman."

"It won't end the association."

Taking a deep breath, he told her the truth. And told her and told her, explaining that he planned to escort Ginny to a few simple affairs, maybe take her to dinner, enhancing his ordinary-guy image, squelching the womanizer talk. He saw little need to explain that he wouldn't feel so lonely with Ginny around every now and then. How could he feel lonely when he was seldom alone?

Aunt Doris was not impressed. He finally had to break off the peace talks; he had a state dinner that evening for a trio of visiting governors from the west who were in Washington to discuss environmental concerns. But he and Aunt Doris went at it again as soon as he returned.

The next morning he climbed aboard Air Force One for a flight to Chicago and a speech before the National Education Association. The teachers could be as feisty a group as he'd ever faced, sometimes more prickly than the British and French combined when it came to discussing specific government policies.

Still, coward that he was, he was glad for the early morning escape. Before they said good night, Aunt Doris had finally agreed that his association with Ginny wasn't necessarily a bad thing, but he wasn't certain she hadn't come up with more questions overnight.

Steve was in a deep sleep in his Chicago hotel room when the telephone rang. Instantly awake, he ran a list of possible emergencies through his mind. His speech had gone well; he'd gotten through even the question-and-answer session without being bombarded with stones. The call had to have more serious implications.

He fumbled for the phone and barked, "What's up?"

"Sorry to disturb you, Mr. President, but we've got a problem out here in the hall and we thought you should know."

He recognized the voice of William Alcorn and devoted a minute to a couple of deep breaths. Okay, so apparently it wasn't World War III, but that didn't mean it wasn't serious. Otherwise, he never would have been disturbed.

"What's the problem"

"You've got a visitor. She says she's expected and she's causing a scene. I didn't think you would want us to drag her away."

"Do you know her?"

"Yes, sir, and so do you."

Steve groaned when he heard the name. "I'll be right with you. Let me throw on some clothes."

"She's being quite loud. I'm surprised you didn't hear her." The chief of security hesitated. "I could coldcock her if you want, Mr. President."

Alcorn was the only Secret Service agent he'd ever met who had a sense of humor. While his offer was tempting, it probably wasn't politically wise.

He tugged on the pajamas he never wore but kept nearby in case the hotel caught on fire, threw on a robe, and stumbled barefoot from the bedroom into the sitting room of his suite and to the hallway door.

Veronica Gray was winking at him on the other side. Flanked by two agents on each side of her and William Alcorn to the rear, she grinned at him as if her midnight appearance was an ordinary thing.

She was wearing some kind of silk-and-feather robe thing that looked as if it came out of a 1930s Joan Crawford movie, the main difference being that hers barely covered her rear while Joan's had always dragged the floor.

The agents had sense enough to look embarrassed.

"She said she had a message from her father, Mr. President," Alcorn said.

"Where's your room, Roni?" Steve asked.

"I forget," she said. She patted herself down with movements that would have done a Bourbon Street stripper proud. "I guess I lost my key."

She swayed ever so slightly, and he caught the distinct scent of expensive Scotch. She was drunk. He considered asking the agents to pitch her in the hotel swimming pool, but he was currently in touchy negotiations with Senator Gray concerning a bill that meant a lot to him. Gray might take offense. He didn't much care what Roni thought.

He stepped aside and gestured for her to come in.

"Don't go far," he ordered Alcorn and his men. "I may need help." He paused. "Unless one of you wants to throw yourself in front of her for me and take her bullets."

The agents almost smiled.

"We frisked her, sir," one of them said with exaggerated solemnity. "She's unarmed."

"Wanna bet?" Roni said as she walked into the room, her hips swaying so broadly, she practically brushed against each side of the doorframe.

There wasn't a one of them who didn't watch and marvel at the twitch in her rear.

"Order up some coffee," Steve said to the agents. "And alert Ford that I may need him. Otherwise, no one is to know she is here. She's going to feel terrible in the morning. Let's not embarrass her any more than we have to."

He was trying to put a positive spin on the situation, as much for her as for himself. What he really wanted to do was give her a swift slap on the butt. But she might enjoy it and insist he do it again.

She'd flirted with him before, hinting broadly that she wanted to comfort him in times of stress, as she put it, rubbing herself against him when the opportunity arose in case he didn't get the message. But she'd never gone this far.

The first thing Steve did was to snap on all the lights in the sitting room. She sat on the sofa and crossed her legs, letting a high-heeled slipper dangle from one foot. She proceeded to pump her leg, so fast and hard that the slipper fell off. Subtlety was not one of Roni's primary traits.

She patted the cushion beside her. "Please, sit here."

"Coffee's on the way."

"I don't want coffee. Unless it comes with lots of sugar." Her eyes fell to his crotch. "And lots and lots of cream."

She lifted her long blond hair away from her

neck. "It's warm in here, don't you think? We're wearing far too many clothes."

Steve studied the way her long-lashed green eyes were looking at him and the way her painted red lips were pouting at him and the way she was arching her breasts at him in case he wanted to get a good look.

"You're not drunk," he said.

She gave him a catlike smile.

"You're smart," she said. "That's what I like about you, Steve. One of the things."

"So why the charade?"

"How else was I to get in here except by causing trouble? This way, I can pretend I don't remember anything that happened. But I'll remember it all."

She uncrossed her legs, leaning down for her slipper and giving him a different, fleshier look at her breasts. When she sat back up, she spread her thighs wide enough apart so that he could get a look at her goody land if he chose. Roni was a celebrated beauty. There were hundreds of men who would sacrifice a great deal to be offered what she was offering him.

Steve wasn't interested . . . well, maybe he was a little interested, being a healthy, virile male, but only because last night he'd had old appetites aroused.

But the senator's daughter was not a dish that offered him what he was wanting. He had selective tastes.

The problem was how to let her down without

making an enemy of her. She could hurt him in ways that she knew all too well.

"You don't want to do this, Roni."

"You have no idea what I want."

"I'm a monk, remember?"

"So why did you have that woman with you last night?"

"What woman?" he asked, playing cool.

"That mechanic creature. Doesn't she work on cars? She must have put out fast."

She spoke with certainty. Somehow she had found out that Ginny had come to call. Not even the *Inside Scoop* had known. He had a spy working for her. When he discovered who he—or she—was, the spy was toast.

"Whether she was there or not is none of your business."

"Oh, you liked it?"

"There was nothing to like."

"I knew she was there," she declared, as if she'd caught him in an admission. "Why don't you compare us? I'm good. You won't be disappointed."

She stood and fluffed her feathers. "Come on, cowboy. How about a real ride?"

And then she came at him, reaching for the belt on his robe. One quick flick and it was untied, and she was studying his pajamas.

"I always pictured you sleeping in the nude," she said, licking her lips.

He grabbed her wrist. With her free hand she grabbed his crotch.

"I can be really good to you, Steve. You have no idea."

"Roni—" Steve was finding it difficult to talk.

"Is that movement I feel? Has the monk come to life?"

She wasn't wrong about his reaction. He wasn't dead. But he also wasn't stupid, and he wasn't in the market for what Roni had to sell.

She wasn't getting the message. Moving close, she parted her legs and rubbed herself hard against his thigh. He could feel her dampness through his pajamas.

"You cooperate with me, I'll get Daddy to cooperate with you," she whispered, letting her breath tickle his cheek.

This wasn't the way he had figured laws were made when he'd first run for Congress.

Getting a firm hold on both her wrists, he put some space between them.

Her eyes narrowed and she stared at him with more calculation than heat. It was the calculation that he found interesting. Veronica wasn't so caught up in lust that her mind had disengaged.

"I'm going to take you to the door and open it and hand you over to William Alcorn, who will handcuff you if he has to, and take you to your room. And then I'm going to forget this ever happened. You're a beautiful, desirable woman, but I'm just not interested."

Her pout turned to a sulk. "You're not a fag, are you?"

Steve was finished being civil.

"No, but I've got some friends who are gay. Watch your mouth."

She twisted free. "And you, Mr. President, ought to watch your back. You may forget tonight happened, but I won't. You've been leading me on for over a year now, and suddenly I'm dumped for a mousy little clerk. Nobody does that to me and gets away with it. Nobody, not even you, Mr. President."

He'd never heard the title pronounced with such scorn, not even on extremist radio. He might have admired her for the dignity she summoned if he didn't know it was as calculated as the lust.

She opened the door just as one of the agents arrived with a tray of coffee. Instantly, she returned to the drunk routine.

"Brandy, that's what we need. I just wanted a little something to help me sleep."

She took a couple of steps into the hall, then glanced at Steve over her shoulder.

"Sorry to disappoint you, Mr. President, but I'm just not in the mood."

The view Steve got of her was a swaying, silk-clad rear moving down the hall between a pair of dark suits. Waving away the coffee, he stripped and went back to bed, but he didn't go back to sleep. He'd been putting Roni off for months, but tonight was the first time he'd actually spurned her. Right now she was probably summoning the furies of a hundred hells.

No, the consequences of this night were definitely

not done, but he didn't want to worry about that right now.

The one image that would get the senator's wily daughter out of his mind was another, this one of a not-so-fancy woman who covered herself in layers of brown and managed to look sexier and more appealing than another woman had in feathers and silk.

Ginny was a good woman. And she was safe. Once he got past all his adolescent fantasies about her, he could comfortably spend time in her company without causing either of them any stress.

Chapter Eight

Ginny took a fortifying swallow of margarita, which sadly wasn't fortifying at all, and set the glass aside. A sense of foreboding was slowly settling over her. She shouldn't have let the guys leave her here alone, even if they were no further away than the rest room. Solitude gave her time to think.

Tonight would be a disaster, regardless of what she did or didn't do, short of running away to Canada. It was a little late in her life for that.

She'd sensed trouble right from the beginning and then, stupidly, she'd allowed herself to forget. But things were going much too smoothly on this balmy evening; too pleasantly, she could almost say. It was a sure sign that trouble really was on the way. And there were other indications, equally subtle; hints that only a woman frequented by trouble would understand.

"Definitely not. Never," she'd said when the dinner invitation was first put to her, and then, after a counterargument, "It's a bad idea. I can't."

Her last desperate effort had been more aggressive: "Why do you keep asking me out to eat? Do you have some kind of food fetish?"

With each response, she'd been using both her heart and her mind. Her tormentor was supposed to laugh and give up, chalking her up as a lost cause, and get back to running the country.

But he hadn't done anything like that. And here she was in the party room of a Georgetown Tex-Mex restaurant, the San Antonio Rose, on a Thursday at the end of April, playing with the thorny stem of a yellow rose, one of which was at every place setting, and waiting for the presidential party to arrive.

Whenever Stephen Marshall was concerned, she was a right-to-the-bone wimp.

"You never eat. That makes you a food challenge," he'd said, "not a fetish. And a challenge is one thing I can't resist."

So that was what she was to him, was she? The guy definitely had a warped sense of humor, along with a few other traits that set him apart from the rest of the world.

And he was smart. It wasn't her weakness or his sexy voice and persuasive banter that had got her here, at least not all by themselves. He'd also suggested she bring her son.

"And your landlord, Professor Morris, too, if you like," he'd added. "Maybe we can fix him up with my aunt."

No wonder Steve had won the presidency in a landslide. The guy was a master politician, and a visionary, too, if he thought Professor Carl and Doris Tanner would ever get along.

But they didn't really matter. Jake was the real reason she was here, and the reason she felt with increasing certainty that tonight something would go catastrophically wrong. They'd ridden to Georgetown in the Professor's '77 Impala, arriving too early, giving her too much time to think.

The past few days had been a special kind of hell for her and, she suspected, for her son as well. They'd hardly spoken, and when they had it was always painfully polite, about when he would be home or whether she would be working late. Nothing about the state of her clothing as it concerned the President or about Jake's paying her a little respect.

Matters hadn't improved any when the flowers arrived, a big, beautiful bouquet of spring blooms with just the one name on the card, *Steve*. Somehow the simplicity of the identification was more personal than the flowers themselves.

They'd sat on the dining table for a day, neither she nor Jake admitting their presence, and then she'd given them to the professor, as thanks, she'd said, for the cookies and muffins he had baked, denying to herself the warm glow she experienced every time she saw the flowers or breathed in their perfume.

The card she carried in her purse.

Ginny could chastise herself for her weakness concerning Steve, even come close to joking about it when she wasn't reliving the way he'd kissed her and the way he'd touched her, but the trouble with Jake was something she couldn't think about without getting sick inside.

And then Steve had made his most recent phone call and Ginny, after a long, futile struggle, had allowed her hopes to rise. Here, she'd thought, was a chance for her son to see the President in a neutral setting and begin to understand that basically he was a nice guy.

Then they could get back to the way things had been.

"The President asked me out for another dinner," she had announced that same evening when Jake came in from practice. "He wants you to come along, too."

She was expecting him to be just as negative about the invitation as she had been, and she was thinking of some arguments to put to him, providing he stayed around to listen.

"Okay," he had said right away.

"Okay?"

"That's what I said. Okay. I'll go."

Taken by surprise, Ginny hadn't been able to leave well enough alone. "There will be no cracks about the oppressor President, understand?"

He'd rolled his eyes. "Mom, I know how to behave."

At the time, she hadn't realized that his reassurance could be taken more than one way.

"All right, then," she had said, lulled by his pleasantness. "It's Thursday night in Georgetown. Mexican food. You like that. Professor Carl is coming, too."

"Okay."

It was the longest conversation they'd had in days. She should have been suspicious about his ready acceptance, as if she were asking him to a ball game, but she was so relieved that they hadn't argued, she refused to push the issue by asking *why*.

So here they were, positioned like a police lineup at the back of the private party room of the San Antonio Rose, in their assigned places on one side of a long table, facing the door that led to the main part of the restaurant, Ginny in the middle, Jake's chair to her left, and the Professor's to her right.

All in all, they must look fairly ordinary and reasonably calm, ordering drinks like any other customers—the margarita for her, sangria for Professor Carl, a Coke for Jake. But looks, as she had learned early in life, could be deceiving, and at last, and far too late, she had begun to see the situation as it was. Jake was being too nice, too cooperative, with a definite hint of tension beneath his bland demeanor. More than the niceness, what got her was the hidden tension that only a mother could detect. He was up to something. Trouble was on the way.

She wanted to leave now, fast, before anything

worse happened than a case of nerves. Steve might not run from a challenge, but she did, every chance she got.

She was debating ordering a second margarita when Jake and Professor Carl returned to take their places beside her. They were followed by her old buddies the Secret Service.

Jake glanced at the four somber men as if he expected them to pull out Uzis and open fire. Instead, they looked around the room, then backed out. The strains of mariachi guitars wafted through the open doorway, and Ginny, nervous, jumpy, got an idea.

"I'll be right back," she said, and she was, after only a few minutes in the main dining room of the Rose. She was settling into her chair just as the presidential party arrived: Doris Tanner, Steve, and, much to Ginny's dismay, Chief of Staff Redford Davidson and a short, brown-haired woman who had to be his wife.

Recalling too well the reception for the British ambassador, she had the feeling Steve's most trusted adviser was not her friend.

Ginny wasn't at all sure of the proper protocol, but she decided she ought to stand. Professor Carl followed suit, but it took a few prods to get her lanky son to unwind his long legs and pull himself upright.

Maybe she shouldn't have prodded. Maybe she should have left him alone.

Steve's eyes went directly to her for a quick once-over. She was wearing a new blouse—a spring green, long-sleeved, looks-like-silk polyester she'd bought for the occasion—and an old skirt, a serviceable khaki that hit her just above the knees. A fake gold belt encircled her waist, and she wore matching dangle earrings and a spangle bracelet Jake had given her for Christmas.

She'd played around with her hair, pulling it back, twisting it up, but in the end had decided down and straight was best. Without a lot of assistance, it didn't hold a curl anyway, and she didn't have the money for a perm.

Still, going by the expression in Steve's eyes, she must not have looked too bad.

He was golden and gorgeous, of course, in a dark blue sports coat, open-throated red shirt, and smoky gray trousers. It was the open throat where he looked best.

And his lips. They looked good, too.

Ginny's stomach started to quiver. She ought to kick herself. She had no shame. And then the mariachi trio made its way into the party room, strumming what was supposed to be the song she had requested, "Hail to the Chief." Unfortunately, it sounded more like a march-tempo version of "Cielito Lindo."

Steve grinned as he took a chair across from her. "Your idea?" he asked with a nod toward the musicians.

Ginny's knees collapsed involuntarily. "Sorry," she said, taking her seat along with the others. "It didn't turn out the way I had planned."

She was about to babble on some more when she sensed rather than heard something that sounded very much like a growl at her left, and all the words jammed up in her throat.

No, Jake, please. Not here. Not now.

Surely he could hear her silent plea. She touched his arm, and Steve turned his attention to the boy.

"You must be Jake," he said. "Your mother has mentioned what a fine baseball player you are. We must talk sometime. It's a great sport."

Jake's response was a brief nod, and Ginny began to breathe again. For the moment. Thank goodness the President hadn't extended his hand. Jake probably wouldn't have taken it.

Steve handled all of the introductions as if nothing were wrong, and for the moment Jake seemed to settle down. Ginny had been right; the extra woman was the chief of staff's wife, Barbara Davidson.

"I'm delighted to meet you," Mrs. Davidson said, then added, "at last."

"I'm pleased to meet you, too," Ginny said. Dumb. She could imagine what her husband must have told her about the woman who had crashed into the Oval Office, then made a mad dash out of the Department of State.

Still, Mrs. Davidson had a kind look in her eye, and Ginny was responding to all the good stuff she could get.

The First Aunt gave her a cursory nod, saving her longest regard for Professor Carl. In his tweed jacket and white shirt, he looked very professorial. Something about the way he returned the woman's regard made her think Steve knew something about the pair of them she didn't.

In his long-sleeved blue denim shirt and jeans, Jake looked all arms and legs, and resentful, too, with his head cocked back, as if daring the world to take him on. When they all sat back down, she squeezed his hand, but he quickly pulled free and she knew for sure the evening would be a disaster.

"I hope you haven't been waiting too long," Steve said. "At the last minute we were unfortunately detained."

"An emergency?" she asked in all innocence, hoping beyond hope he would launch into a very interesting story about how he had saved somebody's life or adopted a litter of homeless kittens or done something, anything, that would make him appear human and not a power-mad, money-hungry head of state.

Davidson shot her a hard look.

"Sorry," she said with a wave of her hands. "Forget I asked."

Picking up her rose, she promptly stuck her thumb on a thorn. She blotted the blood on the napkin in her lap.

"Actually," Steve said, with the beginning of that killer smile on his lips, "we had this tourist run amuck through the place, claiming some kind of physical problem. She caused all kinds of hell."

"Stephen," his aunt said, then looked at the professor as she added, "I don't know what gets into him sometimes."

Inwardly Ginny groaned. The story was just the kind Jake would believe, and not because he had heard it before. He had no idea exactly how she and Steve had met.

"We're deciding right now what to do with her," Steve said, ignoring his aunt, his eyes still on Ginny. "Two times in one month is just too much. We have to make an example of her, wouldn't you say?"

Everyone at the table was watching the two of them, no one more intently than her son. Sixteen-year-olds didn't have the same sense of humor as adults.

She finished off her margarita, then realized what she was doing. "Sorry," she said, her hand shaking as she set down the empty glass. "We went ahead and ordered."

She would have gone on longer, desperate to fill the silence with nonsense that gave no one offense, hoping against all hope that Jake would let her do the talking for them both.

But of course he didn't.

"Don't apologize, Mom."

Ginny closed her eyes for a moment. Here it came. She forced herself to look at her son, who was staring at the man across the table.

"Look, Jake, maybe tonight wasn't such a good idea. We can leave right now if you're uncomfortable. Everyone will understand."

"It was a great idea."

He turned his stare to her, and she felt the room begin to spin.

"Don't apologize," he repeated, emphasizing each word, as though she wouldn't understand otherwise. He was looking at her the way he had when she told him Jonas was moving back in, accepting the fact that his mom was a weak woman who needed guidance, whether she wanted it or not. "Don't say you're sorry. You've done it three times now."

"Son—" Steve began.

"I'm not your son," Jake snapped.

Davidson came halfway out of his chair, but Steve waved him back down.

"You're right. I shouldn't have called you that. Or are all apologies forbidden?"

Steve's face had tightened and the lines fanning out from his eyes deepened, but otherwise he looked as calm as when he'd first walked in.

Much to Ginny's distress, Jake looked just as self-righteous.

"Cut the crap."

"Young man, that is entirely inappropriate," Doris Tanner said, but no one looked her way and Jake didn't stop.

"You can fool my mom, but not me. Don't mess around with her, understand? Leave her alone. She's not too good at picking out men."

For a minute there wasn't a sound in the room. Ginny closed her eyes and prayed to die.

She could feel Steve's eyes on her. She couldn't

imagine what he was thinking—what any of them were thinking, other than what a strange, crazy family the Baxters were. And crude and rude, to boot.

But they weren't, not really, especially not Jake. He was her responsibility and he was her love, and he was hurt and helpful in the only way he knew. He needed her support. Death was too easy an out.

Again the First Aunt spoke. "See here, young man," she sniffed, "that's entirely uncalled for."

Ginny opened her eyes and took up his defense. "You're right, Mrs. Tanner," she said, "but hard as it is for us to believe, it's something that's been worrying him. He's my protector."

She looked at Steve and let her eyes do her pleading as much as her words. "He's the only one I have."

She sensed Steve was about to speak, but she raised a hand to silence him. Where she got the nerve to hush the President, she had no idea, except that she was a mother protecting her child.

"Jake, you're smart," she said. "Think it through. The President can have any woman in the world, if that's what he wants. He's not interested in me. I'm an average citizen. I represent a large portion of the American public. With us, with you and me, he has a chance for personal contact that must be hard for him to get anywhere else."

She sounded reasonable, and so she should. She'd been working on the *why* of his calls since they first began.

But her son was not so easily persuaded. He looked at her with all the defiance and intensity that came of being a sixteen-year-old with a cause.

"Oh, yeah?" Jake asked. "How much has he asked you about your politics?"

"Well . . ." she said, stumbling around for an answer.

"That's what I thought. I know how guys are, Mom. You don't."

"See here, Baxter," Ford Davidson began, then glanced at the President and fell silent.

"Let him have his say," Steve said.

The two—the worldly, controlled leader of the western world and the fatherless, passionate adolescent—stared at one another. The tension in the room must have radiated to the rest of the Rose, for the four Secret Service agents came through the doorway, fanning out across the room. Davidson waved for them to stand back. A waiter entered, a tray of food balanced on one hand, took one look around, took a second look at the agents, and backed out.

Jake shoved back his chair and stood. "Come on, Mom. Let's get out of here."

She stared up at him. He looked so tall and thin and young, so righteous, and so very, very wrong. He was trying as hard as he could to be a man when he wasn't, not quite, and that made him fragile. She truly did not know what to do.

For all her determination to handle this herself, she found herself looking to Steve for help.

"Now," Jake ordered, sounding very much like the father he'd detested. "You've gotta get away from the jerk."

This last was too much. Suddenly everybody was standing and talking at the same time, everyone but her and Steve, and the agents were standing close by, their hands hanging loose, ready to reach for their guns.

It was Professor Carl who came up with the solution.

"I'll take you home, Jake," he said. "Your mom's all right. She'll be along soon."

Jake looked down at her, but he didn't say anything, just let his deep brown eyes do the questioning. He looked at Steve and then back to her. She needed to tell him that while she understood what he was doing, he had hurt her, too. Before she got the chance, he strode past her, down the length of the table, and was gone, the professor hurrying after him, sparing a quick, reassuring nod at Ginny.

"Does Professor Morris have a car?" Steve asked.

Ginny nodded, still staring at the door, remembering the look of betrayal in her son's eyes. She wanted to do nothing else but fold herself into a ball in a dark corner far away and cry. When she tried the hardest to do right was the very time she made her worst mistakes.

What a rotten mother she was. And look who was witness to the proof. To hell with doing the right thing. She stood, ready to rush after Jake and join him in his getaway.

"No, Ginny, please."

Steve spoke softly, but his words rooted her in place.

"Ford," he went on, "can you get my aunt back to the White House? And let my driver know we'll be leaving."

"Now, Stephen," Doris Tanner said, "you know you shouldn't be—"

Ginny focused her eyes on the flower she was rapidly destroying, petal by petal, not knowing what Steve did to hush his aunt. But she hushed fast.

Barbara Davidson came to her side and gave her a hug. "Ford and I never had children. But if we had—"

"Barbara," her husband said behind her, "that's none of Mrs. Baxter's concern."

"But if we had," she continued, ignoring her husband, "I would have wanted him to love me as much as your son loves you."

The words were almost Ginny's undoing. She closed her eyes and heard the sound of her own shallow breathing, a shuffling of feet, a few whispers, and then silence. With a sigh, she looked up, and there was her Golden Man watching her with sympathy but not the least bit of pity.

Everyone else was gone. Everyone, that is, but the Secret Service.

Steve didn't say anything, when there was much he could have said. And he didn't smile and give her false words of encouragement. He just looked at her and let her know that he wasn't going to leave.

Her heart started pounding and she felt a rush of warmth unlike anything she had ever experienced. If she ever fell in love again, she, the biggest mistake-maker in all the world, knew it would be with him.

Chapter Nine

Steve settled into the back seat of the presidential limousine beside Ginny, very close beside her, so close they were practically touching despite all the room they had. Distress left her too weak to move, and too needy for whatever he could offer.

Back in that party room, something had taken place between them, something important. As much as she needed comfort, she also wanted to know what that something was.

Sitting close seemed as good a way as any to find out.

"Let's ride for a while and give him time to settle down," he said.

The suggestion was not unwelcome. It was also wonderfully generous, considering the scene he'd just been through. She didn't know how to begin to thank him, except maybe by throwing her arms around him and covering his face with kisses.

But he'd been assaulted by the Baxters enough for one evening.

"Fine," she said, "if you're sure that's what you want to do." She had to be honest. It was the least he deserved. "I ought to warn you, though. Jake hasn't settled down since he was twelve years old and his father walked out."

"So we ride for a little longer. I need to go to San Francisco this weekend, anyway."

Ginny smiled, something she hadn't expected to do for a year or two. And she became even more aware of the man sitting beside her, not only who he was, which was enough to cow her into a fetal position if she thought about it long enough, but also the what and the how of him, too. Everything from the cowboy-strong lines of his face, which kept him from being a pretty boy, to the width of his shoulders and the way the collar of his shirt rested against the pale hairs at the back of his neck to the length of his legs to the polished shoes that were as perfect as the rest of him.

"Everything's American made," he said, and when she looked away fast, added, "The clothes, I mean. I thought maybe that's what you were wondering."

She took a deep breath. "You figured me out. That's what had me worried, all right."

"If you keep looking at me like that, I may let you check out the labels."

She took two deep breaths. "You're joking, right?"

He didn't answer right away.

"Yeah, I'm joking."

"To help me forget what happened in the restaurant."

"You figured me out."

She looked away from him and out the window. They had left the steady lights of Georgetown and were now on a road that ran alongside the Potomac. She didn't know enough yet about Washington to identify exactly where they were. All she knew was that there were motorcycles in front of the limo and at least one car to the rear, and all traffic was held up at every street they came to, always giving them the right-of-way.

He had power, far more than most people could ever imagine.

And she had her son.

"Jake wants to protect me," she said.

"He's doing a good job. Not many men would have the nerve to speak up the way he did."

She covered her face with her hands. "Don't remind me." With a sigh she added, "Who am I kidding? I'll never forget. He got way out of line and I got sappy, wanting to protect him. I made a mess of the whole thing."

"I know it's none of my business, and you don't have to tell me if you don't want to, but has he done this kind of thing before?"

She peeked at him through her fingers. The passing streetlamps cast light and then shadows across his face, but she saw enough to know he wasn't smiling. And he didn't look the least interested in her in any way other than as a friend.

It was just the kind of look that could be her undoing, and she found herself talking about things she'd never told anyone else, the way she had before, at the White House, only this time it all seemed even more personal.

"I dated only a few times after the divorce, and then not at all after Jonas died. Jake had to throw one man out because he . . . well, he got a little fresh, and the rest of them he just scowled away from the house. For a kid, he knows how to scowl."

"I noticed."

He took her hands and held them in his, settling them on his thigh. If he thought that would calm her down, he was as big a mistake-maker as she.

"You don't have to be nervous, Ginny. I've already been warned about fooling around."

She leaned her head back on the seat and groaned.

"As if you needed the warning," she said.

The truth was, Jake had given his lecture to the wrong person. Right now she was experiencing a powerful desire for a pair of strong, sure hands to fool around in places that hadn't been visited by a man in years.

Steve stroked the back of one of her hands. "How do you know Jake wasn't totally justified?"

Ginny jerked her hands away. "Don't tease."

"He's sixteen, isn't he? He's got some hormones

raging in him. It could be he recognized a few in me."

"The only signs of hormones are his Adam's apple and a few whiskers." And then she realized all that he had said. "I asked you not to tease. Good grief. You could have Veronica Gray back here."

She thought maybe Steve winced, but the light and dark were following one another so fast she couldn't be sure.

She darted a glance at the chauffeur, who was separated from them by a glass partition. "Can he hear us?"

"Not unless I punch the right button."

Steve Marshall was good at punching buttons, no matter what result he was after. He was punching hers just fine.

She groaned again. Some mother she was turning out to be.

"You'd better take me home."

"With all this entourage? It's probably best if you arrive a little less conspicuously. Otherwise it might look as if I'm putting on a big show of power, letting the boy know he can't boss me around."

She looked at him, really looked at his face for the first time since Jake had made his unfortunate pronouncement, not judging the way he looked but the way he was. It didn't matter about the on-and-off lights. She was seeing him just fine.

"You ought to be a father. You'd be a good one."

For the first time since she'd met him, he looked uncomfortable.

"I didn't mean anything by that," she said. "If you can't have a child, or you don't want to, why, that's perfectly understandable."

She fell silent, far, far too late.

He flashed the killer smile, and the love machine's motor engaged. She was too shameless to live.

"Ginny, you are priceless."

"I'm not for sale, if that's what you're getting at."

"I know. You're not bartering the pleasure of your company for anything from me. You're here because I asked you and you were nice enough to say yes."

"I'm here because you also asked Jake, and I hoped he would begin to understand you're not all bad."

"Thanks. I think."

Ginny could see the need for some explanation.

"See, he doesn't like any kind of authority outside of a few baseball coaches, and he's smart enough to understand he needs the referees. He thinks all governments are less than worthless. I'm beginning to understand his attitude now, even if I don't agree with it. It comes from when Jonas was home and was far too strict with him, and then he was gone, taking all his tyranny with him."

"He hit the boy?"

"Oh, no, nothing like that. He just made us feel . . . insignificant. It was like nothing we did mattered. Jake's smart. He figured out right away that someone with control over him was bad. He extended that to anyone in authority. The greater the power, the worse the offender." She tried to smile. "So you can see where that puts you."

Steve touched her hair and then her cheek, so lightly she barely felt his fingers. Still, they burned against her skin.

"What about you?" he asked.

For a minute she couldn't breathe, couldn't remember what they were talking about. Oh yes, Jake, the light of her life.

"He doesn't see me as having any power at all. We helped each other. And we still do."

"Sounds like a great relationship."

"Until we moved here, it was."

"It still is. Trust me. A bond like that doesn't die when two people understand one another the way you and your son do."

She felt a rush of warmth that settled around her heart. Steve could have crushed Jake, humiliated him in the way that only a prideful adolescent male could be humiliated.

But he hadn't. He'd shown understanding. Now he was comforting her. She'd better start looking for flaws in this guy or she was lost.

He dropped an arm around her shoulders, and it was the most natural thing in the world to rest her head against him. She would look later for flaws. He kissed her forehead. She didn't move away. If this was a dream, it was one mixed in the midst of a nightmare, and she'd take them both as long as they lasted.

"You're doing some strange things to me, Ginny. And I swore—"

He broke off, and she wondered exactly what it was he had sworn. And then he was lifting her chin and brushing his lips against hers. It seemed right to accept the comfort and the forgetfulness his kiss brought.

But of course she had to go beyond acceptance, gripping the lapels of his jacket to keep from crashing through the sky roof of the limo and spiraling into space.

He eased away from her and she thought *good*, several times, grateful he hadn't done anything more and wondering why she wanted to cry.

"I'm sorry about that," she said, as afraid of silence as she was of anything condescending that he might say.

"As someone said recently, don't apologize."

He eased out of the jacket and tossed it aside, then took her back in his arms. "Besides, if you're really sorry about the kiss, I'm the king of Spain."

Naturally he would pick royalty. She thought of who he was and who she was, where they were, understanding how insane this was and not caring at all, especially when he started kissing her again, this time the way he had at the White House, with all the enthusiasm she'd begun to think had sprung from her imagination.

She splayed her hands against his chest, yearning to touch bare skin, filled with a great rush of pleasure because he felt so good and strong and hard and substantial. He was opening something inside her that she'd thought closed forever. If he didn't stop soon, she would go more than a little wild.

But stopping would be up to him. She needed this more than anything she could ever remember. He didn't stop her when she unfastened the top button of his shirt, stroking the strong neck and every part of his chest she could reach without tearing his clothes off him.

The last thing she would consider looking for was a label.

Instead, he held her tight and kissed the side of her mouth. "You taste good, Ginny. Pure and sweet."

"I don't feel pure."

"How about down and dirty?"

She shivered from her hair roots to the tips of her toes.

"Oh, yeah. I feel like that."

"Then let's get down."

One very authoritative hand moved down her side, his skin hot against the slippery fabric of her blouse as he paused to give special attention to the side of her breast. She could feel her nipple harden, and it was as if the parts of her body were crying out for more thorough attention than he was giving them, begging him to cut out the teasing and the moving on.

Linger awhile, they sang, taking the lyrics from the old song she'd always loved.

But on he moved, his hand coming to rest at the edge of her skirt.

"I love your legs."

"They're nothing special."

"Quit putting yourself down."

She thought about his hand on her thigh and everything it was close to. "There's that *down* word again."

"I've been thinking of that, too."

Down he went, feeling his way to her knees and around to the backs of them, which had never been a special sensory spot for her but were definitely sensitive tonight.

"Keep going," she whispered. For a man used to being in charge, he certainly needed advice.

Or so she thought for the moment.

His laugh was rich and thick and came from deep in the chest she knew she would never see naked. She had a hard time keeping her hips still and her thighs pressed together, all the while she was cursing the modern torture known as panty hose.

In that smooth, take-charge way of his, he somehow managed to lift her and set her across his lap. She kicked off her shoes, wrapped her arms around his neck, and started rubbing her breasts against his chest, all the while she was licking his lips and enjoying the way he licked hers. She opened up to him and their tongues did a fast two-step, the way their feet might on a western dance floor.

That's what he was right now, her cowboy dream hero, and nobody else, nobody who had any special importance to anyone outside the limo.

Of course, the limo sort of soured the notion of how they were just everyday folks; they should have been in a pickup.

The limo took a sharp left and the kiss was effectively broken. Holding her close, with her lips pressed against the side of his neck, he reached out somewhere at the end of the car seat for something that had nothing to do with any of her body parts and then he was saying, "Keep driving," in a voice she scarcely recognized. "And go slow."

She spared a quick glance out the window and saw a lighted monument go by, but she was too far gone in her own inner light and the heat that came with it to identify anything that she saw other than Steve. She went right back to kissing his neck and tasting him with her tongue.

Washington, glorious by night, was slipping past them and she didn't care.

"Take 'em off," he growled, and she knew he meant those cursed hose.

Here was the moment she ought to protest, but she was human and she was being loved, if only physically—but with this guy physical was far more than she had expected and all she would get.

Quit thinking of who he is.

It was hard to do, but she managed, just the way she managed the offending undergarment. She had to take off her belt first, and while she was at it she went ahead and removed the dangling earrings. They landed somewhere farther down the way in the block-long car in the vicinity of the discarded jacket.

The panty hose removal took some maneuvering, but with the two of them motivated the way they were, they succeeded. For a second her bracelet got caught in the hose, but she ripped it free and kept on.

He didn't say anything about taking off the panties she always wore under the hose, never sure whether or not she was supposed to, wishing the things came with instructions.

Neither did she—come with instructions, that is—but Steve knew what to do. She went crazy when his fingers touched the naked flesh of her thigh. The rasping of his tongue against the side of her neck served to drive her further from sanity, and when his tongue licked down the opening in her blouse to where her cleavage began—with her it was a long way down—she gave up reason as a stupid state of mind.

Her breasts were so tight they were about to explode, and she didn't try any longer to keep her hips from grinding against him, feeling his own hard, protruding reaction against her rear.

She wanted more than anything to pull up her skirt and straddle him. Where she got that idea she didn't know, since she'd never done anything like it before. But touching Steve and rubbing their bodies together and letting the feelings take over was the best way she'd ever found of keeping out the loneliness and the worries that never quite went away.

She was like a teenager again, wrestling in the back seat of a car, only this time she knew the exact sensations to anticipate and she wouldn't be getting scared, stopping the action, asking for assurances of love that couldn't be sincere.

She was a grown-up. She knew what was going on. When his hand moved under her skirt to the inside of her thigh, she made no attempt to play coy or hard to get. For the first time in her life she was easy, and he knew it. Besides, he had clever, wonderful hands, so clever they were teaching her things about herself she hadn't known.

Things like what a wild woman she could be, particularly when his hand stroked her thigh while his tongue licked a nipple through her blouse.

Being a sharer and a nurturer, Ginny wanted to do her part.

She kissed around the edge of his ear and whispered, "You're having all the fun."

"Yeah," he whispered back, but he didn't stop, for which she planned to be eternally grateful.

"I want to touch you," she said, in case he didn't get what she meant. She started to add something about *presidential privates,* but that might bring him to his senses, reminding them both of who he was. She preferred him as lost and abandoned as she.

"Nope," he said.

He put a lot of determination behind the one

word, and she figured she'd best not argue. Besides, the "fun" crack had been a lie. She was having the best time of her life.

Smoothly—he didn't do anything any other way—he eased her back until she was lying on the limo seat, her head against the crook of his arm, the top of his body resting against her top, while his hand kept working at her bottom.

She didn't try to keep still, not her hips and not her hands. Gripping his upper arm, she let her other hand stroke the full length of his chest, playing with his belt buckle, then giving up on its intricacies, moving lower, hearing his sharp intake of breath when she reached ground zero. Frustrated by the trousers, she cupped him as best she could.

Steve suffered no such impediment. One finger eased inside her panties and started roaming around, finding the body part that had been crying out the most for him. He did everything right. She held on tight, kissing his lips, his cheeks, even his eyes, for as long as she could concentrate.

Which wasn't very long. He slipped inside her and was out in an instant, then in and out again, playing with her, and what seemed as close as possible to loving her, even if it was only with his finger. Her blood was pumping hard, but she gave up on breathing, permanently if that's what it took to get where he was taking her.

He got her there in what was for her record time, or so she recalled. It had been so very long since this had happened to her; she couldn't have been twenty years old. She clung to him with all her strength, enjoying the bursts of sensation, the tautness of everything about her, the small grunt of satisfaction she heard come from him. As for herself, she was crying out his name.

He pressed his hand against her damp underwear, as if he could keep the sensations where they belonged for just a while longer. But of course even Stephen Marshall couldn't do that.

And Ginny began to realize just what he had done.

Worse, she remembered everything she had done, too. Everything.

She buried her face against his chest, and he held her. More than anything in the world, besides complete amnesia, she wanted to come up with a smartmouth quip that would get her through the next few minutes and, if necessary, the rest of her life.

But she was brain dead. Too bad the rest of her didn't follow suit.

"Are you all right?" he asked.

He sounded placating. She would have preferred silence.

Keep it light. Keep it casual. She lay still in his arms until she found the nerve.

"You're good, Steve. Why wouldn't I be all right?"

How was that for sassing the President?

The President. What was she doing? What had she done? This was like rising from a deep, dark pool much too fast. She was getting the bends.

And all the while he kept watching her. She

couldn't see his eyes, but she could feel them, the way she'd felt everything else about him that she'd been able to reach.

"Ginny—"

"You don't have to say anything."

They both sat up and she started smoothing her clothes. An outside light revealed a very wrinkled skirt and, more seriously, damp spots on her blouse where he'd put his mouth. Her nipples were still trying to poke through.

Surely they ought to be shriveling up by now. Everything else about her was.

"I don't suppose there's a hair dryer in this thing," she said.

"I could ask."

He sounded cool, almost offended, like she wasn't supposed to come back as strong as he. What he didn't realize was that every syllable she uttered was sapping a very, very small store of strength.

"Please," she said, "don't push any more buttons."

"I have to, or we can't get out of this thing."

It was at that moment she realized that the limo had come to a stop, probably had been stopped for a long time.

She looked through the darkened windows. "We couldn't be—"

"We are. We got back to the White House ten minutes ago."

"You looked at your watch?"

"It's an estimate."

He was probably right on the money. Ten minutes. They'd arrived about the time he was—

She had to learn how to cuss better. She knew no words to express how she felt.

"I'll get out and give you a few minutes to pull yourself together," he said.

And I'll run like hell. He probably wanted to say that, too.

The world outside the limo began to come into focus, the tall, lighted white walls, the columns of one of the porticos, the shadowy figures standing a few yards from the car.

"They must be out there waiting, all those agents and goodness knows who else. They're probably ready to break into this thing and find out what I've done to you."

"An armored tank couldn't get into this thing."

His words were yet another reminder of who he was, as if she needed any more.

She looked down, unable to glance at anything anywhere near him, and her fingers found their inevitable way to her forehead. "I can't believe this. You . . . and me."

"Man and woman, Ginny. I guess we're not too deeply civilized. We both went crazy."

She looked at him from the corner of her eye. "You went crazy, too?"

"Couldn't you tell?"

He shrugged into his jacket. His collar fell right into place without his having to adjust a thing; except for a little mussed hair, he looked as if nothing had happened.

And she looked wanton, confused, and satisfied at the same time. Appearance-wise, she was a mess. Why did guys always seem to have an easier time?

"This wasn't planned," he said.

He didn't sound particularly happy about the situation.

But then, neither was she. At his most ardent, Jonas had never made her feel quite this way. For a little while, she'd felt loved. And she'd felt loving, too. Could it be she really was falling for this guy? Not in a temporary, power-groupy kind of way, but in the manner of true love, the kind she'd begun to think didn't exist.

If she was, she'd better fight it. And there was only one way she knew how, by showing that he might have gotten to her but only in a physical way.

"No harm done," she said. "In fact, I'd say just the opposite. It's just as you said, we went a little crazy with the man/woman thing. I was upset and you tried to console me, and I'd have to say you did a fine job. Believe me, Steve, I'm not upset."

He looked at her for a long time. She didn't blink or look away, or let loose with the stored-up tears that were beginning to give her an executive-sized headache. It was, all in all, a supreme moment in her life.

"Good," he said. "I'll call."

She nodded, thinking he sounded just like the boys in high school.

"It'll be next week sometime. I'm flying to California in the morning."

Another nod. Putting off women with promises must be a universal male-type thing.

She waited until he was halfway out of the limo to get in the last word.

"All I can say, Mr. President, is that you certainly know how to serve the electorate."

Steve waited until Ginny transferred to the Taurus for the ride back to Ballston. Not once did she turn to look for him; probably she'd assumed that he'd already gone inside. He stood in the back driveway of the White House and watched until the taillights disappeared. Then, very slowly, eschewing the elevator, he stopped in a downstairs rest room to wash the scent of Ginny from his hands—not wanting to but knowing he must. Afterward, he walked up the stairs to the privacy of the family quarters.

He had some thinking to do. And some calming down.

But he found no privacy. Ford Davidson, sans wife, and Aunt Doris awaited his return. Added to the mix was Edward Seale.

"You couldn't find Alan Skinner?" he asked as soon as he walked into the room. "Surely we need to get the press in on this."

He went to a side table and, passing up the pitcher of ice water, poured himself a stiff Scotch.

He looked to his aunt to begin the inquisition. She did not disappoint him.

"You took a long time to get back here," she said.

He swallowed half the drink. "Yep."

"Did you take her all the way to Ballston?" Ford asked.

"Nope." A devilish urge made him add, "Since we passed up supper, I took her to the drive-through at McDonald's."

"Humph," Aunt Doris said. "I guess you're going to tell us motorcycles and all went through."

"It was quite a sight," he said.

Ford cleared his throat. "We need to investigate that son more than we have. He could mean trouble."

"Jake Baxter loves his mother," Steve said. "Remember what your wife said. Besides, the boy's a baseball pitcher. You can't get better than that."

"Ford told me what happened at the restaurant," Seale said. "That must have been devastating for Mrs. Baxter. Is she all right?"

Edward was the first one he took seriously. "I hope so." He remembered her "electorate" crack and almost grinned. "She's tough."

She would have to be to hang around him very long. And to put up with her son. But if tough was all she was, he wouldn't be feeling like putting in a call to the Taurus and getting her back here right away. Behind her final words, there had been both courage and a vulnerability she didn't want him to see.

He finished the drink. "Is Florence around anywhere? What the hell, she doesn't have to be. If anyone wants to talk, I'll be in the kitchen."

Of course everyone trooped after him down the corridor to the spacious, well-equipped kitchen that Jackie Kennedy had ordered constructed for family meals. She'd brought in a French chef. With him it was either Florence McKelvey of Bottle, Oklahoma, or do-it-yourself.

Taking off his jacket, he rolled up his sleeves, tied on an apron, and started opening and closing cabinets, looking for flour and baking powder, pulling the eggs and milk out of the refrigerator, finding a small can of Vermont maple syrup behind a jar of sugar-free strawberry preserves.

At one time he'd been handy with a skillet. Tonight was a night for using a variety of long-unused skills.

Tonight he'd been a cad, a beast, a brute, an arrogant bastard, and thoroughly dishonorable, groping around like that in the back seat. He also felt great, better than he had since the election. He'd been ashamed of himself for a while, but Ginny had shown him that she had no regrets; he was honest enough to admit that neither did he.

A Cincinnati girl and an Oklahoma boy—that's all they'd been, and it had been enough.

"What are you doing?" Aunt Doris asked.

"Making pancakes."

"After the Scotch?"

"I know. Back in Bottle, it would have been Jack Daniel's and pancakes, but we're fancier here in the

East. Maple syrup right out of the trees. Double wow."

"What about McDonald's?" Ford asked.

"They use the artificial flavor kind."

"I didn't mean the syrup," Ford said, then with a wave of his hand gave up.

Steve didn't bother to measure anything; tonight he had a sure touch.

"Anyone want to join me?" he asked when the first batch was sizzling in the skillet.

"I will," Seale said, the only one who spoke.

Steve knew his aunt and chief of staff were passing looks, trying to figure out just what had happened after they'd left the San Antonio Rose.

He didn't know himself, except that what had been a disaster had turned into a special night. He could say he didn't feel quite so lonely right now, the way he sometimes did even when a crowd of people were nearby. But that wouldn't cover his friskiness.

He flipped the pancakes. Yep, that's the way he felt, downright frisky. He didn't know where this thing he had with Ginny would lead; he had to let her know right away that he wasn't making any promises—he couldn't, not considering his position—but being so close to a son who hated his guts, she would probably be relieved.

He didn't want anything from her and she didn't want anything from him, except the pleasure of each other's company. Just how far that pleasure would go, he wasn't about to guess. When it came to his relationship with Regina Baxter, every guess he'd made had been wrong.

Chapter Ten

When Ginny arrived home, the door to Jake's room was closed. She took time to change into her nightshirt and to clean up, giving herself a few minutes to decide on an approach before knocking. She took silence as permission to enter.

He was propped up in bed reading. With his hair flopped across his forehead, he looked no older than twelve, but she couldn't let that weaken her. She sat beside him and looked him straight in the eye, which was not an easy thing to do, considering all that had taken place after he left the restaurant.

The whole thing put Ginny on shaky ground. Still, some things needed to be said.

"That was a tough thing you did tonight, Jake. I'm trying to see it from your side, but it's not easy. You protected me, but you embarrassed me, too. And the others. There were people there who didn't need to be involved."

"I don't like you seeing him, that's all. What do you think he wants from you?"

"Whatever it is, I'll handle it. We can't live each other's lives, and we can't always keep each other from harm. Otherwise, all the loving parents in the world would lock up their children at birth."

"But Mom, look at the facts. Look at who he is, and who—"

"Careful. You're swimming in dangerous waters here."

"But of all people, *him*."

"Yeah, imagine." She tried to get a smile out of him, but he wasn't going to make this any easier for her. "All I'm saying is, in this instance I'll have to take care of myself."

"Lots of luck. Don't say I didn't warn you."

"Never." She started to get up, but she wasn't done yet. "I've hated these last few days, with the way things have been around here," she said. "Let's don't fight like that again."

His face softened, and with a grunt he looked away. As close as they were, he was still an adolescent male and not given to open demonstrations of affection, but he didn't push her away when she hugged him good night.

She almost made it out the door before he gave her his best shot.

"Did he take my advice?"

Ginny couldn't pretend to misunderstand.

"Good grief, Jake, I was in the presidential limousine. There must have been a dozen agents surrounding us and a driver right there. Give your mother credit for more sense than that."

"I didn't say you let him. I wanted to know what he tried."

Ginny smiled. "He tried to reassure me that you wouldn't be thrown into irons. There are some places in the world where that would be considered exceedingly generous."

She left before he could figure out that she hadn't actually answered his question. In delicate situations she saw the benefits of *"don't ask, don't tell."*

Walking to and from work on Friday, she got the feeling she was being followed, but she could never spot anyone who looked the least suspicious. Nerves, that was all. Considering the turn her life had taken, she had a few things to be nervous about.

She didn't see her knight errant offspring again until that evening, when Professor Carl joined them for a meatloaf dinner. After Jake went outside to practice pitching, she thanked him for his help at the restaurant.

"The boy began to have a number of doubts on the way home," the professor said.

"I thought he might."

"But that doesn't mean he will refrain from a similar declaration should the occasion arise."

He looked at her with a question in his eyes: Would there be another evening out with the President? She stared back with an equally obvious expression: She hadn't the vaguest idea.

Ginny kept busy over the weekend. Saturday she worked half a day and cleaned the apartment in the afternoon to show her son she still knew how. In the evening the two of them watched a British movie about the hardships of England's industrial north.

Again, whenever she was outside, she felt watchful eyes on her. She must have been listening too much to Jake's talk about Big Brother keeping tabs on everyone.

On Sunday she washed clothes and put in the most energetic session ever at the kickboxing studio. Here she knew who was watching—the other women who were there to work out. She was either doing something very right or very wrong; she'd bet her money on wrong.

In the evening she shared a plate of homemade cookies with the landlord/professor/chef, managing to get down her share with a big bottle of sugary soda.

Whenever she had a moment alone, she was flipping the dial on the TV, looking for reports on the President's California trip. He had several meetings and gave a number of speeches, mostly involving the Pacific Rim.

In one interview outside the Hyatt Regency in San Francisco, he assured the American public that his meetings with the Chinese had absolutely nothing to do with fund-raising of any kind. He looked as sincere as he had when he told her he would call.

He also looked gorgeous, but that was another matter entirely. One moment she was cringing over memories of what they had done, and the next she was treasuring those same memories as something very special in her life.

Sometime between the cleaning and the kickboxing and watching TV, she came to understand what had happened between them in the restaurant, before the limo ride, the change that had sealed her fascination with him for all time. She had learned to lean on him for help and support, and he wasn't pushing her away. If that couldn't lead to some serious emotional entanglements on her part, nothing could.

On Monday, when Ginny showed up at Sam's Auto Repair, déjà vu struck her in full force.

A crowd was around the counter, not so big and boisterous as before, but still it was a crowd. Naturally someone was waving a copy of the *Inside Scoop*. This time the photographer had caught her and Steve coming out of the San Antonio Rose, his arm around her, a distraught look on her face. They had both been so involved, they hadn't noticed the camera flash.

At least she wasn't showing much leg. It was small compensation when she read the headline:

MYSTERY WOMAN IDENTIFIED

NOW THE MYSTERY IS:

WHAT'S GOT HER SO UPSET?

SEE STORY ON PAGE 2

She didn't ask to read it. She didn't want to.

"It's got your name," the woman with the paper said.

"This time it's spelled right, too," another added.

"Did you really have an intimate dinner with the President?"

She looked around at the faces, some of which she knew. Everyone fell quiet. "His aunt and my son were there. We weren't alone."

Her words gave a legitimacy to the story that it hadn't had before. She made her way to the counter, where her boss Ted stood smiling broadly. "Hey, it brings in business. I heard the big boss may drop by one of these days. Sam himself. No one's ever seen him that I know of."

Someone tugged on her sleeve, and she looked down at the round face of a little gray-haired woman who she knew for a fact was eighty-three and in danger of losing her driver's license because of too many speeding tickets.

The woman thrust a small box into her hand.

"I thought you might want one of these. For a souvenir, I mean. Maybe later I could get your autograph on my bill."

Ginny opened her gift. It was the Stephen Marshall for President official campaign badge, a shiny tin star with one word printed boldly across the center in alternating colors of red, white, and blue: MARSHALL.

"Here's something else, dear. I don't know if you saw the story in the *Post* this morning. It was in a

211

back section of the paper. That makes you a real celebrity now. I brought you a clipping in case you didn't have one. Along with the one from the *Scoop*, so you can compare the two."

Thanking her, Ginny took all the offerings and found refuge in the employees only rest room, where she skimmed both stories. They were remarkably similar, both identifying her as a divorcé recently moved to the D.C. area who had been seen several times recently in the company of the President, the world's most eligible bachelor.

In the *Post* a spokesman for the President said he and Mrs. Baxter were casual friends. The *Scoop* said Steve could never again be called a monk. He'd been seen repeatedly with one woman in the East— Ginny supposed the reporter meant her—and on the West Coast a *Scoop* reporter had on several occasions seen Veronica Gray, daughter of California Senator Roger Gray, with the presidential party.

"Until divorcée Regina Baxter appeared on the scene," the tabloid reported, "Miss Gray was considered a possible candidate for First Lady. Rumor has it she was also staying in the same Chicago hotel as the President on his recent trip to the Midwest. Hotel officials refused to confirm or deny."

Ginny wondered how many times the word *divorcée* had to appear before the reader got the idea. She also wondered why the light had gone out of the day. Of course Stephen Marshall was seeing other women. And she could hardly claim he was "seeing" her. So why did she want to cry? She hadn't been led down any primrose path.

Shredding the clippings, she flushed them away, but she kept the Marshall badge as she went out to cope with her day. She did okay, telling herself that she was probably coming down with a bug that caused the constant tightness in her throat.

And then the call came from Jake's school. His counselor wanted to see her as soon as a visit could be arranged.

She was there by midafternoon, Ted being inclined at the moment to agree to most of her requests.

Mrs. Aldrich, counselor for the junior class, greeted her in a small, cluttered office with enough filing cabinets for the Census Bureau. She had about ten years and ten pounds on Veronica Gray, most of the poundage around the middle, but otherwise the two women had a great deal in common: a pretty face, lots of blond hair and makeup, a fitted white dress that understood the shape of the body, and a watchful look in her green eyes, which were especially watchful of Ginny's khaki trousers and white embroidered shirt. Ginny got the feeling she was a disappointment.

She took the chair across the desk. "What's wrong? Is Jake all right?"

"You mean Jonas. He's fine."

Ginny always felt a shock when her son was called by his first name, a reminder of both sides of his heritage. Early in his life she'd gotten the idea he was hers alone.

Mrs. Aldrich glanced down at a slip of paper. "His schedule shows he's in English right now. You know, while I've got you here, I should point out that he ought to be in an advanced class, considering his test scores, but you declined the placement."

"It was Jake's choice, and I honored it. Look, Mrs. Aldrich, when you called me at work, I thought maybe he'd gotten into a fight or something. He's never done that before, not since sixth grade."

"Actually, you're close to the truth. There wasn't a fight exactly. It's just that he's been getting a lot of attention from the other students, and from a few of the teachers, too, since the first picture in the *Inside Scoop*. Not that I read it regularly, you understand, but this latest issue was called to my attention, along with the story that named you. And then there was this morning's *Post*."

She gave a short, embarrassed laugh. "It's not every day we have a celebrity in our school, not at this level, though we've had the children of a general or two and the grandson of a secretary of labor."

"Jake isn't a celebrity. Except in his own right. He's a fine baseball player. Is there anything in his folder about that?"

"Not that I remember. Does he play for the school team?"

Ginny didn't feel like going into how he didn't want to fool with school coaches, good or bad, or rules about grades. Any trouble on the team might reflect on his academic record, and all he wanted was to satisfy his mother's request that he graduate, then get on to his real quest, a place on a major league roster.

"He prefers American Legion ball," she said. "It's where the colleges and pros scout." She began to grow impatient. "You realize I took off work for this, and I still don't understand why I'm here."

"As I said, Jonas was getting a lot of attention, and he doesn't seem to care for it very much. He's been rude and I'm afraid a little obscene at times."

"I'll bet he wasn't rude first. He's a very private person."

"But still, the President—you can imagine how curious everyone is." Mrs. Aldrich fingered a long curl. "I want to be prepared for anything that might come up involving him—your son, that is, not President Marshall."

"Of course. Jake is our primary concern."

"Is there a chance any more stories will come along involving you or the boy? Anything on television? He's so much in the news—the President, that is, not your son."

"I have no idea whether there will be any more stories. Anywhere. And if there are, just remember you shouldn't believe everything you read."

But Mrs. Aldrich was not put off.

"He's such a handsome man, isn't he? Such a . . . fine leader. I imagine he's just as charismatic when you really get to know him as he is on television."

Ginny waved a hand airily. "If you like the type."

By which she meant if you were female and breathing.

Mrs. Aldrich paid no attention to her irritation. "There's also the matter of security. If Jake or someone in his family became very important to the President"—she was choosing each word with great care—"could we expect the Secret Service on campus?"

That would happen only if Ginny became the First Lady. Mrs. Aldrich must be a real dimwit. She didn't know whether to laugh or throw her purse at her. There was also the option of bursting into tears. She chose a quieter course.

"I'll let you know if anything like that seems imminent. And as for the rudeness, I'll speak to Jake, but I suggest you talk to the others who are bothering him. Given the fact that most people around here work for the federal government, these students wouldn't want to cause any trouble that might reflect on their parents and by extension their parents' careers. The President has taken a special interest in my son."

It was a subtle point she was making about the jobs, but Mrs. Aldrich caught it. They shook hands, and Ginny left. She was going out the front door when another woman stopped her, this one middle-aged, tall and sturdy in her black slacks and blazer and blue turtleneck blouse. Her gray-streaked brown hair was short and straight, and a pair of glasses hung from a chain around her neck.

"Mrs. Baxter? I thought I recognized you from . . .

well, you know." She had the grace to look embarrassed. "I'm Cordelia Witherspoon, Jake's American history teacher."

"You call him Jake?"

"He asked me to. I just wanted to tell you what an unusual student he is."

Ginny bristled. "In what way?"

The woman had a way of smiling that crinkled up her face, deepening all the wrinkles and making her look younger at the same time.

"You look just like him right now, ready for combat. I meant the remark as a compliment. He's unusual in that he reads and remembers and understands, and what's better, he can see relationships. You have no idea how rare that is." She hesitated. "He also has some pretty far-out ideas, but I'm hoping he'll get over those as he matures."

"Do you think there's a chance?"

"When I was sixteen, I wore garlands of flowers in my hair and went around chanting 'make love, not war' and swore I would never trust anyone over thirty. If I made it to maturity, there's more than an even chance your son will, too."

All in all, this was the best parent-teacher conference Ginny had ever had, and she proceeded to tell Mrs. Witherspoon exactly that.

"I wish there were more Jakes around to stir things up," Mrs. Witherspoon said. "We must get together sometime and talk. I'd like some insight into guiding his reading and would appreciate any help I could get."

*   *   *

Later in the evening, with Jake outside practicing, having been warned to be Jake the Cool at school, Ginny was trying to forget the events of the day when the phone rang. Somehow she knew who was on the line.

"Have I got a deal for you," Steve said.

She thought she had prepared herself for the call, but the first sound of his voice proved her wrong. She felt betrayed, hurt beyond measure. And that was really dumb.

"I'm not buying a used car from you. I don't know you that well."

Wrong crack. If she'd been more dexterous with his belt buckle, she would have learned things about him she had no right to know.

Never, ever would she know what was in his heart and mind. But that was getting serious. She had to keep this light.

His response was a low, wicked laugh, and Ginny had to sit down.

"No used cars. I meant another dinner."

Thud went one of Jake's hard-thrown baseballs against the back fence.

"You can't be serious," she said.

"I am. Do you accept?"

Ask Veronica. Petty. High school.

"Where is this dinner?"

"What does it matter? We'll be together. We'll have a good time."

She wanted to ask him to define "*good time*," but she hadn't the nerve. "Where?"

"Here."

"The Big Here?"

"I like that. The Big Here. Maybe I can use it in a speech."

Ginny looked down at her Bengals sweatshirt and cutoffs. Her hair was in pigtails and she was barefoot. No matter what Steve was wearing, he would look a hundred times better.

"I don't know why you want me around. I'm really not as easy as you think." She paused. "All right, maybe I was the other night, but it's just that I'm so—"

She couldn't think of what she was except ordinary, and she was getting tired of using that one. Besides, it wasn't accurate anymore. How many women got regular calls from the President?

A depressing thought struck. What if their numbers were in the hundreds? Two were more than she could handle.

"Regina Baxter, if you think getting to see you is easy, you have no idea what my life is like. Because of the legacy I inherited from my predecessor, I live in a fishbowl. The little time we had together in the limo was a miracle."

She sat farther back on the sofa, her legs folded Indian-style, and picked at the loose fibers in the upholstery.

"A miracle?" she asked, forgetting the rest of the world.

"Genuine, bona-fide, twenty-four karat."

Ginny had thought so, too, when she wasn't consumed with embarrassment over a few details, but hearing him say it set her blood to pumping. Neither of them said anything, and she knew they were both remembering.

"Are you there?" he asked after an agonizing minute.

"Oh, yes."

"You're a tough negotiator. I should have had you with me in San Francisco."

"Yes, you should."

"You're forcing the truth out of me," he added. "This dinner is also a reception for a few senators and their spouses. Not formal. Definitely not formal."

She heard another *thud* from outside.

"No way."

"Please."

"No."

"I was afraid you'd say that. So I came up with another proposal, being a clever politician and all. If I can get away, and I probably can, how about riding with me Sunday afternoon?"

She couldn't believe he was suggesting it.

"You want me in the back of the limo again? This time, I promise you, there will not be another miracle. Besides, I've had my fill of news stories and pictures."

"You saw the *Scoop*?"

"It was brought to my attention. Along with the *Post*."

"Oops."

"Well said."

"I need to teach you to ignore those things." He had the nerve to laugh. "Besides, I wasn't referring to the limo. I was talking about horseback riding."

She would have been embarrassed except that she was immediately seized by terror. "I've never been on a horse. I've never even seen one up close."

"There's a first time for everything."

He put a lot of meaning in his *everything*. Neither of them spoke for a moment.

"I'll be gentle," he said. More meaning. "You may be a little sore afterwards, but you won't be hurt."

"Do you talk like this to anyone else?"

"Never. I wouldn't feel comfortable talking like this to anyone else, and besides, I don't want to. If it makes you feel uncomfortable, let me know."

It made her feel uncomfortable, all right, but not in the way he meant, not in any way bad.

"Horses are very, very big," she said.

"Big isn't necessarily bad."

"There you go again."

"Yeah. And at my age. I ought to know better."

"I'll bet you were a lot of fun when you went through puberty."

"That's not the way I remember it," he said. His voice had lost its coaxing warmth, and she realized how very little she knew about him.

"I didn't mean to pry."

"You weren't prying."

Still, she felt guilty, which was the only reason she said, "Okay, I'll go." Guilt and the fact that she wanted to say yes more than she wanted to breathe.

And so she found herself on a beautiful May day taking the Red Line to Maryland, at her insistence, having refused to be picked up by Edward Seale again. Getting to the train proved tricky. The watchful eyes she'd sensed last weekend now came with a body—that of a reporter who, wanting to interview her, had twice shown up at her door. Jake and the professor had convinced him that she didn't want to be disturbed. But she knew he continued to lurk somewhere outside her apartment, and if not him, someone just like him.

Professor Carl smuggled her to the Metro stop in the Impala. She rode all the way to the end, where she caught a cab and, with Secret Service cars fore and aft, rode through Gaithersburg, then headed west on River Road, passing mansions the likes of which she had never seen, and lush, grassy land that rolled in descending hillocks to the Potomac.

The President's rented farm was not so fancy as the rest, but it would do. Besides, as the all-knowing cab driver pointed out, he didn't rent the whole thing, primarily the stables that lay in a neat white row at the end of a long, winding drive. Beyond the stables there were horses grazing in the distance behind a white picket fence, but she had eyes for only the small gathering of men and women watching her arrival. Except for Steve, all of them were dressed in dark suits, as if they were going to a funeral.

When the cab rolled to a stop, she paid the driver an amount that guaranteed no lunches for a month. Getting out took as much courage as the D-Day landing on Normandy Beach.

She was wearing jeans, a red pullover sweater, and knockoff Ferragamo high-heeled, low-top dress boots, which was as close to western wear as she could get. The jeans were too tight and the heels too high, but what the heck. It was the best she could do. Let the suits think what they would. She was watching Steve.

The look on his face when she walked toward him told her that she wasn't too anything as far as he was concerned.

Neither was he. Jeans, boots, a white shirt, and a denim jacket, his gait John Wayne rolling as he walked toward her, his jaw square, his eyes so blue they blinded her—the guy knew how to stop a girl's heart.

Minding her manners, she nodded to Ford Davidson and Edward Seale. Leading her back to them, Steve introduced his press secretary, Alan Skinner, a man she recognized from newscasts; the director of the Office of Management and Budget, David Browner; a special assistant to the Council of Economic Advisers, Pamela Macauley; and another man whose title and name she didn't catch, having already taken in all her brain could manage, especially with Steve staring at her.

"Did I get here too early?" she asked.

"Not at all," Davidson said.

"Just winding up a little business," Steve said.

The rest of them watched her, no one more intently than the press secretary. Edward Seale was the only one who smiled. She stepped out of earshot and waited nervously for them to finish. Despite herself, she heard isolated words like *budget* and *committee* and *Senator Gray*. After five minutes they were heading for a couple of limousines parked in the driveway, and then it was just her and Steve and the agents she knew were watching, out of view.

"Sorry," Steve said. "It really is hard to get away."

"I know what you mean. I left a pile of laundry at home."

She got the killer smile as he looked her over again. "Ready to ride, cowgirl?"

"I'm ready, cowboy."

He made her feel good, flirty and cute and, when she could forget the Secret Service, like a woman going out on a date with a good-looking guy. To heck with White House advisers and senator's daughters and lurking reporters. She was determined to have fun.

And then Steve led her to the horse, a black beast the size of her apartment whose reins were looped to a post outside the stables.

"We're both riding geldings," he said. "They're the gentlest animals. Besides, geldings like women."

"Do they like us for dinner?"

Steve grinned. "They do if they've got any sense."

Oh, dear.

"Your horse is named Thunder."

"I hate to tell you this, Steve, but it's not a gentle name."

"It goes with Lightning." He gestured to a white horse tied up down the way. "I get to ride the white one. It's part of my image."

"Thunder and Lightning. I'm in trouble," she said.

"You have nothing to fear but fear itself."

"You told me that once before. I'm not sure you were right."

Turning his back on the horses, he took her in his arms and kissed her, gently, not holding on tight or letting his hands move anywhere except against her shoulders, not caring about who was watching, just making her feel like she was the most desired woman in the world.

"Put yourself in my hands, Ginny," he said. "I promise you won't be disappointed."

Chapter Eleven

"The first thing you have to do is pull Thunder's head close to yours, cup his nostrils, and breathe into them."

Ginny stared at Steve long and hard, fast forgetting the kiss.

"I hate to tell you this, cowboy, but I'm disappointed already," she said.

"It takes only a second or two."

"You didn't say anything about my touching the beast so intimately."

"Nostrils aren't intimate."

"They are when one of you is a horse."

"Ginny, Ginny, Ginny," he said, giving her his straight-on, full-force, rethink-your-foolishness stare, the one that must bring heads of state to heel. "Believe me, you're going to love him by the end of the day."

But she wasn't buying. She looked at Thunder from stem to stern. "Just tell me I'll still be alive."

He eased closer. "More alive than you ever imagined."

Too late. She was already that.

"I'll give you your gloves in a minute. Just hold him with your bare hands and breathe the way I told you. Nose to nose. He needs to know your scent."

"That's not the way humans do it."

"He's great, but he's still a horse. Although he will nuzzle you if the two of you get along."

"Couldn't he just tolerate me? No nuzzling, no loving."

Steve stepped aside. "Quit stalling."

"What if he hates my smell?"

"He'll curl his upper lip."

"And if he likes it?"

"The lip will stay down."

That sounded simple enough. She took a deep breath, stepping close and praying one of Thunder's front hoofs didn't land on a fake Ferragamo, and rested her hands on the ferocious head right where Steve indicated. And she breathed. Oh, how she breathed, right into those huge, quivering nostrils.

Thunder snorted, spraying her with snot, and she jumped back.

Steve pulled a blue bandanna out of a coat pocket and handed it to her. Of course he'd have a bandanna. Cowboys always did.

"Smile, girl. He likes the way you smell."

"You knew he would do that. You were ready."

She dabbed at her face. "Remind me to change perfumes."

Steve nuzzled her. "No way."

She slanted her neck, giving him what little encouragement she could. "I like you better than the horse. You don't sneeze on me."

"You're stalling again." He pulled one pair of leather gloves from a back hip pocket and a second pair from another. "One for me and one for you."

"They may not fit."

"They should. I had a pretty good idea the size of your hands."

He looked innocent, but from experience she knew otherwise.

Of course he proved himself right; the fit was perfect.

The horse shifted around, all the leather on him creaking, and his tail swished.

"Ready to mount?" Steve asked. Like a good passenger, she circled around the beast and headed for the right side. He took her by the waist and guided her back to the horse's left.

Mistake number one. She'd better cut out the counting right up front. There was no telling how high she could go.

"Put your left foot in the stirrup and swing your right leg over the saddle. Then all you have to do is sit and I'll hand you the reins."

She knew there would be more to it than that. For one thing, the stirrup hit her practically at waist level. He was asking a great deal for her to get her foot that high. But then she felt his hands on her rear, giving her a boost, and she decided he gave a great deal, too. She felt weightless as she moved upwards, swinging her leg with such enthusiasm she almost pitched off the other side.

But he had a hold on her thigh, and she balanced her weight, telling herself there was nothing wrong in the way the horse shifted, not much, just a little. Still, it was enough to stop her pulse.

Shifting wasn't her only worry. Her legs were spread so wide, she feared for the seams in her jeans. Thunder needed some low-fat feed.

Steve spent a couple of minutes adjusting the stirrups. "If you feel the urge to pet him, go for his withers. Definitely don't touch his stomach."

She stared at the horse's wiry mane, determined not to look straight down. "His stomach is safe from me." And so were his withers, wherever they were.

"And his ears. That's another thing. They don't like having their ears touched."

"When I'm flying over his head, I'll try not to grab them." She glanced down at the saddle, which was little larger than the seat of her kitchen chairs. "There's nothing to hold on to."

"Sorry about the English saddle. It's all I have. Anyway, it's bad form to hold on to the saddle horn."

Bad form was not a major worry for her.

"You're doing great," he said, freeing the reins from the post and lifting them over Thunder's head, showing her how to hold them loosely in her hands.

"There is one little thing," he added. "You're squeezing your knees. Relax your thighs around the barrel."

"I'll fall off."

"No, you won't. I promise."

She decided to believe him. It made breathing easier. Sure enough, she relaxed and remained upright.

He began to walk away.

"Where are you going?"

"To mount Lightning. All you have to do is what you're doing. Thunder may take a step or two, but that's all. He's well trained."

Veronica Gray can do this, she told herself. It was enough to still the rising panic as she watched Steve desert her. At least he offered her a chance to look at his backside and watch the way he walked in boots.

Sure enough, Thunder took a couple of steps.

Veronica wouldn't scream.

So neither did she, giving full attention to the way Steve mounted Lightning, in one fluid motion, with no one pushing at his behind. She could have watched the movement forever, though she would have preferred the view from ground level.

He rode the white gelding back to her. "Let's go."

"How do I start him?"

"A flick of the reins ought to do it."

He took a moment to explain what else she could

do with the reins, tying them around her not being an option.

"Remember to move with him. Go with his rhythm. Don't fight it. And when you bounce—don't look like that, Ginny, you're going to bounce—hold yourself loose. Let things on you bounce, not all of you. Otherwise, you're going to have a very sore rear when you're done."

"Let things on me bounce?"

He stared at her sweater. "Yeah."

She thought of the lacy little slip of a bra that for some strange reason she'd chosen to wear. "I don't see that I have a choice."

She was so lost in his devilish smile, she forgot where she was until Thunder started moving forward. Gripping the reins, then loosening them at Steve's instruction, she rode alongside him, telling herself to go with the horse's rhythm.

This really wasn't so bad, she told herself, and then she got to the end of the stables and into an open field. Lightning started to move faster, and copycat Thunder did the same. And she started bouncing, all of her, not just parts, her rear slamming down onto the brick-hard saddle with each bounce.

This was not fun.

"Are you all right?" Steve asked. "Remember to relax."

"I'm f-fine." She decided to make the lie a really big one. "I'm relaxed."

They ended up on a path at the side of the field;

she had no idea how, since she really hadn't picked up on exactly how to steer. Steve dropped back. "The path narrows up ahead. Go in front. I'm right here behind you."

Thunder trotted ahead just as Steve asked, Ginny holding on, the horse completely in control. She attempted to relax, she honestly did, but she and the gelding moved to entirely different beats. When she was up, he was down, and vice versa. She tried looking at the grass, the hills, the trees, the beautiful countryside. Mostly she tried to remain in the saddle without squeezing her knees. She had no idea what would happen if she weakened and squeezed them tight, but she knew it would be bad.

An inadvertent signal she must have given the horse quickened his speed as they headed up a hill. She bounced big, squeezed her knees, and pulled back on the reins, all at the same time. Thunder came to a halt. Not so Ginny, who flew over his head and landed hard in the summit grass, spread-eagled on her back.

Steve was kneeling beside her in an instant, checking her over with his expert hands.

"Sweetheart, I'm sorry."

Ginny looked up at him. Sweetheart? She forgot the indignity of her fall.

She struggled to sit up. "I'm fine, Steve. Really. I don't think I touched his ears."

He grinned. "You're in terrible danger, Mrs. Baxter, and I don't mean from the horse. He's the gelding. I'm not."

He put his arms around her and she prepared for another kiss. Instead, he helped her to her feet. "I want to make sure you're all right. Walk around."

She did as he asked. Didn't she always?

"I'm fine, really, except that my legs don't want to go back together."

"That could prove convenient."

He was great at deadpan one-liners.

"Mr. President!" she said, trying to act shocked.

"You are absolutely forbidden to refer to me like that, ever. You and Aunt Doris are the only two people left on the face of the earth who call me Steve."

"Ah ha, so that's why you keep phoning me. I remind you of your aunt."

He stood on the top of the hill and looked beyond her to the picture-perfect countryside. When his gaze returned to her, he was a different man, the hints of humor in his eyes and on his lips gone. His solemnity warmed and frightened her at the same time.

"I keep calling you because I don't seem to have any choice. I like being with you. You're entirely separate from what I do all day every day, innocent of government, innocent of deals. You don't suck up because of who I am. Instead, you give me sass. You have no idea how refreshing that is."

"I sound like comic relief."

"No way. Maybe I'm not saying this right. You don't want anything from me. You have no cause to pursue. The one time you seemed to need me, the other night in the restaurant, it was because I

233

could give you help as another human being. No one's asked that of me in a long, long time."

Ginny's heart swelled to bursting and her eyes burned. Right then and there, under a clear Maryland sky, with God and the Secret Service watching, she fell in love for all time. This was new. This was different from how she'd been with Jonas. Stephen Marshall filled all the lonely spaces in her heart and in her soul.

Sure, she wanted to touch him and kiss him and do some pretty raunchy things, but mostly she wanted to exist on the same planet, to breath the same air he did.

All this flashed through her mind in an instant, and she looked away. The man was smart. He would read the love in her eyes.

"I think Jake regretted what he said. At least the phrasing." She made a C-plus stab at laughing. "His verbal skills need a little work."

"I've got some speech writers he can use."

She dared a corner-of-the-eye glance. "I'll bet you have someone for just about all your needs."

"Not quite." The look in his eyes scorched the soles of her boots. "Let's ride back in."

"We didn't get very far."

"That depends on where we're going."

She rubbed her gloved hands against her thighs, so nervous she was about to explode, over him, his look, his words. And, of course, there was also the horse. She wasn't so far gone that she totally forgot reality.

"I don't want to get back on Thunder."

He smiled at her and winked. She watched as he walked down the far side of the hill to where Thunder and Lightning were grazing. She watched even more closely as he led Thunder back up to her.

Please, Steve, don't make this a crusade. She would, she knew, sacrifice her life for him, but she preferred it to be in a nobler cause.

He secured the reins in a knot over the horse's neck. "Go on home, boy," he said, slapping Thunder's rump. And to her, "He'll make it back to the stables. He knows the way."

He whistled, and Lightning came at a run. "We'll ride double."

That had a nice, safe sound to it, the *double* part more than the *ride*. It also sounded intimate, the kind of intimate she could throw herself into. He helped her mount as easily as he had done before, then eased into the saddle behind her, thighs pressed against hers, arms around her waist, breath stirring her hair, and she tried to remember what was so terrible about horseback riding.

"We can go for a while longer if you'd like," he said.

"I'd like."

Who knew what crises awaited him back at the stables? She'd take him however she could, whenever she could, even on the back of Lightning.

They moved at a leisurely gait, their bodies swaying together in the rhythm of the horse. It was practically like a dance, or sex. She couldn't help making the connection. It was definitely close to sex, very, very nice, but maybe not quite close enough.

"This is beautiful country," she said.

"If you can't get Oklahoma."

"There's no place like home."

"And yours is Ohio."

"I guess. There's nobody back there to go see except for a few friends." This was getting too depressing. "So tell me what your ranch is like." It was an old trick, one of the few her mother had taught her. To get through an awkward situation, ask a man about himself.

Steve proved her mother right, describing the small town of Bottle and the BB Ranch. Reluctantly he admitted the initials stood for Black Bart. The opportunity was there to ask about his father, but Ginny wasn't totally stupid. Despite his denial, she was in part comic relief, and his father was serious stuff.

He talked on and she lost track of where they were. Suddenly Lightning broke into a trot. "We're coming up on the stables from the other side," Steve explained.

"I'm s-sorry I'm bouncing," she said.

"No problem. Just lean back a little more and I'll cushion each fall."

She wiggled her bottom against him. "You make a nice cushion."

"You do a great fall."

Slowing the horse, he rested one hand on her

thigh and ran his thumb along the inside seam of her jeans.

"Whoa, cowboy," she said, but she didn't put much force behind it.

The thumb moved higher, edging toward very dangerous territory, and he kissed the side of her neck. "No way."

A dozen muscles in her stomach-to-knee territory went into play. "You always get to have the fun," she said.

"This isn't fun for you?"

"It . . . has its moments."

She was fighting to keep from grabbing his hand and putting it exactly where she wanted it, but she was still on the horse and they were still who they were, and, worse, where they were, approaching the stables with no telling how many men watching, using binoculars, probably, if they were doing their job right.

So she grabbed his hand and moved it away from her leg. He muttered something very unpresidential and very satisfying to a woman who wanted very much to be loved.

When they got back, he turned the gelding over to a stablehand who materialized out of nowhere. "Put him out to graze with Thunder."

"Yes, Mr. President."

Steve shrugged as the horse was led away. "Mr. President. See what I mean?"

She shrugged right back at him. "I'm sorry you

didn't get your ride. At least not the one you planned."

"How do you know what I planned?"

She took a deep breath. "I guess I don't. It's just that I read in *Newspeak* that riding is how you exercise."

"It's one of the ways." He looked her over. "How do you stay in such good shape?"

She could have walked on the tension between them. "Want me to show you?"

"Oh, yeah."

She led him into one of the stables. Hay was scattered on the hard-packed dirt ground. Two gated stalls stood empty, one on either side of the low-ceilinged room. Bridles and other leather stuff and strange-looking tools hung on the walls. Everything smelled of horse or horse droppings, but it wasn't an unpleasant odor.

"I guess you know what all this is," she said.

"I can show you, if you'd like. A few might have interesting uses."

"Don't tempt me." When they were all the way inside the semidark interior, she turned to face him. "Put up your dukes."

"Words to warm a man's heart."

"It's something I've always want to say to the Pres . . . to a man. I'm a kickboxer. Don't look like that. I'm not a very good one. It's exercise, and a little self-defense, too. I usually work with a partner holding a pad, but you'll do."

She proceeded to pretend-box, striking out with

her fists, stopping just short of hitting him.

"What about the kick part?" he asked.

"I don't know about it in these jeans and boots."

"Take 'em off."

"You're full of ideas."

"Yeah."

He wanted kicks? He'd get kicks. She made them low, then high, to the side and to the back. She was combining the kicks with another blow from her fist just as he moved in. She caught him right in the eye.

"Oh, my God," she cried. "I've hit you."

He touched his eye. "I'll live."

"Oh, my God." She flew to him, tearing off the leather riding gloves, gingerly exploring his injury. "You may have a black eye."

"Really?"

He was grinning. He had no sense.

"Why did you come at me?"

"If you had seen the way you looked in those jeans, you'd understand."

"We need some ice."

"I hate to disappoint you, Ginny, but you didn't hit me that hard."

He took a step forward, she took a step backward, they repeated the steps, the gate to the horse stall gave way, and she found herself in the smaller enclosure with him, standing on a pile of hay, wishing she could see his eye better.

"Don't you have a lantern around here?"

"You've been watching too many westerns. We've

got electricity. Do you really want me to turn on the light?"

She let out a long, slow breath. "I guess not."

The side wall of the stall was shoulder high. He took off his jacket and, along with his gloves, tossed it across the top.

She fluttered her hands, not knowing where to put them. No, that wasn't exactly the truth. She knew where she wanted to put them; she just didn't know how to get them there.

She stared down at her feet, retaining enough sense to be embarrassed.

"The hay's clean," Steve said. "I mucked it out earlier today."

"Mucked?"

"I raked it."

"Oh."

She was busy trying to figure out what to do or say next when Steve took her in his arms and kissed her. Her hands found their way to his arms. He started slow, but he built fast, whispering "Ginny" against her lips one second, ravishing them the next, and she kept busy rubbing her hands across his chest and opening her mouth anytime he wanted to go inside.

When he broke the kiss, she swallowed a protest, but he was still holding her so close that she couldn't take offense.

His fingers threaded their way through her hair. "You don't have to do this," he said.

"I know."

He kissed the side of her neck. "Tell me to stop."

"Go."

"I like a woman who knows what she wants."

Ginny was far more than that, but he would never know it. The trick was to love him with all her heart and her body and do it with sass.

"I want you naked," she said.

"That may prove a little tricky."

"Okay, not all of you. I'll settle for parts."

"I guess I don't have to ask which ones."

She pushed away from him. "Now you're the one who's stalling. I know what I'm doing."

Her heart was beating so fast she thought it might explode. Every part of her, mind and soul, yearned to tell him the truth, but that would be dumb. She couldn't play this dumb or it might all end here and now.

So she smiled and told what truth she could.

"You're the best-looking guy I've ever known, and the smartest, but at the moment smart isn't all that important. You're as separate from my life as I am from yours, and I like that. I like you. Very much."

Her voice broke, but that wouldn't have been sassy, so she covered with a laugh.

"There's also the fact that being with you is a real rush," she added. "I've been alone a long time. Right now I'm about as unalone as I could ever want. So, Stephen Marshall, Mr. Nobody, get naked."

"You like me?"

She rolled her eyes. "Is that what you got out of

241

all that? Egotist. Get those parts naked or I'll bop you again."

"Okay, slugger. You first."

"Pulling rank; I should have known." Stepping back, she pulled off her sweater and pitched it aside.

"Don't move," he said. "Hold that thought."

He left her, but only to close the door to the stable—good grief, she'd forgotten about the outside world—and to snap on a dim light that couldn't have been more than sixty watts. But it was enough.

He came back to her with long, determined strides, and stood in front of her looking at the lacy bra, a brilliant crimson that made her skin glow. Now she remembered why she'd worn it, in case such a moment arose.

The glint in his eyes made her glad of her choice. And then she took a closer look at him. "Good grief, your eye really is turning red."

"So don't look at it."

She dropped her gaze to the opening of his shirt, and then lower, to where the seams of his trousers were being tested the most.

"You're right. This is better."

He didn't say anything for a moment, and she felt a strong urge to put her sweater back on.

"It really has been a long time, Ginny. Those monk remarks weren't wrong."

She tried not to think of Veronica Gray in San Francisco and, worse, in a Chicago hotel. Maybe he was telling her the truth. Politicians didn't always lie.

"Then we shouldn't worry about giving each other anything. Except a good time."

"And babies. Don't worry. I came prepared."

He was looking at her with such concentration, first her eyes and then her breasts, she found it impossible to think that one through.

"I guess we ought to find out if everything's still working," he said.

"I've got a feeling it is."

He stroked the rise of her breasts, and her nipples snapped to attention.

"So far, so good," He said. He put a palm to each breast. "Very good."

She felt languorous and charged at the same time, her head resting to one side while the rest of her body went on alert. Some long-unused instinct of survival told her that no matter what happened between them, she must never be the submissive, passive partner. It could be that had been her mistake before.

The bra had a front hook. Easing his hands aside, she did the necessary unfastening and added this latest item of her clothing to the growing pile at her feet.

Steve let out a long, slow, "Oh," and then added to the compliment: "Ginny, you're beautiful."

"It has been a long time for you," she flipped back, knowing she was on the small side of voluptuous, but she couldn't keep from arching her back a fraction to show herself at a better advantage.

"Stop putting yourself down or I'll leave."

"No, you won't."

He grinned and cupped her breasts. "Okay, you win. I won't leave."

She tried to think of another smart-mouth remark, but all she could think of was how much she loved him and wanted him, hard and fast, down and dirty, before that stable door flew open and the world marched in.

Showing was better than telling. Unfastening her jeans, she eased down the zipper until he could get a view of the top edge of her bikini panties, red to match the bra. She gave him a couple of seconds to look, then unsnapped his jeans.

"I don't know how we're going to manage this," she said. "You'll have to tell me what to do."

His answer was to take her in his arms and bend his head to lick her nipples, then kiss his way back to her lips, all the while his hands were tugging at her jeans until they bunched at her ankles. He shifted right away to the panties, concentrating on the rear, snapping the elastic like a kid with a new toy, then cupping her buttocks and holding her hard against him, her high heels bringing her important parts against his important parts.

It wasn't enough. He had on too many clothes. Forcing her hand between them—she didn't have to force too much before he got the idea—she rubbed him hard, giving little cries of impatience that he picked up on right away.

He dropped his jeans, and she was holding him through his briefs, cupping him the way he had cupped her. He filled her hand, and more. She was throbbing and pulsing, forgetting to breathe, needing so much from him, willing to give everything.

"You need satin sheets," he whispered against her ear, "not groping in a barn."

"I'll tell you what I need."

Slipping her hand inside his undershorts, she stroked him skin to skin, her hand shaping itself firmly to the long, hard shaft, her thumb teasing him until she felt droplets of moisture at the tip.

"Sweetheart," he said, "you've got it."

He pulled her hand away and took control. Kneeling down, he pulled off her boots and the rest of her clothes. Then, to her surprise, he eased her feet back into her boots and stepped back, looking at her standing there in nothing but the knockoff Ferragamos. He didn't seem to care that the boots were fake.

"Triple wow."

"I'm cold, Steve," she said. "I need you to hold me."

And to love me anyway you can.

"This won't be pretty," he said, dropping his undershorts.

"Wrong, cowboy."

"I meant the way we'll have to do this. Next time I definitely promise satin sheets."

"I'll hold you to it," she said and was rewarded with a grin.

He pulled a condom from a shirt pocket and slipped it on. She watched, wishing she could help.

He ran his hands along the outside of her thighs, then moved to the inside, fondling her and finding her ready.

"Put your arms around my neck."

She did, but not before she unbuttoned his shirt, licked his nipples, and then pressed her breasts against his chest. It was, of course, a glorious chest, lightly dusted with golden hair.

"Wench," he whispered.

"What happened to sweetheart?"

"That, too."

She held on to him tight as he lifted her off the ground. She wrapped her legs around his waist, and he eased her down onto him. He hurt her at first—it had been a long time—but then he wasn't hurting her at all. Bracing himself against the side wall, he held her and did what was natural and necessary. So did she. Miracle of miracles, with the wall shaking and the world whirling, they came at the same time. Just before she went completely over the edge, she thought how skilled her true love was at creating miracles.

Chapter Twelve

Ford Davidson dropped the Monday edition of the Washington *Post* on top of the Oval Office desk.

"Ah, the paper to go with my coffee," Steve said with a smile. "Thanks. You're a good man."

He was at his desk early this morning, feeling great, alive, charged, and he thought everyone else should be, too.

"It's not my goodness in question," Ford said, tapping the paper.

Steve stared at the front-page color photograph of himself looking down from the second-floor balcony of the South Portico. It must have been taken with a telephoto lens late yesterday afternoon, when he'd gotten restless and strolled outside. Such a lens would have been necessary to capture the image of his black eye.

He'd had some things he wanted to recall in particular detail, things that required being alone, away from his nosy, too-loving aunt. Doris hadn't been pleased with his explanation of the bruise—"I was struck by Lightning"—for which he could hardly blame her. Unfortunately, when she wasn't pleased, she couldn't let the matter rest.

He should have remembered that he was never alone. The light had been dim. Whatever camera was used, it was a good one. Probably developed by the CIA.

"You want to tell me *now* how you got the shiner?" Ford asked. "After this morning the rest of the world will be speculating which door you'll claim you walked into. It would be nice if your chief of staff knew the truth."

Ford had a point. Giving up on the Lightning crack, Steve had put him off earlier by saying it was nothing and he didn't want to talk about it. He'd never lied outright to his old friend. He debated starting now, then decided he wasn't ashamed of what had happened. On the contrary, he was downright proud.

"Ginny hit me."

He could have also said "Ginny kissed me," like the old song, but he didn't think it was anybody's business but the two participants in the kiss.

Besides, describing yesterday's encounter as kissing was like calling Niagara Falls a little stream.

"You'll need to come up with something more believable than that," Ford said.

"Truth is stranger than fiction."

"He who lives by the sword, Mr. President, dies

by the sword. I can come up with as many bromides as you."

How about all the world loves a lover? Better not throw that one out. From the look in Ford's eye, he figured it wouldn't be appreciated, or especially true.

"Ginny hit me," he repeated.

Ford stared at him. "She did, didn't she?"

"Fist in the eye. I didn't see it coming."

"What did you do to her?"

He shrugged, all innocence. Actually, the fist had landed before he'd done anything. Besides, saying it was something he had done to her was ignoring the equally active things she had done to him.

Tit for tat. Wasn't that how Aunt Doris would put it? He could figure out what a *tit* was, but he'd always been vague on the *tat*.

He put his politician's brain to work. "Is there a kickboxing lobby in Washington? Maybe we could get some good out of this. Give 'em free press while we get their support, say, on the day-care bill."

Ford backed up and sat down in one of the facing love seats. "Regina Baxter is a kickboxer?"

"She says she's not very good. Thank goodness, otherwise I'd look like Rocky at the end of a bad bout."

"And I was worried you two were starting an affair. But no, you have to start a fistfight."

"At least it's different. A little kinky, but different."

"Kinky we don't need. Hell, we don't even need different."

Steve skimmed through the cutline under the photo, grateful there was no speculation as to how the blackeye came to be, just the unanswered question about how the youthful bachelor President had spent his Sunday afternoon. Pundits for the television networks, news magazines, and every other form of media known to the western world would take care of the speculating.

"Look," Steve said, "Ginny was giving me a demonstration, at my request, after I gave her a riding lesson. I moved left when I should have moved right. She was very apologetic." Wow, was she ever. "Tell Alan to come up with something when I face the public at the"—he skimmed down his calendar—"signing of the national parks bill this afternoon. Get Seale in on it. If the Three Musketeers can't come up with a positive spin on this, no one can."

He hated this part of his job, always having to be in the right, which wasn't the same thing as always being truthful. He would have preferred telling exactly what had happened . . . well, not exactly, but close. But then Ginny would be dragged into public view again, and she hated that. It was one of her major charms.

The thought brought to mind the woman's other charms. Let Ford wonder why he was smiling. He came up with another bromide: He was not a man to kiss and tell.

"Get as close as you can to the truth, all right? Now, don't we have a Cabinet meeting to go to?"

"Wait a minute," Ford said. "I've got it. We'll tell the Cabinet and the press that a representative of the National Kickboxing Association was giving you a demonstration."

"I've never heard of the National Kickboxing Association."

"There's got to be one. There's a national everything. You've decided it's a wonderful form of exercise, but for the good of the country you're sticking with horseback riding. You're so damned perfect, sometimes you're frightening. Show 'em you can be a klutz."

"Great. That's why you're my man," Steve said, and the two of them made their way to the Cabinet Room for the Monday morning meeting. When he got there, he would be ready for business, discussing legislation that he particularly wanted to push, the congressmen and congresswomen who were on his side, the names of the ones who were not but who could maybe be won over.

In the meantime, it wasn't a man or a bill that was on his mind. It was Ginny. Sweet, simple Ginny. Thank goodness she wanted nothing from him—she was almost insulting in her insistence that she didn't—nothing, that is, but more of what they had already shared.

She couldn't know it, but he didn't have more to give. In his wheeling and dealing, Black Bart had taught him how to handle Cabinets and foreign potentates, but he'd never learned how to handle one woman on this-is-forever terms. He knew it; it was why he'd thrown himself into public works.

But that didn't mean when a good and understanding woman like Regina Baxter came along, he couldn't enjoy a for-as-long-as-it-lasts relationship, especially when she wanted the same thing.

Ginny hung up the phone, feeling good and bad about what was going on with the man in her life. She knew he didn't have more to give than he was already giving, but then, considering she was giving him everything, neither did she. All in life, it seemed, was relative.

She snapped on the evening news. Her first view of the President made her smile; he was still her Golden Man. The second made her wince. Good grief, what a shiner. She wanted to crawl under the sofa and hide. His explanation brought her out of her private humiliation. National Kickboxing Association indeed. She'd never heard of such an organization, but that didn't mean one didn't exist.

Who knew the real story? What exactly had Steve told? He promised her confidentiality, but she couldn't believe the term meant the same thing to them both.

To her, confidentiality meant taking secrets to the grave. To him, it probably meant sharing them with his dozen closest advisers.

She fingered her MARSHALL badge. With or without a black eye, the guy looked great on TV. He looked better in a horse stall. The fact that she knew it to be true made her feel powerful. As did the fact that she had just turned him down.

"Take that, Mr. President," she said to his screen image.

She still couldn't believe it. Not five minutes ago this hero of the media had called and asked her to the White House for an intimate dinner. Intimate dinner: That had been his phrasing.

"Not there," she said. "Anywhere but there. It's a special place to me and should be to everybody."

Her implied criticism hadn't been too subtle for him.

"It's my home. Right now it's the only one I've got."

"It's not mine."

"Then we'll make it your place."

"You'll get soggy pasta and a romp on a lumpy sofa bed."

"Right now that sounds wonderful."

"Forget the romp. We probably won't be alone."

"Okay, we're back to my place, but we'll make it not so intimate."

"Get real." She startled herself, being so blunt. "I mean, look at it realistically. We get together and we're not intimate?"

"You have a point. I'll think of something else and get back to you."

This time she had no doubt he would. In the meantime she would watch him on television, gloat more than a little, and fall in love a little more deeply, even though yesterday on that hill she'd thought her feelings were as deep as they could get.

There was much to remember about yesterday. Afterwards, the big AFTERWARDS, he'd given her time to pull herself together, then escorted her to a nondescript car that would take her back to the Metro station—he'd given in to her insistence on using public transportation after realizing she wouldn't change her mind about taking care of herself. There had been no sign of a reporter anywhere on her route, for which she was truly grateful.

Today at work, a quiet Monday for a change, she'd thrown herself into cleaning up the back files, updating the posting of bills, and in general being such a paragon of virtuous endeavor that everyone looked at her suspiciously, even Ted. It was a great day for the mysterious Sam to show up, but naturally he didn't.

So here she was, slumped down on the sofa in the late afternoon, exhaustion catching up with her while she postponed all thoughts of cooking supper. At least she could catch a moment of rest.

The screen door slammed and Jake came in. She started, as if watching Steve on the newscast was a crime. Guiltily she thrust the tin star election badge in the pocket of her cutoffs.

"We live in Washington now," she said. "We have to keep up with current events."

"Mom," he said with a wave of his hand toward the screen, "it's all lies. They don't want us to know the truth."

"Which is?"

"Who knows?"

He didn't give her much to argue with, so she just smiled and shrugged, acceptance of the inevitable being her new code of survival in this complicated life that had come her way.

Supper was part of that acceptance. While Jake changed clothes and went out to practice, she started the water for pasta and got out cans of soup and tuna. She needed to do better in the cooking department, especially this Saturday. Not only was it Jake's seventeenth birthday, but it was also the day of the tryouts for the local American Legion team. Takeout Chinese sounded good.

Jake was taking his birthday in stride, but not the tryouts. The first game was just two weeks away, in early June, right after the school year was over. He was great, but this was a new town and a new league, and neither of them would be content until he had definitely made the team.

More than two weeks passed before she had a chance to see Steve again. Life kept getting in the way: for him, things like a prolonged visit from the President of Brazil and world conferences and speaking engagements in other parts of the country. Her things were simpler: work and a son, who had not only made his team but had started out the two-month season pitching like a star.

When Steve was finally able to set something up, it was in a place she never would have guessed: a suite in a historic luxury hotel two blocks north of the White House. It was Sunday; as a birthday gift and reward for making the team, the professor had taken Jake on an overnight trip to Baltimore to see Roger Clemens pitch for the Orioles against the Yankees. Steve had a dinner engagement at the home of the secretary of the Department of the Interior. The dinner wasn't supposed to run late. It was about as free a time as either of them could come up with.

She got to the hotel on her own, but Edward Seale was downstairs to take her through the back hallways to a service elevator.

"This thing is well-named," she said as she stepped into the big padded interior.

Seale smiled and punched the button for the top floor. "The President's a lucky man."

"You'd better tell him so in case he hasn't realized it."

He spared her a quick glance. She was wearing a navy blue washable silk above-the-knee dress and matching jacket. A single strand of artificial pearls were at her throat and navy pumps with sensible heels were on her feet. Her oversized purse served as a mini-suitcase, holding a change of underwear and a toothbrush, some makeup, and money with which to get back home.

Nothing like chains and whips, or even handcuffs and whipped cream. The closest she came to racy was a travel-size tube of toothpaste and an under-wire bra.

Her outfit was hardly that of a seductress. She would have called it her middle-class working-mother disguise, but it was the second-best dress she owned.

She'd saved the sexy stuff for underneath. But Seale wouldn't know that.

"As I said, Mrs. Baxter, the President is a lucky man. I can't speak for him, of course, but I think he knows it."

She had a thousand questions she wanted to throw at him: Who else knows what's going on between us? Does he talk about me? Is he seeing anyone else? Seale wasn't the sort of employee expected to lay down his life for the President, but she felt pretty sure he would lie.

He would definitely report what she'd said. Best keep the questions to herself.

The room where he led her looked like something out of the Department of State reception rooms, with thick carpets and chandeliers, antique cabinets and graceful, tapestry-covered furniture from periods she couldn't begin to identify. Seale pointed out an array of stemware and crystal decanters on a side table, with silver-domed platters next to the liquor.

"The President didn't know what you wanted to eat or drink. I took a guess."

She dropped her purse on a burgundy-and-beige-striped wing chair. "I'll be fine."

"He won't be long. I can stay if you'd like."

"No, really, I can take care of myself."

After he'd gone, she realized he had taken the key with him. Oh, well, she hadn't planned to leave and come back. Once she was gone, she was gone.

Besides the sitting room, the suite had two bedrooms, each with a king-sized bed and its own bath. Had he planned for them to make love and then sleep in different beds? She was staring at one of the beds, standing at the foot and contemplating the possibilities when suddenly he spoke.

"What are you thinking?"

"Oh," she said, whirling, "I didn't hear you come in."

He stood in the doorway, still dressed in the tuxedo he'd worn to the dinner, but the jacket was unbuttoned and the black tie was hanging loose under the open, stark-white collar. She stared at him for a moment, drinking in the image of him. She'd been on a TV starvation diet for days now. Stephen Marshall in the flesh was a feast to behold.

"You didn't answer me," he said.

"I was wondering about the two beds. Are we going to sleep alone?"

"I'll be alone with you, unless you had a third party in mind. But I have to tell you, we simple Oklahoma boys have trouble with a ménage à trois."

"Simple Oklahoma boys don't even know the phrase."

"You'd be surprised."

He tugged his tie free and got out of his jacket before she realized what he was doing. Then he was on her, holding her, cupping her face and kissing her cheeks, her eyes, her throat, just about everywhere but her lips, whispering her name between each kiss.

"I missed you," he said between kisses.

"I missed you."

"Big as an ocean?"

"Bigger."

He licked her lips. "Ain't nothing bigger than an ocean."

"The—the sky."

"Oh, yeah." He went back to her eyes. "I forgot the sky." He looked down at her. "When I'm with you, I forget just about everything."

"Me, too."

In unspoken harmony, they began grabbing and tugging at their own and each other's clothing, kicking off shoes, throwing garments aside until he was down to a very small pair of black briefs and she had on her red lace underwear. Plus the latest purchases she'd made for him: old-fashioned hosiery and red garters to hold them up.

He backed off, both hands in the air as if in surrender. "Whoa," he said, "what's this?"

"It was supposed to turn you on."

"The key in the lock did that."

"So I guess this stuff isn't necessary."

"Guess again."

She nodded toward his briefs, which gave ample evidence that he didn't lie.

"Even your underwear looks formal."

"Yours looks sexy as hell."

She was beginning to feel awkward, just standing there in next to nothing, her arms hanging loose at her sides while he stared.

He ratcheted the awkwardness up a notch. "Take it off. Not the hose and garters. The other stuff."

She managed the brassiere all right. Her breasts were firm enough to hold their shape, despite her age and motherhood, and he seemed to take interest in the fact that her nipples were already in position for his mouth.

But when her thumbs caught in the sides of her panties, she couldn't get them to tug.

"Ginny," he said and winked.

It was all the encouragement she needed. Her panties hit the floor in a flash, and she kicked them aside.

"Mamma mia."

"Are you turning into a linguist?"

"Yeah, if that means I get to use my tongue."

She opened her mouth to say yes, but he was already tackling her onto the bed, putting that tongue to work on her ears and her mouth, holding her, touching her, stroking her from her throat to her knees.

Ginny showed how much she loved him in the only way he allowed. She touched and stroked right back, rubbing herself against him when she could, fondling his sex, backing away long enough to order him to finish undressing for her, and when the small black briefs were hanging from the bedside lampshade, going back at it with a fervor that bordered on desperation, she wanted and needed him so much.

"I can't wait," he said, and he was on her, plunging inside. She closed her eyes, and in the red velvet darkness they made the big fancy bed rock.

Much too soon he was covering her cries with his own frenzied whisperings of her name. It took a long, sweet while for the rocking to stop and the room to quit spinning. When it did, she held on to him extra tight, not thinking about what he looked like or who he was, but how good it was to be with him, how kind and funny he was with her, how gentle yet rough in all the right ways.

He made her feel not only good about him but good about herself. He made her feel complete and satisfied in a way she'd never known, as if her destiny had always been to be with him for however long she could.

No man could give her more.

When he finally pulled away from her, she saw that he was wearing a condom.

"How did you get that on?"

"They don't call me slippery hands for nothing."

She was not inclined to ask who *they* were.

He went into the bathroom for a minute, and when he returned she had folded back the heavy bedcovers and was lying under a sheet.

"They were supposed to be satin," he said. "I ordered satin."

"Maybe they're satin on the other bed."

"Don't go away." He was back in a flash. "Nope. You know, could be I forgot. What with the President of Brazil—" He stopped himself. "You don't want to hear about that."

He was wrong; she wanted to know everything she could that wasn't classified, wanted to know how he spent his days, the pressures on him, the little ways he found to relax.

But he thought she didn't care. He wanted her separate from his work. No matter how kind and funny and considerate he was, Stephen Marshall was a man who got what he wanted.

"Tell me something," she said. "That scar on your hip—how did you get it?"

"That's my war wound. From the Middle East."

"Of course. I had forgotten. You served as a foot soldier, didn't you?"

"I wasn't the only one."

He was probably the only millionaire Yalie who left college to join up, but he *would* find a way to put down the courage and patriotism he'd shown. She paid him a great disservice in thinking he always got his way, just because he always got it with her. Maybe not right away, but eventually.

"You didn't take off the garters while I was gone, did you?" he asked, looking genuinely alarmed, neatly turning the conversation away from himself.

"Find out for yourself, big boy."

Easing under the sheet beside her, he took a peek. "Good, you didn't."

"They're beginning to bind."

"We'll just have to do something about that."

Folding back the sheets, he lay on his side and snapped the elastic.

"That's supposed to help?"

He leaned down and kissed where he'd snapped.

"You're awfully playful tonight."

Taking his time, he kissed his way back up her body, nipping at some very private places with his teeth, lingering at the hollow in her throat. Ginny had a hard time holding still.

"Yeah, I'm playful all right," he said when he finally got back to her lips. "It's been a rough two weeks."

She shoved him onto his back. "Then lie still and watch."

Scrambling to the far side of the bed, which seemed an acre away, she propped one foot on the edge of the mattress and began to roll the garter and hose down her leg.

"I ought to have some music for this, but I guess you can't have everything."

"I've got everything."

From his viewpoint, he did. The thing was, he had even more than he knew.

When she was finished with the second garter, he crooked his finger for her to join him in the bed. Of course she did, and with all the enthusiasm she could have ever wanted, he gave her as much of himself as he could.

*   *   *

They made love one more time before he fell asleep. Ginny managed to doze in his arms, but she never went into the deep trance that characterized her usual nightly sleep. Sometime after three she eased from his arms and put on the thick terry robe she found hanging in the closet, taking care to hang up the dress and jacket she would be putting on in a few hours.

Ted had given her the day off, the woman she'd replaced needing some part-time work, but she still had to get home on the Metro.

Restless, unsettled, she also gathered up her undergarments, unwound the hose and garters, and tossed them all over a chair, operating by the light slanting through the partially opened bathroom door.

In the bathroom, she stared into the mirror, trying to figure out whether she looked any different from when she'd first arrived. Not different because her makeup had worn off and her hair was tangled. She was looking for differences that came from inside.

She stared at herself a long while, trying to figure out what was bothering her. She ought to be satisfied; she ought to be deliriously happy. She and Steve were both single, consenting adults. What they were doing hurt no one. It was right and natural to want what they gave each other. Except for her son, little happiness had come her way for a long, long while.

And it wasn't that she had regrets; she would be

with Steve again if they could make the arrangements. But the fancy hotel suite and the expensive robe and the stolen hours didn't add up to anything that was her. Maybe in time, if their affair lasted, they would. She didn't know if that would be a good thing or a bad one.

Ginny rubbed at her eyes. She'd come a long way from the woman who'd lusted over a magazine cover while waiting for the White House tour, the woman who'd joked about being a love machine turned on by a Golden Man. Love wasn't a joke, and lust, for all the happiness it brought, could also be a trap.

Stepping into the triple-sized shower, she turned on the water as hot as she could stand and let it beat down on her face and chest, rivulets of water running down all the places he had touched and kissed. The water came down so hard, it was impossible to distinguish it from her tears.

Gradually steam filled the enclosure, so thick she barely was able to see him when he stepped inside. The moment he put his hands on her shoulders, she forgot the doubts, the worries, and thought only of how her heart swelled every time he came near. She was being needlessly foolish and foolishly needful of something he could never give; but then, a woman in love didn't always make a lot of sense.

"Are you all right?" he asked.

"I couldn't sleep."

"You're the smart one. Sleep's a waste of time."

He dragged a soapy washcloth across her shoulders, down her spine, her buttocks, between her legs.

"I'm having a hard time standing," she said.

"Tough."

He turned her to face him and began to work on her throat and breasts. By the time he reached her abdomen, she was holding on to his arms for support. When he dipped lower, she leaned against him and gave in to what he was determined to do. A soapy rag in the hands of a skillful man was as effective a stimulant as anything in her experience. Steve was very skillful indeed.

He caught her as she climaxed, held her close, and then tossed the rag aside, starting again with the lovemaking, little touches and kisses, gradually convincing her that she was ready for him again. When she reached the point of crying out in frustration, telling him that she was more than convinced, he backed her up to the slick tile wall of the shower and eased inside her the most erotic stimulant of them all.

Later, when they were toweled dry and back in bed, Steve brought up the matter that had been at the back of his mind all night.

"I want you to do me a favor," he said.

"Haven't I already?"

"Come on, Ginny, you love what's going on here as much as I do."

"You win. I do."

She sounded as brash as ever, yet he couldn't help

thinking there was an edge to her voice that he hadn't heard before. When he looked across the pillow at her and she winked back at him, her skin still rosy from the heat in the shower, he decided it must be his imagination. She was a very special woman, and he was as lucky as a man could be.

He pushed his luck a little further.

"So promise you'll grant the favor."

"No way, cowboy, not until I hear what it is."

"It's getting harder and harder these days to put something over on women. Don't you dare tell the NOW people I said that, or I'll tell them I'm your love slave and you put words, among other things, in my mouth."

Fighting dirty, he rested a hand on her breast. "I want you to be my date for the congressional reception."

She stiffened, and not just the part he was holding. "Isn't that thing over with yet?"

"Nope. If you don't go with me, I'll be the only person there without a date."

"You're a real wallflower."

He shifted his hand from breast to abdomen. "I mean it, Ginny. I want you there."

"I can't. You're asking too much." She hesitated. "For one thing, I don't have anything to wear."

His thumb played around a little bit from its position on her stomach, and it took him a few seconds to focus on his plea.

"Here comes the tricky part. I figured you would say that. I'd like to buy you a dress."

She thrust his hand away. "Definitely not."

"You know I'm rich. Why can't I spend a little money on you?"

"I won't let you pay my Metro fare home; I'm certainly not letting you buy me something as personal as a dress."

"It would be a real crime if we got personal."

That stopped her, but only for a minute.

"Why do you want me there?"

"I feel better when you're near, more myself. And I don't like this sneaking around all the time, as if we have something to be ashamed of. We have to do it, I know, to avoid the press, and any unwanted publicity that might come down on you. But every now and then I'd like people to know that I have a very special, wonderful friend."

"You must have a thousand special, wonderful friends."

"I have a few, and I'll have others when I leave office, but for now, no one is closer to me than you, and no one means more."

He hadn't meant to go that far, but the words came out naturally and he knew they were true. What wasn't the complete truth was the part about wanting *people* to know about her. Mostly he was concerned with Veronica Gray. She was getting harder and harder to put off, just as his negotiations with her father were heating up. She'd found out about the riding lesson and had sent him a note saying she'd like to ride him, too. He didn't think her phrasing was a mistake.

He wasn't using Ginny as a shield, exactly—he truly wanted her by his side—but if she showed up on his arm in public, maybe Roni would cool her hot body for a while. And maybe Daddy the senator would realize that the President wasn't leading his baby daughter on.

Hell, the main truth was, he simply wanted to be with Ginny. In a room full of seasoned politicians, she would be a breath of fresh air.

Only the last part did he put into words.

"A breath of fresh air?" she asked. "More like a destructive hurricane. Or have you forgotten the ambassador's reception?"

"This one is simpler, smaller, in the East Wing of the White House. All of Congress won't be there, just a few senators and representatives who are working on the appropriations bill. We've put in long hours trying to hammer things out. This is my way of showing my appreciation."

"You said I was innocent of government and deals. That's what you liked about me."

"You won't be corrupted, I promise. Besides, it seems to me one person in the room ought to be innocent."

He could almost see her mind working, coming up with another argument. When she did, it was a good one.

"Jake may have a game."

Damn. He hadn't asked about the boy. He'd meant to, over the phone and when he got here tonight, but he'd had other matters on his mind.

"He made the team? I remember you mentioned tryouts."

"They were on his birthday. My baby is seventeen."

"You should have told me," he said, irritated, "about the tryouts and the birthday."

"I may be innocent, Steve, but I'm not stupid. You've got enough on your mind. Not only did he make it, he pitched a shutout in the first game."

"That's great, Ginny. It really is. Does he play on Wednesday nights?"

"No. Tuesdays, Thursdays, Saturdays, and Sunday afternoons."

"Sounds like your destiny is to be with me. The reception is a week from Wednesday. Someone will pick you up at six."

"There will be photographers, won't there?"

"I was waiting for you to get around to that. Much as I hate it, for you more than for me, I can't do anything about it. I've done a lot of thinking about the problem and I've come to the conclusion that if we continue to see one another, sooner or later they are bound to catch us. And we are going to see one another. I'd rather it not be big news. The only way to keep that from happening is to show we have nothing to hide."

"But we do."

"No system's perfect. I'll protect you as best I can. Alan Skinner can handle the questions from the press, should there be any. If we're casual and open enough, it really shouldn't be a problem."

He could sense her weakening.

"Tell you what, sweetheart. I'll order us up a big, giant, huge breakfast complete with pancakes and Vermont syrup. By the time it gets here I'll bet you'll have changed your mind."

Chapter Thirteen

Ginny couldn't believe she'd agreed to go. Steve made a big deal about ordering breakfast, the way he'd promised, but she found out later that Edward Seale already had it on the way. Still, he made it seem like a joke, and somehow or other she'd heard herself agreeing to attend the reception.

The more serious doubts, the unexplained middle-of-the-night worries, had been thrust aside, or at least pushed to the back of her mind, where she could deal with them later. Crying like that in the shower had been a silly PMS thing. The tears hadn't lasted for long.

At least she'd had enough gumption to insist on an out. The acceptance was contingent upon her finding a dress.

"I'll loan you one. No strings."

"No dice. All I want from you is reassurance that a long gown is proper," she said. "If I cover my legs, all the other women won't be baring theirs, right?"

"There's a social secretary at the White House who handles that stuff. I'll have her call you."

The guy had an answer for everything . . . as long as her questions didn't get too close to the heart.

The secretary did call, that same afternoon, with the news that the occasion was formal, long dress, fancy. The little black number was out, which was just as well, considering the memories attached to it.

At work Tuesday, feeling a little reckless, she confided her problem to Ted Waclawski, admitting that she was going to see the President again. He would find out about it anyway, and she would rather it not be from a telecast or from the front page of a tabloid. She even told a few of the customers, including the woman who had given her the badge.

"I knew that tin star would bring you luck," the woman said, "just the way it did that nice Mr. Marshall. You must tell us everything that happens, dear. We're all so proud of you."

If the woman only knew the whole truth.

Ted's wife helped her out with the dress, telling him to tell her about a resale shop in Arlington. On Wednesday afternoon, one week from D-Day (Disaster Day), she rode the bus there and found a blue sequined number that was simple and elegant at the same time and almost fit. Her next-door neighbor claimed to be great at alterations. Ginny bought the dress before she chickened out.

The cost, even of a preowned gown, was substantial, but she figured she could sell it back there or to another shop and recoup some of her loss. It was the kind of gown she would never wear again.

The dress truly was lovely, sleeveless, with a high neck that emphasized her slender throat, cutting in deeply to reveal her shoulders, then skimming down her body to the floor—or at least it would skim to the floor once her neighbor got to work, took in the seams, and turned up the hem.

Silver shoes and purse and control-top pantyhose would get her ready to go. Now she needed a physician who would load her up on Prozac and all would be well.

She said the same to Jake, who was taking the news of her plans fairly well, being more sanguine about life now, after passing another grade in school and heading toward his senior year, getting to see Roger Clemens, and especially after doing so spectacularly well on his new team.

She suspected Professor Carl, with his low-key, reasonable approach to everything, was having a calming effect on him, for which she was truly grateful.

"Cold turkey," Jake said at the mention of the Prozac. "That's the only way. They're just a bunch of bureaucrats, anyway. You're worth a hundred of any of them."

Ah, a son's love for his mother was a wondrous thing to behold, except that he put the strongest emphasis on the *bunch of bureaucrats*. Beside those scoundrels, he seemed to be saying, anyone would look good.

He did mention one thing that truly disturbed her.

"You know, Mom, you don't babble anymore."

"I hadn't realized it, but you're right. I don't suppose I do. Is that good or bad?"

For a minute he was his grim, take-on-the-world self.

"If he hurts you, he'd better watch out."

Ginny shuddered, remembering the Secret Service guns.

"I know it's hard for you to believe, but he really is a friend. You like me, don't you? Why shouldn't an Oklahoma cowboy? Remember, he's working here at a temporary job. Now maybe if he were someone important, like Roger Clemens, you'd have reason for concern."

His only comeback was a disgusted shrug.

Saturday morning she did something she had been meaning to do ever since moving to the D.C. area: she went to the Smithsonian. In particular, she went to the National Museum of American History, or more precisely, to the exhibition entitled "First Ladies: Political Role and Public Image."

She would have died if Steve had had any idea she was there. She wasn't angling to be First Lady; she would make the worst one ever, and besides, it would never happen. But she couldn't help being curious about the women who had taken on the role.

Even with a quick first study, she learned more than she wanted to know, walking through the winding exhibit with its photographs and quotations and comments on the times. These women were tough, had to have been, considering the demands put upon them.

She was on her second walk through, picking up on nuances she'd missed on the initial viewing, when the first voice came.

They said I was insane. But I wasn't.

Ginny was standing in front of a display about Mary Todd Lincoln. She looked around at the other museum visitors, but no one seemed to have heard anything. Neither did they seem to be paying any attention to her.

"Mrs. Lincoln?" she asked the First Lady's portrait, feeling about as foolish as she'd ever felt. She shot furtive glances to right and left, but still no attention came her way. Maybe the display featured a recording she hadn't noticed before. It was unlikely, but more possible than any alternative she could come up with.

Yes, my dear. Thank you for listening. It's been a while since a sympathetic soul paused here. I'm so often overlooked or scorned.

There was a personal, between-me-and-you quality to the voice that seemed to preclude a recording, and she found herself compelled to respond in the same tone.

"I'm listening." A few more furtive glances. "Go on."

The sigh from the portrait was as audible as the words.

I saw my husband shot down before my eyes and buried my beloved son Tad, and then had to endure the indignity of commitment. Few of my memories are happy ones.

Ginny leaned close to the picture, feeling that maybe she was the one who should be committed, and whispered, "Didn't you hate being on display all the time?"

If anyone finally noticed, she hoped they would think she moved her lips while she read the captions on the wall.

Of course. But I lived in a time of war. My privacy was little to sacrifice when so many others gave so much more. I could easily sacrifice myself, but not my loved ones. They claimed I squandered federal funds on foolishness such as Presidential china, but later Julia Grant spent equally and more. She was popular, you see, the wife of a war hero, and I far more a symbol of loss.

The portrait fell silent. Feeling more than a little like Alice after she fell down the rabbit hole, Ginny found herself being drawn to another portrait.

Mary tends to remember herself as noble. I'm not saying she wasn't, considering the terrible losses she suffered, but willingness to sacrifice was not her strong point.

Ginny looked at the grim-faced visage of Abigail Adams, wife of the second President.

"Do you two talk?" she asked, giving up all hope of sanity.

We all do, those of us who have gone to meet our

Creator. It passes the time. I was called upon to run a farm while John fought for independence. Ours was also the first family to live in what was then called the President's house. What a dreadful place it was, big and drafty and inaccessible. We had to hang wash in what you call the East Room.

"How did you handle the public exposure?"

I thrived on it. Men tended then as they still do to prefer absolute power over their wives. I thank the Good Lord John and I were partners. They called me Mrs. President, you know, and none too kindly. But I gave him sensible advice and he was sensible enough to take it.

Abigail Adams was definitely a woman before her time.

Abigail's manner was harsh, blunt, not like mine.

Here was another voice to be heard. Ginny sought out Dolley Madison, looking serene, confident, and regal in her Gilbert Stuart portrait, her voice soft and winning.

I found a gentle touch, a compliment, a laugh served far better to win support for both Thomas, who asked me to serve as his hostess, and my own dear James.

Thomas Jefferson and James Madison, such glorious names, but Mrs. Madison had been glorious in her own right.

"Did you know who to court, who to influence, exactly what to say and do?"

We all had to know those things.

Ginny turned to find Martha Washington's full-length portrait close by. Again, here was a First Lady who looked confident and dignified.

I set the pattern for the wives who would follow. Mr. Washington insisted that I hold a weekly open house. I served as hostess for our new nation. Of course I knew who to court and whose influence would best serve the President's needs. It was a nev-erending task, but it had its compensations. Did you know that before the election, I visited the troops in the field of battle, ofttimes at great peril? But Mr. Washington was a special man and the office to which he was eventually elected, a position unique in all the world. I did nothing I would not do again. Except perhaps tolerate a certain friendship that he held . . . but that's another story many of us have had to face, some friendships far more flagrant than Mr. Washington's.

Ginny heard the clearing of a throat and found herself looking at a portrait of the seated Ruther-ford B. Hayes, with his wife, Lucy, standing behind him.

Do you want to know the real secret of their suc-cess? Alcohol.

"Alcohol?"

It was simple to serve as hostess if you kept filling the guests' wineglasses. I said nay to such folderol. It's true I became the object of ridicule, but I was also a beacon of hope for the Woman's Christian Tem-perance Union and for all those women and children across our great land who suffered at the hands of Demon Rum.

Evelyn Rogers

Disinclined to linger before Mrs. Hayes's portrait, yet not disagreeing with her entirely, Ginny walked on, not stopping until she came to a portrait of Eleanor Roosevelt serving in a soup kitchen during the early, dark days of her husband's first administration.

They talk of serving as hostess as though that were our primary responsibility. But our country has greater need of us. Seek out the others—Mrs. Wilson, who ran the presidency when her husband fell ill, and Florence Harding, a divorcée abandoned by her n'er-do-well first husband. Did she lie upon a fainting couch and cry for smelling salts? No; she turned a failing newspaper into a success and then spoke out for women's suffrage. And please do not neglect Mrs. Nixon, who, dear soul, made needed friends for us in South America and Africa. Talk to them all and you will find strong women with a social conscience and the spirit to fight for the causes in which they believed.

Ginny was ready to hear a drumroll and a fanfare of trumpets when Mrs. Roosevelt was done. She was also ready to crawl on her belly out of the exhibit, realizing more than ever her own inadequacies. These women had waged crusades, ridden into war, faced criticism that would have destroyed many a man. And all this did not include the good work and brave deeds of the First Ladies who had not yet, as Abigail Adams put it, gone to meet their Creator.

Why had they spoken to her, as if they shared some kind of bond?

She took one last stroll through the exhibit, looking at the clothing and the artifacts, seeking an answer to her question, but all she heard was the chatter of a school group tromping through, glancing at the pictures, giggling at the quaint forms of dress. If the First Ladies had truly spoken to her, they were silent now, and Ginny began to wonder if she had imagined it all.

Puzzled though she was by the talk, she understood all too well the message the women brought, a message of courage and intelligence and public spiritedness. These women had known not only how to stand by their men, but also by their country.

As she made her way down the steps of the museum and headed across the Mall toward the Smithsonian Metro stop, clutching a copy of a book on First Ladies she'd bought at the Museum Shop, a sobering thought would not leave her mind. The services and support she provided the current President of the United States would never be ones she could boast about from a Smithsonian wall, unless the museum curators opened a new wing for a First Mistresses exhibit.

Why that should depress her so much, she didn't know. But she had the same dark sense of doubt she'd experienced in the bathroom at the hotel. She loved Steve and understood him and the limitations of what they shared, yet she couldn't shake the feeling that, though her temporary relationship with him was both right and inevitable, in some way she had not yet fathomed, it was also very wrong.

"Jake Baxter's pitching. I'm going to the game."

William Alcorn stared at the President in disbelief.

"Impossible. There is no way I can guarantee your safety."

"I'll go in disguise."

Ford Davidson snorted. "You're the most photographed man in the world. Are you planning to go in drag?"

"Good idea. Get me RuPaul on the phone. He should be able to help."

Edward Seale was grinning, Ford was scowling, Alan the intrepid press secretary was figuring out the spin, and his chief of White House security was staring at him in an especially rigid, stone-faced way, making Steve feel as if he'd spilled something on his tie.

He leaned back in his Oval Office chair. They could all go to the devil. Jake Baxter was pitching tomorrow. He was going to that game if he had to run away to do it. He owed it to Ginny. She was going to the congressional reception, something she was predetermined not to enjoy. He, on the other hand, liked baseball and would enjoy the game.

And he liked Ginny. More and more. He couldn't get her out of his mind, from the quick, unintimidated way she had of throwing words at him, to the sudden smile that showed she understood him, even to the way her brow furrowed when something troubled her mind.

Remembering all this and more, he smiled during inappropriate moments, like when General Patton Cartright was expounding on the latest nuclear-powered weapon that could annihilate half the known world, thereby guaranteeing for all time U.S. military supremacy, and at a cost of no more than six trillion dollars.

Or when Vice President Posey was reporting on the latest state funeral he had attended, this one in Singapore.

He looked at his watch. It was three p.m. Saturday afternoon. That left him less than twenty-four hours to figure out how to get to the bleachers at an Arlington high school for a one p.m. Sunday American Legion baseball game, and get there without taking away from the game's star. It didn't look as if the Three Adviser Musketeers would come up with anything helpful. He knew for sure that William Alcorn would play the obstructionist right down the line.

He waved them away, as if agreeing with their arguments, giving up, trying to look disappointed but accepting of a verdict he didn't like.

But inwardly he smiled.

It was time to call upon the Black Bart side of his nature, the devious, devilish streak that got him to date Ginny Baxter in the first place, the same streak that was getting her to the reception, the same streak that would in a manner yet to be determined get him to that game.

Ginny settled down on the bleacher seat next to Professor Carl and watched Jake warming up on the sidelines. In his red, white, and blue uniform, he looked older than seventeen, especially when he wound up and let fly with one of his zingers. The crowd of parents and young people around her murmured after each pitch. She wanted to tell them to hold their admiration until he let loose with one of his eighty-mile-an-hour fastballs.

She was so proud of him, she was ready to explode.

And then it was time for the teams from the opposing American Legion posts to stand along the baselines for the Sportsmanship Prayer. Like the others, Jake stood with hat over heart, head bowed. Ginny had heard the prayer so often, she knew it by heart, but she always sent up a little prayer of her own in thanks for whatever kept Jake from protesting this very important ritual.

The stands were only three-fourths filled, with lots of empty spaces in the rows below, but Ginny liked to sit up high where she could get a good view of all the action.

She squeezed the professor's arm. "Thanks for being here. I've watched so many games alone, it's nice to have someone to cheer with."

"You're like family, Ginny. I wouldn't be any-where else."

"I don't know anything about your family."

"They're all gone."

"I'm sorry. Like mine, I guess."

He didn't answer right away, but she could read nothing in his expression to hint at what he was thinking.

"Yes," he said. "Like yours."

She might have asked more, but a latecomer was working his way past the spectators two rows be-low. He was wearing jeans and a leather jacket, his oversized gut hanging over his belt. An Orioles baseball cap was pulled low on his forehead, and aviator sunglasses hid his eyes. The collar of the jacket was pulled up, blocking the back of his neck and half his face.

If his hair had been dark and the jacket studded with brass, he would have looked like Elvis Presley.

Despite all the covering and the pillow he must have stuffed down his shirt, he didn't fool her for a minute. She'd seen him from too many angles too many times, knew too well the slope of his head and shoulders, even the way he sat, easing himself down until he was at rest, crossing one leg over the other, resting a hand on his boot.

How she kept from screaming out *Steve!* she had no idea. It had to be shock that shut her up. What she did know was that the rascal—the darling ras-cal—sensed she was watching him. He'd probably chosen that particular row so she could get a good view of his being a good sport. Payback for the up-coming reception. It was another reason she never should have said she would go.

As he took a seat directly in line with her, she clutched Professor Carl's arm.

"What's wrong?" he asked.

She blinked twice in the direction of the cap, afraid to point and say anything. After a minute the professor picked up on the blinking.

"So?" he asked, looking downward.

"Interesting crowd here today," she said, smiling, darting her eyes to the latecomer and wriggling her brows.

Professor Carl nodded, glanced down again, and then his eyes widened.

"*Mein Gott!*"

He, too, understood. The President of the United States was at Jake's game.

Ginny didn't know whether to propel herself across two rows and thank him with hugs and kisses or to recoil in horror at the potential disaster of the scene, there being no sign of a Secret Service agent anywhere. They were good at disappearing into the President's surroundings when it suited them, but nobody was this good.

She was so busy worrying and trying not to look at Steve that she missed Jake's first pitch.

"Strike one," the umpire called.

This was the same umpire who had officiated at Jake's first game. The dramatic kind, he liked to yell out his calls. A burly man in sweats sitting next to

Steve gestured his disagreement at the call, and Ginny got a sick feeling in the pit of her stomach.

Whistles and catcalls from the stands preceded the second pitch.

"Strike two!"

Another gesture from Burly Man, and Ginny got sicker. Usually the fans were polite in their enthusiasm. Why did a loudmouth have to show up today?

Tugging at the professor's sleeve, she got him to move down a few places on their row to where she could get an angle on Steve's face and better read his expression. He was looking cool, an everyday kind of guy watching a Sunday afternoon game, seemingly oblivious to the fact that the temperature was close to eighty. He had to be dying in that leather jacket.

The third pitch was a pop fly, caught by the third baseman. The next batter grounded out, the third was called out on strikes, and the team from Post 139 came in from the field for its turn at bat. They got a runner on but no one crossed the plate, and at the end of the first inning the score was 0–0.

For the next hour the game turned into a genuine pitchers' duel, Post 139 ahead 1–0 at the end of the fifth, with Jake having a no-hitter going. American Legion games went nine innings, as opposed to the seven in high school. At one of the practices, Jake's coach had explained to her that few pitchers went the full nine innings. Ginny had thought but not said that the man didn't know Jake.

She'd been a baseball mom too long to argue with a coach.

This would have been a glorious day for her and her son if it weren't for two things: Steve's presence and the growing agitation of Burly Man, who was obviously a supporter of the other team.

But that was like the old joke, "Other than that, Mrs. Lincoln, how did you enjoy the play?"

The joke had always been decidedly unfunny to her, and was especially so now that she was on speaking terms with the tragic First Lady.

Two more innings passed and Jake's no-hitter still held, Steve was still playing Joe Cool, and Burly Man was still playing the boor, yelling out every time Jake was winding up.

Once Steve leaned toward him and whispered something; the boor growled back at him, but Ginny wasn't able to pick up what either man said.

Okay, guys, cool it with the testosterone.

She prayed they got the message.

At the top of the eighth, as Jake trotted out toward the pitcher's mound, the coach followed. A relief pitcher warmed up at the side. Her mother's heart was torn in two directions: pull him and rest his arm; let him go for the no-hitter.

The crowd got into the argument, with most of the opinions coming from the high schoolers in the stands. When the coach headed back to the sidelines, leaving Jake on the mound, mostly cheers went up. Burly Man chose to protest, loud and clear, that the pitcher was a bum, the umpire was in the tank, and just about every \$%@ˆ*&˜! person who cheered against his boy (Ginny had figured out the unfortunate lad was the opposing catcher) sucked.

Ginny hadn't heard the like since middle school days in Ohio. Steve stood and in an unmistakable voice that carried across a major section of the bleachers told the guy to watch his mouth or get the hell gone. Just how many people recognized him at this point Ginny didn't know, but the word *President* rippled across the rows around her. The boor shoved and socked him in the pillow, which unfortunately shifted to a position high on Steve's chest.

Steve had his fist drawn back when a third combatant flew between the two—William Alcorn in jeans and T-shirt, coming from nowhere, doing his job. At least he wasn't firing a gun.

Two other jeans-clad agents dragged the man down, while the White House chief of security hustled his President to the end of the row and up the bleacher steps to the main stairway. As Steve passed her, he pushed down his glasses a fraction and winked.

She collapsed against the professor and the place went wild, not so much on the field but in the stands. It took fifteen minutes for order to be restored. Ginny didn't know whether to run after Steve or stay in place. By then he was probably long gone, in an armored limo Alcorn would have had waiting. She stayed and watched the rest of the game in a daze. Jake lasted the next two innings, losing his no-hitter in the top of the ninth on a single to right, winning the game one to zip.

Later, on the ride home in the professor's Impala, he also got in the last word about the disturbance in the stands.

"So what if he came to the game? He didn't hang around to the end. I'm telling you, Mom, he's not any different from the other guys you picked. When you need him most, he's not going to be around."

Carl Morris was sitting at his cluttered dining room table pecking away on the old manual typewriter he'd owned for thirty years when he heard the knock at his door. He growled over the disturbance. After decades of putting off writing his memoirs, he had finally taken a summer off from teaching to get the cursed thing started, and he did not suffer interruptions graciously.

Writing was hard, especially writing the kind of narrative he was dealing with, where the memories were seldom benign.

Shuffling to the front door in his slippers, he glanced at the clock over the mantel in the living room. Ten on a Monday night seemed late for a caller.

He opened the door and Doris Tanner barged in. On the stoop behind her were a couple of Secret Service agents. He gestured for them to come in, too. They did, took a quick look around, then returned to the stoop, closing the door behind them.

Wearing a pink silk dress and gray shoes, with a matching purse dangling from her arm, the President's aunt stood in the middle of the living room and tapped her foot.

Carl straightened his suspenders and tucked in his shirt. "I assume this isn't a social call."

"We've got to do something," she snapped. "This is getting out of hand."

"Let me take a guess. You refer to your nephew and Mrs. Baxter."

"Of course. Who else?"

"Please," he said, "let me fix us a cup of tea and we can talk."

She opened her mouth to protest, but he already had her by the arm and was gesturing to the kitchen at the back of the house.

He took his time preparing the tea, putting a half dozen sugar cookies on a platter and setting it on the kitchen table, pouring cream into a pitcher, spooning sugar into a bowl, while his guest tapped her foot, drummed her fingers on the table, and fumed.

She muttered, too, but he made no attempt to pick out what she said. His hearing wasn't what it used to be and, besides, he knew he would hear it all again.

Fingering the lace-trimmed linen napkin he set beside her plate, she quieted a moment. "Nice." She ran a finger around the Dresden plate with its intricate rendering of lilies of the valley. "Nice."

"Cream? Sugar?" he asked.

She said yes to both.

When she opened her mouth to begin, he offered her a cookie.

"Nice," she said after a couple of nibbles. He'd been especially worried about this batch; it hadn't seemed to please the Baxters.

"Now then," he said, "what must we deal with in particular?"

"He's been seeing her."

No need to identify the *he* and *her*.

"And?"

"She causes trouble. I know she had something to do with his black eye, but he keeps telling me something stupid about his horse Lightning. And then yesterday he went to that game." She shuddered, as if he'd paid a visit to hell. "I suppose you heard about it. She was probably bragging to everyone who would listen about how he showed up and all because of her."

"I was there, but I don't recall her bragging. As a matter of fact—"

"You saw it? The brawl? The public disgrace?"

"He came out the hero. If I'm not mistaken, he could easily have picked up a vote or two."

"I don't care about votes. I care about his safety. He sneaked out. Sneaked out! Like an adolescent. Borrowed that dreadful jacket from someone downstairs, and those glasses. He looked like something out of a biker movie."

"What do you know about biker movies, Mrs. Tanner?"

"Why, nothing," she said, giving every appearance of being nervous. "But I've heard."

Ah-ha, he thought, a closet movie junkie. He was one, himself.

She finished off the cookie and helped herself to a second one, pausing to take a swallow of tea.

"He gave everyone the slip. I think he went through one of those tunnels under the White House. If Mr. Alcorn hadn't gotten suspicious and gone to the game with a few agents, there's no telling how things might have ended."

"And all this is Regina Baxter's fault."

"She's cast some sort of spell over him. He hasn't been the same since she forced her way into his office."

Carl suspected the President was happier, but he doubted Mrs. Tanner would agree.

"Doris—you don't mind if I call you Doris, do you? Please, call me Carl. We should be on a first-name basis if we're to work together on this problem."

Doris smoothed the back of her hair.

"It would probably be best."

"More tea?"

"Why, yes."

Again, Carl took his time.

"Don't think I don't realize what you're doing," she said as he poured the hot water into the teapot.

"What, recycling the leaves? I always do."

She sighed. "I mean all of this. You're calming me down so that we can talk reasonably."

"How successful am I?"

She looked as if she wanted to smile, and would, if only she didn't have so much on her mind.

Her hands fluttered and settled in her lap. "I'm worried about him, nothing more. He's all I have in the world. I want someday to leave all this behind and get him safely back to Oklahoma, away from danger and the public glare."

"He has three more years here and, I suspect, another four after that."

"It's what he wants, I know, and of course that makes it what I want. But after these years in Washington, that's when he needs to go home." She went back to drumming her fingers. "I'm afraid for him. I don't know why, but I am."

Carl covered her hand with his; she didn't pull away. What she feared was losing him to someone else, to wit a single working mother with a problem teenager as her only child. Ginny doubted that would happen; she'd as much as told him so.

But people didn't always read the signs right when predicting the future. He had only to read through his own memoirs to be convinced of that.

"She plans to marry him," Doris said, looking up at Carl with genuine worry in her eyes.

"I don't think so."

"Oh, but she does. Did you know she went to the Smithsonian First Ladies exhibit last Saturday? She was in there for hours. Steve doesn't know I know, but I heard one of the agents reporting to him."

"He's had her followed?"

"There was some sort of threat—it was nothing, I'm sure, there are always threats—but he wanted to know she was safe. Not because he's emotionally involved, you realize, but he feels responsible for her for some unfathomable reason."

"It could be because he asked her on a date."

"Well, that was a special situation, that first time. I'd really rather not go into it, if you don't mind."

"What exactly was his reaction to her visit to the exhibit?"

"He was more bemused than anything. I don't believe he knew how to react. He's not used to brazen women, you see. Where women are concerned, he's led a protected life."

Carl almost laughed. Ginny Baxter was one of the most unassuming women he had ever met, and one of the nicest.

But laughter was not the way to court Doris Tanner's good graces, especially laughter that wasn't shared.

"As I see it, Doris, we have two options—to throw them together so that they realize they don't suit, or to keep them apart so that affection doesn't have time to grow. It might be necessary for us to consult on a regular basis to come up with an adequate plan."

Chapter Fourteen

At five minutes before six Wednesday evening, Ginny opened the door to her apartment expecting to greet Edward Seale. What she saw knocked her back on her very high heels—the most gorgeous man in the world looking as if he'd just stepped off the cover of *Gentlemen's Quarterly*, saving his grin just for her.

"Hi," he said. "Hope I'm not too early."

She had to swallow her heart. "Steve, I didn't expect you. Where's Edward?"

"There are some things, my dear, a man has to do for himself. May I come in?"

She peered around him. "Are you alone?"

"Get serious. My guys are everywhere. After Sunday, finding privacy in the bathroom is tricky."

"We need to talk about Sunday."

"Can we do it inside? The agents get antsy when I stand around in one place too long. They've been sweeping the area for the past two hours and still aren't convinced it's safe."

He came in and she stood aside, nervous, seeing the small, plain room as he must see it, the sofa and TV, the Formica kitchen table with its centerpiece paper napkin holder, the four mismatched chairs, the antebellum stove.

"So that's the lumpy sofa bed," he said.

"I might have known you would pick that out first."

"Tell the truth. It's what you like about me."

He took a long, slow, round-trip survey of her. She didn't mind, feeling good about the way she looked. She was wearing her hair straight, no jewelry, the sequined top of the gown taking the place of any rhinestones she might have come up with. If she did say so herself, the dress skimmed everything just fine.

She hated the exposed freckles on her shoulders, but it wasn't as if he hadn't seen them before.

"Triple wow. For a woman with nothing to wear, you fixed up real fine."

He moved toward her, the picture of sophistication despite the affected drawl, bringing with him the clean, lemonlike scent of his aftershave, looking like Everywoman's ultimate fantasy in his tuxedo. Forget Everywoman. Right now belonged to her and her alone.

And right now was all that mattered, she told herself, and she believed it, too.

She turned her cheek to him. "The mouth is out. I finally got the lipstick just right."

He brushed his lips against her cheek. "Everything's just right."

"With you, too, Big Guy." She looked at the sofa bed. "We'd better leave or we'll never get out."

"Where's Jake? I figured on a lecture from him before we made it through the door."

"He's at practice."

"I meant to tell you right off, that kid of yours is great. I played a little baseball when I was a kid, third base, lead-off batter—"

"Naturally lead-off."

"Yeah, I was pretty good in seventh grade, but remember, I had a father who expected perfection. It was a good thing I never faced a pitcher like Jake, or it would have been the orphanage for me."

"There are no pitchers like Jake."

Where her son was concerned, Ginny didn't fool around with false modesty.

"But about Sunday—" she tried to add.

"Sweetheart, you can't tell me anything I haven't already heard. And you want to know what? I don't regret going there at all."

"Not even the leather jacket and shades?"

"Especially not those. I was cool."

Ginny gave up. For a world leader who prided himself on honor and dependability, he did Bad Boy very well.

He led her down the drive toward the limousine, which was parked in the street, motorcycles to the front, automobiles to the rear. The convoy took up most of the block, and a host of agents were crowded along a large portion of the driveway.

With the sun shining down so brightly, Ginny could imagine everyone in every house around peering out their windows to get a look at the proceedings. They wouldn't have to wonder what was going on, not with the Presidential seal on the door of the limo and the two flags flapping on the front fender.

The question in their minds wouldn't be *what* but *why*. She figured over the next few days she would hold open house, ask Professor Carl to bake the refreshments, and answer the questions as best she could, keeping the lies to a minimum.

Surrendering to the inevitable was a lesson Steve had taught her well.

Pitching her purse in ahead of her, she eased cautiously into the back seat. Her neighbor had done a splendid alteration job on the gown, but she'd used measurements taken when Ginny was standing. They had both forgotten that on occasion she would have to sit down.

Steve sat close beside her and took her hand.

"Tell me, cowgirl, is tonight easier or harder than riding Thunder?"

"I don't know. Is anyone planning to throw me?"

The quip was supposed to bring a laugh, or at least a smile. It was the best she could come up with, given her Prozac-free condition.

Steve's frown was not at all a comforting reaction.

"Steve, what are you hiding?"

"Nothing."

He was all golden innocence, but she was getting to know him very well. Something was wrong.

"If you don't tell me, I'll give you another black eye."

"Oh, boy, you're forcing the truth out of me. It's nothing really, nothing you can't handle."

"That does it. I'm out of here. Tell the driver to turn around and take me home."

"Just wait. There are several senators I'll be talking to, and some representatives, too, so maybe I won't be right with you as much as I'd like."

"When will you stray? From the time we get there until the time we leave?"

"It won't be that bad, I promise. Ford and Barbara will be with you if you need them. You liked Barbara, didn't you?"

Ginny thought back to the San Antonio Rose, and to the scene she usually managed to keep from her mind.

"She was very kind about Jake at the restaurant."

"That's no surprise. She has a weakness for mother-and-son situations. I know she and Ford wanted children, but it just didn't happen."

Ginny also remembered how Steve had behaved, staying calm, using his considerable charm to smooth a situation that could very easily have gotten out of hand.

"What about you?" The question popped out of nowhere. She couldn't believe what she was saying. But that didn't mean she could stop. "Haven't you ever wanted children?"

She felt him stiffen. Letting go of her hand, he looked away, staring out at the passing view from the George Washington Parkway.

"I wouldn't make a very good father. I wouldn't know how."

Ginny wanted to scream. Here was some more of the legacy that had made a seventh-grade third baseman afraid to fail. Steve was so incredibly wrong about himself, she couldn't believe what she was hearing. But what could she say? *Come on, why not give it a try? And by the way, if you need a mother for the baby, I've got a healthy womb going to waste.*

"Just asking," she said.

He turned back to her. "My turn. It seems a year since I've seen you, except for the game. What have you been doing with yourself lately?"

Here was something else she couldn't say.

I visited with a few former First Ladies and found they were out of my class.

"The usual stuff," she said. "Working, you know. Overcooking the pasta."

He ran a finger across her bare shoulder and down her arm. She closed her eyes and let the nerves tingle and ripple all they wanted, which was a lot. Fighting fire with fire, she rested her hand on his thigh, way up and slightly to the inside. From his quick intake of breath, she figured he was tingling and rippling, too. And when Stephen Marshall tingled, he got dangerous. She moved her hand away from the risky zone.

"Do you ever come into D.C.?" he asked. "Are you around sometimes, not far away, and I don't know it?"

She felt sure his questions were innocent; he couldn't have known about her trip to the Smithsonian, and if he did, she could say she was looking at the "All in the Family" chair or Dorothy's *Wizard of Oz* red shoes, both of which were, like the First Ladies exhibit, housed in the American History museum.

Still, she didn't like his asking.

"This is a great town for sightseeing. Sometimes I make the trip. That's how I met you."

Opening her purse, she pulled out a mirror and smoothed her hair, but for all she saw of her reflection she could very well be bald.

"Don't worry," he said. "You look great."

"What does a guy know? The first real test will come when the women look me over. Not that they'll notice me, you understand, not with you around. I'm going to try for that corner of the room I could never get to at the Department of State."

For just a second she could have sworn she saw his look of concern come back. But he smiled, said, "Lots of luck," then went on to tell her the way the evening should play out. She decided to suck up her worries and quit giving him a hard time.

This time she was appropriately dressed. Edward

Seale and Barbara Davidson would be there. What could go wrong? Nothing, if she kept her eyes and ears open and her mouth shut.

Steve called the beginning of the evening right, step by step. She was met in the curving north driveway of the White House by Seale, who guided her through the doors into the large entrance hall, resplendent with its marble walls and pillars. The last time she had been here was on the White House tour. In fact, it was from this point that she'd made her fateful dash for a ladies' room.

If she found herself at a loss for conversation over the next couple of hours, she could always discuss that day.

It seemed at least a hundred people were milling about, all of them as glittery as she remembered them from the ambassador's reception. A quick glance didn't reveal the one glittery woman she didn't want to see, the beauty whose name she refused to even think. She'd considered asking Steve if what's-her-name would be present, but she'd been afraid of what he would say.

He had taken another way, going upstairs for his grand entrance, which, according to him, was de rigueur. He promised to get down to her as soon as he could. He would have his aunt at his side.

Nothing he had told her had been especially comforting.

When she entered the hall, she drew a few looks, but nothing harsh, merely curiosity, beautiful people wondering the identity of the stranger in their midst. If any had been at the ambassador's reception, they gave no sign that they recognized her. And certainly no one remembered her from the cover of the *Inside Scoop*. The issue had come out weeks ago; she was old news.

When she saw Barbara Davidson's smiling face, Ginny wanted to rush across the hall and kiss her. Much to her pleasure, Mrs. Davidson came to her instead, brushed her lips across her cheek, and squeezed her hands.

"You look lovely," Barbara said.

"Thanks, I needed that," she said, and then belatedly added, "So do you," meaning it. The chief of staff's wife had been severely dressed at the restaurant. Tonight she wore a pale green, loose-flowing gown that sort of undulated around her and brought out the glow of her skin.

Ginny forced her attention to the chief of staff himself. He eyed her with an unmistakable frown.

"I know what you're thinking," she said, deciding to be direct. "But I had nothing to do with the President's showing up at that game on Sunday. No one was more surprised than I when he walked in. Or more upset."

Ford Davidson gave her a reluctant smile. "Am I so obvious?"

"Yes, dear," Barbara said. "You could be wearing a neon sign."

"He gave us a scare," Ford said.

"I'm sure he did," Ginny said. "You can imagine

how bad it was in the bleachers. I didn't know William Alcorn was anywhere around."

"You must tell me all about it," Barbara said, linking her arm in Ginny's. The Marine Band chose that moment to strike up "Hail to the Chief," and Barbara whispered, "Later. Our Steve is about to arrive."

He might be Barbara and Ford's Steve, but he wasn't Ginny's, outside of certain circumstances and places she could not allow herself to think of. Still, she couldn't suppress a proprietary rush of pride as the music swelled.

The pride didn't last long. As he walked down the center of the red-carpeted stairway, Aunt Doris on his arm, he was a man she didn't know personally, regal, commanding, very much in charge as he looked over the gathering. When his eyes found her and he smiled, her stomach clenched and she forgot to breathe.

The only way she could keep from lowering herself in humble adoration was to picture him, not in the stable or in the hotel bed, but in the bleachers, wearing the mock Elvis outfit and getting his pillow belly punched by Burly Man.

Shaking hands, greeting people, he made his way to her side. Aunt Doris, tending to her own share of greetings, didn't let him get too far ahead.

"Ginny, hello," he said, shaking her hand as casually as he had the others. "You remember my aunt."

"Of course. Good evening, Miss Tanner."

How polite they were, the guest and the President, slight acquaintances to anyone watching, but only Ginny caught the tickle of his finger against her palm.

The First Aunt gave her a brisk nod before turning a warmer smile on the Davidsons. From the look on Steve's face, Ginny got the idea that he'd instructed Doris to be on her most civil behavior. From what Ginny recalled of her, she was probably doing the best she could.

Ginny didn't know how he managed it, but Steve got everyone flowing into the East Room, which opened off the Cross Hall, a long corridor that led from the East Room to the State Dining Room and backed up to the closed doors of the beautiful Red, Blue, and Green rooms. From her tour she could have drawn a map, including some areas she was certain not many people even knew about, much less had actually seen.

There was, for instance, that rather dingy, closetlike cubicle where William Alcorn and his minions had questioned her and, finally, removed the cuffs.

The inside knowledge made her feel strangely more at ease.

Ford Davidson excused himself, and with music playing in the background, Ginny and Barbara sipped wine and walked among the crowd, listening to snippets of conversation that sounded very much like government business.

"Don't they leave their work behind at the office?" Ginny asked.

"Their work is their life. What else are they going to talk about?"

"I don't know. Family? Movies? Books?"

"Sometimes they do, but not often. And you can bet the lovely dress you're wearing that the books and movies will have a political theme. The problem is, they're all strangers here, temporary residents from different parts of the country. It's hard to make real friends inside the Beltway because everybody's after something. Support for legislation, an appointment, a contribution, there's always a cause."

"I don't have one." At least not the kind Barbara meant.

"I know. I believe that's why the President enjoys your company. You don't want him for anything."

It wasn't exactly the truth, but Ginny let the comment pass.

"Your husband and the President have known each other for a long time," she said, feeling awkward calling the men by name in this setting. Steve could howl all he wanted; in the White House he was Mr. President.

"When the President first decided to run for Congress from his district in Oklahoma, he wasn't long out of Yale Law School. Ford's a lawyer, too, and had been a visiting lecturer at the school. The President hired him to help with his campaign, and they've been close ever since."

"Your husband is very protective of the President."

Barbara patted her hand. "He's not always right in his judgments."

"But usually he is."

Barbara looked up at her with kindly eyes. "So am I. Come on, girl. Let's schmooze." She looked around. "Ah, Congressman Smithers," she said, dragging Ginny by the arm toward a tall, distinguished-looking elderly gentleman with a head of thick white hair and rosy cheeks. Tiny veins showed through the papery skin on his nose and cheeks. The congressman was a drinker. He'd been at the wine awhile.

"I'd like you to meet a friend of mine," Barbara said. "And of the President's."

Ginny really, truly, honestly wished she had left out the last.

"Ginny, this is Congressman Ormond Smithers of Georgia, isn't that right?"

The congressman nodded. "You know it is, Mrs. Davidson. You're never wrong about such matters."

"Congressman, this is Regina Baxter. She's recently moved to the area."

The Georgian might be a little blurry-eyed, but he still managed to give Ginny a sharp, quick-judge look, and not solely as a politician.

"A friend of the President's, are you? He's a lucky man."

What was it Dolley Madison had said? *A gentle touch, a compliment, a laugh.*

308

Ginny shook his hand, then eased away from the hold of his damp palm.

It was compliment time, but she couldn't think of a thing to say.

"Have you been to Georgia?" he asked.

Okay, he was feeding her a straight line.

"No, but I saw *Gone with the Wind* three times."

Dumb. Worse than dumb. Insane. She was speaking to a congressman, for crying out loud.

Sure enough, she didn't get so much as the hint of a smile.

"I guess you've heard that before," she said.

"Far more than three times," he said, looking around for one of the waiters bearing a tray of drinks.

Dragging her away, Barbara muttered something about the man being a fool and certainly ill-mannered. Ginny was more inclined to credit him with good taste.

They stopped before another distinguished-looking gentleman, this one short and round and bald. Or maybe it was the matron on his arm that gave him the distinguished air. Tall and formidable in size, she was dressed in a gray satin suit with a floor-length skirt, and the look in her eye was sharp enough to carve ice.

"Senator Williamson, good evening," Barbara said.

Ginny smiled at the man.

"I'm the senator," the woman said.

So Ginny smiled at her as Barbara made the introductions.

"A friend of the President's?" the Senator asked, and Ginny understood more than ever that it was the most interesting thing about her. "Are you in government? I know that's a foolish question. Everyone here is. Either that or a family member or a very close acquaintance of someone who is."

Hint, hint. *Are you someone important?* was what the senator meant.

"I vote and pay taxes," Ginny said. "That's about it."

The woman's smile was fleeting. "Don't we all?" And then to Barbara, clearly dismissing the unimportant upstart, "I've been wanting to talk to Ford about setting up a meeting with the President. I know he's quite concerned about the passage of legislation concerning day-care help for working mothers. I feel the same, and I think I might be of help to him. We are, after all, in the same party."

She went on to talk about the legislation, as if Ginny the working mother wouldn't know anything about the issue, while the senator's husband listened and nodded.

She glanced around the room, saw the representative from Georgia helping himself to another glass of wine, and thought of Lucy Hayes. Lucy would have known what to do with the decidedly inebriated congressman. She would have knocked the glass from his hand.

Ginny continued to look around, at the crowd of

people talking animatedly, catching bits of conversation, all of it concerned with government or Washington at a level she would never know or understand. She also saw Steve with Ford Davidson, standing in the midst of a half dozen men and women, grinning and talking and getting them all to nod.

How could anyone turn him down, no matter what he asked?

She couldn't.

Or maybe she could. Never would she attend another function like this one tonight. You could put a saddle and bridle on a sow and call her a Thoroughbred, but beneath the trappings she would always be a pig.

And then a bad time became worse. She spotted Veronica Gray not twenty feet away, all blond and gorgeous in a black low-necked, figure-hugging gown, a matching stole draped over her arm. She was looking right at Ginny, and she was gesturing and laughing, behavior Ginny's mother would have called outhouse manners.

To Ginny's horror the senator's daughter came toward her, at her side one of the women with whom she'd been laughing. Barbara Davidson, lost in conversation with Senator Williamson, didn't seem to notice.

Ginny was on her own.

"Mrs. Baxter, isn't it?" Veronica asked. "We met once before, I believe. Don't think me rude, but I was admiring your gown. It looks exactly like one

I used to own. When I wore garish colors."

Blood rushed to Ginny's face.

"Oh, does it?" was the best comeback she could manage.

"Yes. Mine was supposed to be an exclusive design. Tell me who your couturier is, if you don't mind."

The woman wasn't speaking softly. Gradually, the conversations in the immediate vicinity died.

"But first," Veronica said, "I need to get Daddy over here. He bought the dress for me as a one-of-a-kind. If it's been copied, he ought to know. There are far too many unscrupulous people in the world, wouldn't you say?"

But Ginny wasn't up to saying anything.

"Of course," the intrepid senator's daughter went on, "I did pass it on, since it never seemed quite the thing. I have no idea where it ended up."

She waved over her shoulder, no doubt summoning Daddy, but Ginny couldn't see the advantage in waiting for more Gray troops to arrive.

She took a step back.

"I didn't catch the name of the couturier," Veronica said, then added, "the designer," as if Ginny wouldn't know what *couturier* meant.

All the blood that had been rushing around in her began to boil.

"As far as this dress is concerned, I don't know. The label had been cut out before it got to the resale shop, which probably makes it yours at one time, if you're into selling your clothes."

"I—"

But Ginny wasn't done.

"This is nothing I could afford new, but I'm sure you know that. I work at Sam's Auto Repair, which I highly recommend if you ever need a tune-up. And as for couturiers"—she put her best high school French behind the pronunciation—"usually I depend on whoever is buying for the discount stores."

It was not what Dolley Madison or Martha Washington or Eleanor Roosevelt would have said, even had there been such stores in their day. But then, Veronica Gray would never have dared be so offensive to those august women. Ginny was fair game.

If she could have taken off the hated dress, she would have, but she'd already made a big enough fool of herself. From the corner of her eye she caught Barbara Davidson moving in, the cavalry riding to the rescue, ready to save her day.

Ginny was in no mood to be saved.

Easing her way through the crowd, at least half of whom had blessedly *not* heard the exchange, she hurried out to the entrance hall. Edward Seale was not in sight, for which she was grateful. That made one less witness to her habitual retreat.

If she could find that closet where William Alcorn had interrogated her, she would gladly duck inside and avoid all the witnesses. Her only other choice was the north door, the portico, the curved drive with the waiting limousines. A doorman/Secret Service agent/somebody stood at the top of the stairs.

"Can I get a taxi?" she asked.

"Of course. There will be one waiting at the end of the drive. Just outside the gate. I'll find you an escort."

"Please, no. The way is lighted. I'll be fine."

Barbara caught her halfway down the steps.

"Veronica Gray has been trying to trap Steve ever since he came to Washington as a congressman. Don't let her send you running."

"She isn't. Not by herself. Look, Barbara, you weren't at the ambassador's reception. It was pretty much like this; not quite so bad, but close. Believe it or not, I used to be fun at parties. But that was a long time ago, and I never went to one like this."

She hugged the woman. "Thanks for being a friend. But you've got other work to do in there. Believe me, I'll be all right. I've learned how to take care of myself."

Ginny made it to the taxi without being accosted by anyone else. Steve might not even realize she was gone. He would soon, and he would be upset, but he would never say anything harsh to her, or critical. That wasn't his way.

He was killing her with kindness, surrounding her with so much temptation she hadn't had a clear thought in days.

But she was thinking clearly now. As much as she loved him—or rather, because she loved him—she would have to tell him good-bye. She made the decision dry-eyed. It was the way she must make all her decisions from now on.

*   *   *

Ginny escaped all the way to her Ballston driveway before he caught up with her.

As soon as she got out of the taxi, she heard the tires squeal behind her and glanced over her shoulder at a pickup with Steve behind the wheel. She sprinted toward her apartment, but she couldn't move fast enough to get inside and lock the door.

He caught her by the arm and swung her around, at the same time the taxi driver floor-boarded it and peeled out. The coward.

"Let me go, Steve."

"No." He pulled her into the shadows beside the professor's house. "What in the hell do you think you're doing?"

"I'm trying to go inside and get out of this dress and forget tonight ever happened. And not only tonight."

"What is that supposed to mean?"

"Exactly what it sounds like. I don't like those people, and they don't like me. You'll have to get another tootsie for your fun and games."

"Tootsie? Is that what you think you are?"

"Whatever name you want to put to it. It doesn't matter." She pulled herself free of his grasp. "I quit."

"I won't let you."

"You don't have a choice. I'm sure you can find candidates by the dozen. Start with Veronica Gray. She looks willing and ripe enough."

"Roni has been trying to fill that role for the past

two years. I don't like the woman. I like you."

If he thought he was smoothing things over, he was a fool. Nothing could have hurt her more than *I like you*. He liked barbecue, too.

"Let me alone. Please. I can't handle this anymore."

She felt the burn of tears. Her most fervent prayer was that not one single teardrop would fall before she was alone.

"This is all my fault," he said. "I should never have left you alone with that witch in the room."

"She wasn't the only one. Didn't Barbara tell you what a fool I made of myself?"

"She said a couple of self-important politicians gave you a hard time."

"They did. But I deserved it. I played the whole scene dumb."

She tossed her purse into the grass and stepped out of the shadows, her arms open wide so that in the moonlight he could get a good look at her.

"This is a used dress, Steve. Secondhand. Don't you recognize it? It belonged to the beautiful Veronica, who took great delight in announcing the news."

"So take it off. I'll help."

She cried out in exasperation. "Don't you understand? Everyone back there must be laughing at me. But that's not the worst part. They're laughing at you, for being fool enough to invite me."

"You didn't hang around long enough for the applause. Roni isn't the most popular woman around."

"So maybe they thought the whole thing was a setup to get her. Good. That way I come across as simply a bad actress instead of stupid."

She turned to go.

"No," he said, and he took her into his arms, so quickly, so smoothly, she had no chance to run. "We're not done. There's too much good between us to let it go."

He kissed her, hard and without a hint of the coaxing sweetness she was used to. And he held her hard, so hard she couldn't breathe. She couldn't fight; she couldn't even scream. She tried holding herself stiff against him, but he was too strong for even that small protest.

One hand cupped her buttocks and held her tight against him.

"I'll take you here and now if that's what it takes to convince you," he said.

Oh, God, she didn't know what to do. He frightened her, as much as she frightened herself, wanting him to do exactly what he threatened even while she knew it was insane. She found herself grinding her body against his, acting like the tramp she felt herself to be, not caring about anything but the raw passion he had aroused.

Tugging at her skirt, bunching it at her waist, he ripped a seam, but that only made the tugging easier. When he thrust his hands inside her panty hose and squeezed, he made her burn.

In the silver moonlight at the side of the house, loving him, hating him, she rubbed herself against him, as if what protruded hard from between his legs was all that mattered in the world.

The sudden, desperate, illicit nature of the assault, wanted and hated at the same time, affected her in wild, unimaginable ways and started her spiraling. She exploded and cried out, at the moment the world around her did the same with another, far more dreadful assault, the unmistakable flash of a camera, the sound of her son's voice yelling, "Mom," the screech of brakes out on the street.

Confused, shaken by the climax, she clung to Steve. He eased his embrace, letting her torn dress fall into place, and shifted to place himself between her and the source of the flash.

Footsteps pounded down the driveway, and they were surrounded by his protectors, arriving too late to protect her.

"Mr. President, are you all right?" someone snapped.

And there was Jake, still yelling "Mom," then cursing as he, too, was surrounded by the agents of the President.

"Don't let them hurt him," she said, crying against Steve's jacket, letting all the tears fall in a rush, knowing she was powerless to do anything else.

Chapter Fifteen

"Marry me."

Ginny had expected Steve to come up with a way out of their disaster, but not this. Never this.

She closed her eyes to his earnest gaze. When Stephen Marshall looked earnest, the way he did now, she did crazy things, like riding Thunder and taking on Veronica Gray.

But marriage? No way. That was like trading one terrible situation for another. She wasn't that insane.

"This is your idea of a solution?" she asked. "You'll have to do better than that."

"Then I'll get on my knees and promise you the biggest diamond you've ever seen, and a honeymoon that'll knock your socks off. Whatever it takes to get you to say yes, consider it yours."

She looked at him in disbelief. "You think I want—"

She broke off with a sigh of disgust. What was

the point in going on? She rubbed at her throbbing head. The nightmare of last night not only wasn't ending, it was taking darker, more devilish turns.

The two of them were in the private living room upstairs at the White House, a place she had vowed never to enter again; but then, she had broken so many vows to herself that she couldn't see one more as making much of a difference.

Outside the door, waiting in the regal hallway that led to countless regal rooms, were his aunt and Ford Davidson, along with Professor Carl and a very reluctant, if not surly, Jake. They had all started out together, but it was Steve's idea to talk to her alone.

She got up from the leather sofa and went around to look at the Thomas Moran painting, but its grandeur made her feel more tawdry than ever, and she moved to the large window that opened onto the Capitol.

"Let's skip your Plan A," she said, focusing on a distant patch of green. "What's Plan B?"

"We run away to South America."

She shook her head, shuddering, still able to smell the screeching brakes and see the flash of lights, and worst of all, to hear the cry of her son and his yell when the agents surrounded him, all of it coming at a moment when, to put it mildly, she was most vulnerable.

Had it been only last night? It seemed her senses had been assaulted by the horrors all her life.

"Please don't joke," she said. "This is too serious."

"I pretty much figured that out. Marriage is the most serious part, the only part that matters. We'll do well together, Ginny. You know we will."

She had to fight to hold back the tears. She—a woman who seldom cried, not when Jonas asked for the divorce, not when he got sick, not when he died—had vowed only hours before to continue dry-eyed where Stephen Marshall was concerned. The vow came after hours of sobbing off and on, ever since the moment last night when disaster struck.

She'd been either sobbing or sitting zombielike while Jake talked or Professor Carl or even her neighbor, who came over to see what all the commotion was about.

She had started to tell her to read Sunday's *Inside Scoop*, where the illustrated version would be laid out for all to see.

But the Secret Service had hustled her away before Ginny could get in a word. And they had hustled Steve away and, after a rough night, brought the Baxter duo, mother and son, to the White House on this criminally beautiful day so that everyone could wring their hands and work at damage control.

But Steve wanted to talk only to her.

Marry me. She wanted to make a joke about it, something like he'd fallen off his horse too many times and landed on his head, but the proposal hurt too much for her to say anything much, other than what she'd already said.

"I've never wanted anything from you," she said.

"I know."

"I never angled for anything like this."

"I never thought you had. You're free of deals."

"It's not only the picture. Marriage is a good idea. My only regret is that I didn't think of it until this happened. I've never been around anyone I'm more comfortable with."

For a politician, he sometimes had a cruelly inept way with words.

"You mean the sex," she said.

"Comfortable doesn't describe that. If the sex got any better, I'd never let you out of bed."

Ginny had no idea how she was supposed to respond to that. So she kept quiet and let the hurt go on. He would never say what she wanted to hear and she could never say what she wanted to say, so she kept quiet. And the hurt went on.

He came up close behind her. "I'm not enough for you?"

If he could fight dirty, so could she.

"Not at the reception last night. No, you weren't enough."

"Guilty as charged. More guilty than you realize. I knew Roni would be there. I'd hoped that if she saw us together, she would back off."

"I don't understand. Back off from what?"

"She's got the mistaken idea I've been leading her on. She's been wanting her father to refuse cooperation on the White House budget, but when that didn't work, she went through you to embarrass me. I had no idea she would go so far. By the time I saw the two of you, it was too late. I promise, Ginny, you won't be alone with her again."

"What kind of a devious place is Washington?"

"You have no idea."

He touched her arm and she pulled away.

"It wasn't just her and you know it. I played the whole scene dumb, but we've already been over this. What do you plan to do, keep me hidden away? I'll be like the wife in *Jane Eyre*, screaming away in the attic, needing a keeper to lock me up. You'll have to hire someone with muscle, considering my defensive skills. I can't see your aunt taking the job."

"Ginny, you are smart and quick and funny, everything that is needed at one of those affairs. You just need a little practice and guidance, which you'll get in spades. Besides, when you're the First Lady, no one will dare treat you with anything but respect. Believe me, if there's one thing politicians respect, it's power. And power you will have."

And what would be her words from the Smithsonian wall?

The President and I were about to screw, as a sort of consolation for the way I messed things up for him at the White House, and then a photographer came along and we were forced into wedlock. Thank God the guy was good in bed.

"What's holding you back?" he asked. "What's in your life that you can't leave behind?"

"Jake."

"You think I'm asking you to leave him behind?"

"I don't know. You haven't mentioned him."

"Give me more credit than that. I haven't had a chance. The boy's out there right now with Doris and the professor, worrying about you, and you're in here worrying about him. Do you think I won't do all that is in my power to see that he is taken care of? That you two will be together as much as you can? It won't be the same, of course. Nothing for any of us will be. It'll be better. You brought him here to show him how government works, to help heal his wounds. Sweetheart, he won't get a better chance at seeing and healing than he will from the view I can give him."

She felt herself slipping. There was nothing for her to hold on to. Every time she found some place to grab, he chipped away at it. He was not only her love, he was an expert at getting his way.

"Do you have the *Scoop* picture here?"

"You don't want to see it."

She turned to face him. With the sunlight streaming through the window, she could see the shadows beneath his eyes, and the strained lines around his lips. Her Golden Man was not so golden today, and she loved him all the more for it. Her heart cried out for her to touch him. But she couldn't, else she was lost.

"What you mean is, you don't want me to see it. Already we're having secrets between us and we're not even engaged."

They looked at each other for a long time.

"You win," he said at last. Going to one of the side tables, he took a folder from a drawer, then brought it to her and pulled out a glossy black-and-white eight-by-ten.

She couldn't look at it for more than a minute. There she was, back to the camera, skirt bunched at her waist, her rear exposed except for the parts covered by the President's hands, and in the background Jake was coming at them, obviously yelling, obviously distraught.

The photographer had caught Steve just as he lifted his head from her shoulder, his eyes directed straight into the camera lens, looking like a thief caught in the commission of a crime.

"My God," she whispered, and he took the photo from her hand. "The *Scoop* will run it on Sunday?" she asked.

"Front page. I think they plan to put a black band across where I'm touching you, but the readers will get the idea."

She covered her face with her hands. "It's worse than I thought."

"They said they would give me the negative if I give them exclusive rights to the wedding pictures. I said exclusive was impossible, but they can be there along with a few selected members of the press, and the publisher agreed. If that thing runs, life for you will never be the same anyway. And there's damned little I can do about it."

Except make me your wife.

Ginny sighed. "You're such an honorable man.

325

You really are." She looked toward the door. "And Jake. He's been hurt so much in life, and now this."

"You asked if I wanted to be a father, and I said no. But I answered too soon. Give me a chance with Jake. Maybe I won't be so bad after all."

In all this talk about her and Jake, he hadn't said a word about what the scandal would do to him. But he had to be worried. Somebody had to be, besides Ford Davidson and his aunt and the countless staff and supporters who would suffer the fallout, too. Not to mention the country, which would view with increasing cynicism the fall of another hero.

The best somebody to worry was one who had the power to do something about the situation, the honorable, face-saving thing. And that pretty much came down to her.

Right now she felt as far from honorable as she could get. And it wasn't because she had let Steve grope her last night. That, at least, had been honest lust at play. They hadn't been hurting anyone except, eventually, her, but that was something she was learning to expect.

If only Jake and the rest of the world had left them alone, today would be a different kind of day, and the rest of her days a different kind of life.

Her beloved son had protected her, true, as best he could, but the protection came as he saw it was needed. He didn't pay a lot of attention to her needs and wants.

And Steve. Honorable Steve. He was beginning to irritate her a lot. He had power. Why didn't he use it? Why didn't he kick some journalistic butt? Surely he could find a way, legal or not, to bring the *Inside Scoop* to heel.

She could hear his howls of protest if she suggested anything so underhanded. Or worse, his patient explanation of how she would have to trust that his way was the only way.

Sometimes it had been easier to handle her two-timing husband's dishonesty. At least it had taught her not to care.

What she wanted—what she really, truly wanted—was for Steve to say he loved her beyond anything this rotten world had to offer, and the sorry bastards who objected could stick their protests where they would never be seen again.

Then maybe, just maybe, under those conditions, if he proposed marriage, she would, without pressure, gladly and unconditionally say yes.

But today wasn't a day for getting her way. She felt as if someone had taken a stiletto to her insides and sliced out all her dreams. A forced marriage to a man who didn't love her was the last thing in the world she wanted, and public life as Steve offered it, her dignity and privacy always on the line, would surely prove to be her most horrendous nightmare.

And yet there was only one answer she could give him. She had enough sass, as Steve would put it, to give her submission a few personal twists, but only after she took a very deep breath.

"I'll take a gold band, nothing flashy."

The words came out more easily than she had

expected, and the worry lines around his mouth eased. He looked as if he wanted to protest, but all he said was, "Done."

"And I'll want a prenuptial agreement that the professor can look over for me."

"Whatever I have is yours. That goes without saying."

"I don't want anything. That's what the agreement will spell out."

"What the hell do you mean, you don't want anything?"

"Just what I said. What I bring to the marriage, I take away. Should things not work out."

"That's my little optimist. So what if things do work? What if by some wild miracle, we live a long and happy life together?"

"It won't be because you spent a lot on me. I'm not high maintenance. I buy used clothes."

"Forget it. I can't go along with that."

"You'll have to. There are so few areas of our lives where I'll get my way, and I know it. But in this, I'm not changing my mind. I need it for my own self-respect. Before any announcement is made, I want your promise as an honorable man to give me the agreement I want."

"You'll be my wife, Ginny. In every way. This may be something that's done where you come from, but not in Bottle, Oklahoma, which is where we'll eventually live."

"I'll bet it is done there. You just don't know about it."

"What if we have children? It's possible. It's even likely."

That stopped her for a moment, and told her how far he was willing to go to get through this disaster.

She wrapped her arms around her middle. Condoms weren't one hundred percent safe, and she wasn't sure he had taken the right precautions when they'd been in the shower. She could already be expecting his child.

And wouldn't that be cute, everyone in the world with access to a calendar counting the months till Stephen Junior was born.

She didn't care. A child, a baby, was what mattered, and not the day when the infant was conceived.

Steve had no idea how much the sweetness and the promise of the possibility shook her.

"Of course you'll take care of your children," she said. "If we have them."

He nodded once. Briskly. "And Jake."

"And Jake," she said. For a minute, concentrating on the agreement as it concerned her, she'd forgotten about him. But there was so much to think of, to decide.

"One last thing," she said.

Steve stood straight and still, his normally summer warm eyes turned winter cool, a man for all seasons, a powerful, worldly man who wanted to get his way.

"I can't fault you for being overly sentimental, can I?" he said.

"Is that what you want? Sentiment?"

"I want you to say yes."

Of course he did, but not for the right reasons. If only she could go back and say yes to his offer of the bended knee, he would see more sentiment than he could ever imagine. Too late. He was withdrawing from her, not so much physically, but inside, where it mattered most, turning more harshly analytical as the specifics were spelled out. Tough. She couldn't allow herself to care. Not right now.

"The agreement must be kept a secret between you and me and the lawyer. Let the world think what it will. I'll know the truth."

It was clear he wanted to protest some more, but he kept his response to a brief nod.

She closed her eyes a minute, then looked at him, straight on and clear-eyed. "Then the answer is yes. I'll marry you."

No soaring music, no violins, no floating on air accompanied her acceptance. The only thing she heard was the heavy pounding of her heart.

"You drive a hard bargain, Mrs. Soon-to-be-Marshall."

"And you thought I was easy."

"Nothing between us has ever been easy, Ginny. Except how we are when it's just the two of us."

"How often is that likely to be?"

His expression was all the answer she needed: seldom, and then not for very long.

She would have laughed, but that would let loose all the emotions she was holding inside. She, who was getting what any single woman on the face of the earth would want—and half the married ones—felt a return of her tears.

But the time for crying was past.

He moved in to kiss her.

"Please" she said. "I promise we'll be doing a lot of that later. But not right now. It's what got us into trouble in the first place."

In this, she did not get her way. Sweeping her into his arms, he kissed her, then kissed her again. And of course she kissed him right back. This was still fine between them, and always would be. Never would she put a condition on their making love.

"We're going to be good together, I promise," he said, as if he could read her thoughts, once again the Steve she saw most often, the most powerful man in the world. "Now let's go out there and tell our family the good news. Aunt Doris wanted a June wedding in the Rose Garden. We've got what, two weeks? It looks as if she's going to get her wish."

The Rose Garden in June? It was more wish fulfillment for the women of the world. Right now, holding her hand, remembering how she had given in to his kiss, he looked so certain he could control things. But she knew he couldn't, not everything. The knowledge made her smarter than he.

And infinitely sadder, too.

"I warned him not to fool around with you. Now look what's happened."

Jake's crude insult didn't shock Ginny the way it had the first time, nor did it seem to bother anyone else. In the past hours they had all been through too much for mere words to give offense.

At least his reaction was honest, not like Doris's tearful, "Stephen, if this is what you truly want, then you have my blessing," or Ford Davidson's halfhearted, "Congratulations, Mr. President, and best wishes to you, Mrs. Baxter."

It could be she was beyond all shock.

Professor Carl distressed her the most, because his reaction came closest to her own private truth.

"I assume you have thought this through, Ginny. The change for you will be profound."

"I've thought it through. I'll make it all right."

Doris shot her a look, as if to ask how she could possibly think otherwise. Wasn't she getting the world's most eligible bachelor as her groom?

They were all gathered in the sitting room. Other advisers, including the press secretary, Alan Skinner, waited outside. Steve's social secretary, the one who had called her about the right dress for last night, had also been summoned. She doubted the woman could come up with rules to handle Jake.

He was standing by the window, away from the others, separating himself as he had so many other times in his life. She sensed more than saw Steve begin to go over to him. This time she needed to handle the situation herself.

"In a way, you're right, Jake," she said, holding her place beside the sofa, gesturing Steve to back off. "If Steve and I had stayed away from each other, this wouldn't have happened. But that didn't seem to be an option for us. I care for him very much. He didn't do anything I didn't want him to do. I'd be lying to you if I said otherwise, and between us there have never been lies."

For the first time since Steve made the announcement, Jake looked straight at her.

"You kept telling me you wouldn't be seeing him again."

"I kept thinking I wouldn't. But I was lonelier than I realized."

She forgot about the aunt and the adviser and even the professor, the one person in the room completely and unselfishly on her side. Steve and Jake were all that mattered; they were the men in her life. No matter how much they irritated her.

Right now Jake took precedence. He'd been in her life first.

"We don't need him, Mom. It's just the two of us, remember? That's how it's always been."

"Not always. Before you, there was your father. Please, don't look at me that way. I loved him. Otherwise you wouldn't be here. And before him there were my parents. People always have people moving in and out of their lives. Times change. Before long, you'll be gone, too. There will be games in your life that don't include me. There already are. I'm just a spectator in the thing that means the most to you."

Jake was smart. He was listening.

But he was also callused against outside interference in their lives. Professor Carl was as close to them as anyone had gotten in years.

Somehow Steve must get that close. He wouldn't succeed if the decision was up to Jake.

"I need and want your blessing," she said, "but I'm marrying Stephen Marshall as soon as we can make the arrangements." There was a rustling in the room behind her, but Ginny ignored it. "I told you that we were moving here to Washington. I didn't give you much of a choice. Today I'm asking for something else. I want you at the wedding, a part of it, if you can bring yourself to do it, and I want you to continue to love me as much as I will always love you. He's not pulling us apart. He'll bring us together as a family in ways we've never known."

Jake wasn't buying it; she read the rejection in his eyes. But neither was he putting up an argument or ranting about government bullies or the men his mother chose. He just shrugged, as if he was giving up on her, and in that shrug she had to place the hope that fluttered tenuously in her heart.

The wedding, private but with a larger reception afterwards in the East Room, was scheduled for the last Sunday in June in the Rose Garden, fulfilling Doris Tanner's wish. Perhaps not every wish— Ginny was certain she never would have chosen a divorced auto shop worker with an almost-grown, harshly critical son as the life's companion for her beloved nephew—but there was nothing either of them could do about it.

Jake refused to give Ginny away. The honor—at least he swore it was an honor—fell to Professor Carl. But her son did agree to attend the wedding, and in a newly purchased suit, which Ginny assured him he would need from time to time during his senior year.

She didn't bother to tell him that his would be the only suit in Arlington created especially by the President's own tailor. He was smart enough to figure it out for himself.

She would not have believed the event could be planned with such detail in so short a time, but she hadn't counted on the advantages of a crew of calligraphy specialists to handle the invitations and announcements, a White House floral department to arrange the flowers, a social secretary to answer every possible question that anyone could bring up—with the possible exception of accommodating the *Inside Scoop*—and a well-staffed press secretary to field inquiries from the public and the press.

Her first press conference, called in the East Room so that Steve could announce the engagement and wedding, was not a success. He, naturally, was calm and in control, telling the assemblage that his life was now complete because he had found the woman he wanted as his wife. Then he ruined it all by calling her up on the platform and holding her at his side behind the podium, allowing her a wide-angle view of the microphones, the sea of astonished faces and waving hands, the tape recorders, the calls of "Mr. President!"

Her speech, short and very First Ladylike, had been prepared for her by one of Steve's speechwriters. She had memorized it in order to appear more natural, but when the flashbulbs popped and the cameras rolled, she forgot every word.

"You know how Stephen is," she said. "It's hard to tell him no."

The quote got picked up and made the headlines across the United States: IT'S HARD TO TELL HIM NO. Some of the crasser publications speculated as to when and under what circumstances she began to tell him yes.

The late-night talk shows were filled with similar comments. Jay Leno, David Letterman, Conan O'Brien all got in their observations, as did their guests, most of the comments centering on what she did for a living:

"Have you heard that the new First Lady works in an auto repair shop? She took one look at the President and decided his battery needed recharging."

"Regina Baxter will be very handy to have as a First Lady. When the President needs some body work done, there she is."

"The President impressed Mrs. Baxter with his knowledge of auto mechanics. The word is, she admired his tools."

Ginny neither viewed nor allowed anyone to tell

her about the comments on the daytime shows. After all that had gone on in the White House over the past few years, where personal issues were concerned it was next to impossible to get respect.

But not totally so. Steve was very popular, and the White House was flooded with calls and telegrams and e-mails of congratulations and best wishes, and gifts.

And the late-night commentators, too, ended their barbs with kind comments and generous thoughts. None of them mentioned that she was divorced; none of them mentioned Jake.

When she finally made it one last time to Sam's, already under the escort of the Secret Service, the crowd was small, her presence being uncertain, but the mysterious Sam was there. Years before, he had turned the hands-on running of the company to a hired CEO and retired to Florida, but he had flown up to shake her hand. He also hinted that any good word she could put in about the shop's servicing the White House fleet would be appreciated, the implication being that she would be rewarded in whatever way she wished.

Steve said she would have power. He was right, and this was only the beginning. But power came with a price. She had to get an unlisted telephone number and post one of the agents at her apartment door to keep unwanted guests from arriving. She felt like a prisoner in her own home.

And if she felt that way, she shuddered to think how all this must be affecting Jake. Secret Service agents accompanied him everywhere. Usually he took the bus or walked to practice; not anymore. She didn't know if it was Steve or William Alcorn who made the arrangements, but the agent assigned to drive him and stay closest beside him was a genuine baseball fan. Boy and agent settled into an uneasy truce.

The next game in which he was the pitcher required special security to handle the crowd. Steve wasn't there—at Ginny's request—but she made it, never yet having missed a Jake Baxter pitch.

Later she wondered if she should have stayed away. With all the hoopla going on around him, Jake gave up one run on three hits, was pulled in the seventh, and Post 139 suffered its first loss of the year, 2–1.

One of the most difficult assignments that Ginny had to face was dealing with the First Aunt. Doris loved Steve as much as Ginny did, but she operated under a handicap: She didn't know how her nephew's fiancée felt. In Doris's view, she had to be an opportunist, probably had made sure the *Scoop* photographer was in place should a chance come along for a once-in-a-lifetime shot.

She hadn't seen the photo—Steve assured Ginny several times that few people had—but she knew about it, and she knew it was the basis for the marriage.

The best way Ginny could find to get along with Doris was to let her have her way. And that meant letting her take over the ordering of her wedding dress and her trousseau, bringing in recommended experts to supervise every aspect of her appearance.

The dark brown of her hair was highlighted, which Ginny kind of liked, then pinned in an up-sweep with tendrils framing her face, which Ginny hated. She was always blowing them out of her eyes, except when Doris was watching, which seemed to be much of the time.

She also took over the hiring of a personal secretary for Ginny, as well as a social secretary, but when she started talking about the separate bedrooms the newlyweds would use, Steve got word and in his gentle-but-no-arguments-accepted way told her to butt out.

Ginny never got to see Steve alone, except for brief, stolen moments when they could kiss. He tried to make a date with her in the back of the limousine, and she was about to agree, when one of her secretaries—she had a difficult time telling them apart—came in with a stack of letters that needed her signature, and somehow the date never came about.

She knew Steve was busy with a thousand demands far more important than hers, so she didn't complain, except about the failed date. She wanted to be his helpmeet, the best kind of First Lady she could be. She also wanted to get back to the Smithsonian and put some very pointed questions to her predecessors. Sadly, she knew she would be surrounded by the press and Secret Service and by the public, which, under a barrage of happy-couple photos both official and otherwise, were beginning to recognize her whenever she ventured outside.

Mostly, when she wasn't at fittings or in the new office Doris was setting up for her in the White House, she was at Professor Carl's. It was there she found out that he was working on a book.

"That's wonderful. Is it about economics? A textbook?"

"No," he said, stroking his white beard, "it's personal."

Something in his voice told her to let the matter go. But she couldn't resist one last comment.

"If you want me to read it, I would be happy to. I'm not an expert on grammar or literature, of course, but I'm interested, and maybe that's enough."

"Later, perhaps. When I'm done."

At last came the day before the wedding. She was spending the night at the White House, in the Queens' Room, so named because of the royalty who had stayed there, including the Queen of Great Britain and Princess Anne. Churchill, too, according to her personal secretary, who seemed a font of information Ginny hoped would eventually prove useful. Decorated in shades of rose and white, with a high, wide, canopied bed, the room was elegantly intimidating when she compared it to her sofa bed.

But who was she to complain? Everyone said the room was appropriate, since her name was Regina.

Doris made elaborate plans so that on the day of the wedding Steve wouldn't see her until the ceremony. But on the night before, she did get together with him after the private dinner for family and friends. Steve had offered to fly in anyone from Cincinnati whom she chose, but her closest friend had taken ill and couldn't make it, so she said Jake and Professor Carl would be all the support she needed.

Not that Jake was providing much support. He hardly spoke during the meal and ate nothing as far as she could see, even though Steve had arranged for barbecue and all the trimmings. She didn't know whether to drag him from the table like a willful child or reach over and cut his meat.

When everyone had gone, she was walking down the corridor toward the Queens' Room, trying to stop worrying about Jake, trying to quit thinking about all the dangers of tomorrow, when a hand snaked out of the open door to a storage closet and jerked her inside.

All was dark and close and crowded, but she didn't need a light to recognize the hand, or the mouth that brushed against hers, or the body against which she was held. And she certainly didn't need more room.

"It'll be all right, Ginny. I promise."

"You don't know how much I want to believe you."

"I missed you," he said, kissing her face, her lips, her eyes, her throat.

"I missed you," she said, letting the heat and the sweetness absorb all her doubts.

That was all the talking that took place, but not

all the kissing and the fondling and the groping, and the shallow, fast breathing, which left her dizzy and drugged with the need for more.

"I want you," he said.

"I figured that," she said, but the words didn't have as much snap and sass to them as she would have liked. She was wanting him so much, she thought she might scream.

"All right, then," he said pulling up her skirt.

"In here?"

"After the stable, this is nothing."

He was better at panty hose than she. He had them halfway to her knees before a knock sounded on the door.

"I hate to interrupt you, Stephen, I truly do, but Ford needs to see you about Vice President Posey. It seems someone important has died somewhere in Africa and he's needed there for the funeral. It means he will miss the wedding. Ford said he's insisting on talking to you."

By the time Doris got to the point, Steve had the panty hose back in place.

But he continued to hold her tight.

"I'll be right there," he said with amazing calm, and then to Ginny, "She's leaving right after the reception for a trip back to Oklahoma. While she's taking off, I'll be screwing you into the bed. Any objections?"

Now here was the Steve she loved.

"None."

"We could get started tonight. Your royal bed is liable to be lonely, don't you think?"

"I'm sure it will be. But that will make tomorrow night all the sweeter. Just hold me for a minute, and then go take care of whoever is calling. I promise, cowboy, that no matter what you want to do to me after we're married, no matter how down and dirty, it will be just fine. Just remember, I ask the same cooperation from you."

Chapter Sixteen

Not once during the night did Queen Elizabeth II sound off with advice on how she handled all the pressure she'd had to face in the past few years. Likewise Princess Anne was a no-show on tips for riding Thunder, should Ginny ever be stupid enough to get on the beast again.

She didn't even get Churchill's *I have nothing to offer but blood, toil, tears and sweat,* which was something she could have said herself if she were eloquent enough.

So she tossed and turned in her Queens' Room bed; then, when dawn finally filtered around the edges of the heavy, drawn draperies, she struggled to sit up on the soft mattress while the butler delivered her breakfast on a tray. Mrs. Eisenhower had begun each day in this manner, he reported with a sniff, a practice he considered quite civilized, implying that she ought to make the right kind of start and copy Mamie.

Ginny didn't especially like the man, but she liked the Oklahoma cook, Florence. If she'd been able to breathe a little more regularly, she might have enjoyed the pancakes more and lifted her glass of orange juice in memory of the late general-turned-President's wife.

But the food reminded her of breakfast in the hotel, one of the several places where she had decided once and for all to break away from Steve.

So what was she doing here in the grandest house in the grandest land waiting to marry the country's grandest man?

Trying to hold on to her sanity while she wondered if there was any way she could run.

By the time the tray was removed, she was pretty much a basket case.

Doris didn't help.

"We're going on a tour," she announced, breezing into the bedroom after a single knock on the door. "Stephen's confined to downstairs with a host of well-wishers from back home. You're safe."

Little did the woman know.

The tour started in the East Wing with the Lincoln Bedroom and Sitting Room, went to the Treaty Room, and more meeting and sitting rooms, each more mind-bendingly gorgeous than the last. By the time Doris was done, having concluded the torture in the huge third-floor recreation area with its collection of every exercise gadget known to modern man—"I ordered them myself for Stephen, and it's a shame he can't find time to use them"—Ginny didn't have a sparkplug's worth of confidence left.

Then it was back to the Queens' Room for a nap, scheduled, of course, by the First Aunt. She spent the time looking over the book on First Ladies that she'd bought in the Smithsonian museum shop, treating it like a self-help manual for Women Who Run with Presidents.

She wasn't the first First Lady to get married in the White House—that honor went to Frances Cleveland, in a ceremony as small as hers would be.

Not, she felt certain, for the same hurry-to-avoid-a-scandal-reason, however.

Nor was she the first divorcée, having been preceded by Florence Harding and Betty Ford. She would bet her trousseau that neither of them could hotwire a car, despite the latter woman's last name. Perhaps the destiny of the newest addition to the book was to have that listed as her "first."

It took an assembly-line crew of specialists to get her ready for the ceremony, from hairdresser to pedicurist. Ginny was beginning to look at Steve's aunt as the boss from hell, but the woman had been living in this rarefied air for over a year and was about to be supplanted, so Ginny gave her her head.

Besides, she couldn't have stopped her if she'd wanted. What she ought to be doing was taking notes.

Her wedding attire consisted of a daffodil-yellow suit, the lined skirt midcalf length, matching shoes and purse, matching hat with a half-veil, pearl necklace and earrings that were Doris's wedding gift. Her hair was tucked under the hat, except for the cursed tendrils, which gave Ginny something else to blow at besides the veil.

The color was not her best, and neither was the style. She felt like a recycled Jackie Kennedy with none of the class.

The Rose Garden, flanked on two sides by the pristine columns of the Colonnade, looked a lot better: flower beds with white and pink lilies, caladiums, geraniums, hollyhocks; on the open sides of the garden, thick shrubs and tall trees; and in the middle of it, the best-looking thing of all, her husband-to-be.

He was wearing a dark blue suit and a red tie, and sported a red geranium in his lapel. With his shirt white as a newborn star, she felt like saluting him. When he watched her walk toward him down the red carpet that had been laid over the grass, her heart swelled so much that she thought it would burst . . . when she wasn't thinking she ought to take a sharp right turn and run like hell.

But someone would catch her. Someone always did.

Jake watched from the side, along with Barbara Davidson and the guests. She didn't look at her son straight on. She didn't have the nerve.

She barely heard the ecumenical ceremony, murmuring her responses after a nudge from Steve, and when it was done she didn't feel married, not even after his kiss, which, though legal and proper, seemed as forbidden as all the others they had shared, but strangely not so sweet.

He didn't linger over the embrace or the kiss; he just stared down at her in a searching way and then let her go.

Professor Carl gave her away; Ford Davidson served as best man; Doris Tanner was her only attendant. The other guests were advisers, cabinet members, and their spouses, plus the Oklahomans, who'd been flown in as Doris's surprise. Except for the out-of-towners, she'd memorized all the names from a photo album her personal—or was it her social—secretary had prepared. It was, she told herself, like learning the parts of a car, though not quite so much fun.

She was reminded of a childhood fear that if she didn't make her block letters just right, she would fail second grade.

Instead of throwing her bouquet of white and yellow roses, she handed it to Doris; then, at Steve's urging, she smiled into the cameras, glad she didn't know which one came from the *Scoop*. After a champagne toast and the signing of papers and a thousand more photographs and a few wishes for their happiness, the sincerest coming from Barbara, the guests excused themselves while she and the wedding party went back upstairs, along the corridor, and down the stairs to the Entrance Hall in the East Wing, where the reception was being held.

This time when Steve walked down the stairs, she

was on his arm, with the wedding party following, and the cheers that went up as they came into sight drowned out the Marine Band. For the first time she was grateful for the dowdy length of the skirt—no one could see her knocking knees.

Steve had been right about one thing: as First Lady, she was treated with absolute and total respect. She didn't have to think of what to say except, "Thank you," a thousand times, and by the time she heard "Mr. President" another thousand times, she started thinking of him that way herself.

How many famous people were in the room? She didn't want to know. At her first wedding there had been her two best friends from high school, Jason's mother, now long gone, and a fellow auctioneer who'd kept up such a running patter, the justice of the peace had been forced to shush him.

Now she was greeting the justices of the Supreme Court.

She had invited everyone at Sam's and their dates, including Sam himself—getting in some positive licks for her boss Ted—along with the neighbors who had befriended her during the past few months. They bunched together, not even joining the Oklahoma contingent, and when the music started, seemed reluctant to go out onto the East Room dance floor.

Steve and Ginny had the first dance, the first time they had danced together. When his hand took hers and he pulled her close, she had a glimpse of satin sheets and just maybe a steamy night ahead. But with so many people watching she couldn't bring the picture into focus, and so once again she became a woman playing a part.

"Try to smile, Ginny," he said as he whirled her around the room. "Look like you're happy."

She wanted to ask him what he meant, why there was sharpness in his voice, but with the world watching, she simply smiled. And thought, *Happy? It's hard to be happy when you're feeling lost and alone.*

Next she danced with Jake, which was not the highlight of the evening, not because he couldn't do a mean jig when he had to—she'd taught him herself—but because he didn't say a word. He was cooperating. One of these days she knew he would explode.

It was a measure of his regard for her that he held off today.

Next came the professor, and then Ted Waclawski. When the band struck up a polka, he surprised everyone by asking her to dance. On a dance floor Ted was livelier than he was at work. Ginny was glad she'd taken off the hat; as it was, a few more tendrils abandoned their uncomfortable hairpins.

And then she was back in Steve's arms, and in the midst of another round of applause he was guiding her down the stairs toward the South Lawn and the helicopter that would take them to their honeymoon location: Camp David, Maryland, the presidential retreat in the nearby Catoctin Mountains. It wasn't fancy, he had said, but it was close and it was private. He promised to take her to Paris or wherever in the world she wanted to go as soon as time would permit.

Maybe later she would care about Paris. Right now, with his hand on her back and the brush of his shoulder against hers sending familiar shivers down her spine, she wished they were headed for his pickup and a quick ride to a nearby motel.

This was not, she knew in her heart, the way First Ladies ought to behave. But she loved him so much that she didn't care, not right now, not for a while. The thing was not to show it, a terrible burden for a new bride.

Outside the White House a butler handed their luggage over to a military aide, who loaded it on board, and they were off for the short, noisy flight to the landing pad by the main house at the presidential retreat. The awkwardness between them began as soon as they were inside the house and alone. She had wanted, foolishly, to be carried over the threshold, but she refused to ask and he didn't offer, so she just strode inside as if she went to Camp David every weekend, and then she stood there wondering what she was expected to do next.

Theirs had not been an ordinary wedding; they were not an ordinary husband and wife. And, her heavy heart told her, they never would be.

The helicopter had borne the presidential seal on its side; the same seal was embedded above the cold stone fireplace. Going closer to inspect it, Ginny wondered if she was supposed to wear it, too.

But that was unfair to Steve. He couldn't help being who he was, any more than she could help loving him.

For a moment she just stood there, feeling awkward and out-of-place, unable to think of a thing to say, twisting the plain gold band around her finger, looking at the overstuffed furniture and the scatter rugs and the homey, rustic interior, knowing he was looking at her. She couldn't remember the last time she'd babbled. The woman who had stumbled into the Oval Office less than three months ago was not a woman she knew.

Had he changed? She didn't know. But he hadn't planned to get married. Then she had come along to stir up his primal instincts, and now they were bride and groom.

He had to be just as stunned as she. But not as insecure. He had another life. Today, and in the years ahead, she would have only him.

"Are you all right?" he asked.

"I'm fine."

"You don't look it."

"It's been a busy day, that's all."

"And it's not over yet."

"True," she managed, feeling her temperature rise.

With his summer-sun eyes and his golden hair tousled by the ride, he looked almost like *her* Steve, the one she'd socked in the horsestall the first time they'd made love. But he also looked cautious, as if he'd brought home a stray kitten he hadn't planned on keeping and was wondering about her breed.

Love me. She wanted to cry out the words. *Let me love you*.

But she just stood there and looked at him and kept the words to herself.

The paneled and stone walls closed in. Suddenly she wanted more than anything to get out of the cursed yellow suit, and sex had nothing to do with it. Unbuttoning the jacket, she tossed it aside and kicked off the yellow pumps, the matching yellow purse having already been thrown she knew not where.

She was working at the buttons of her blouse when Steve's voice stopped her.

"I don't think you're doing that for me."

He said it as an accusation.

She dropped her hands and stared at him in surprise, her mouth dry.

"Everything I've done the past few months I've done for you."

"Like hell you have."

He tossed the lapel flower onto the coffee table in front of the fireplace and shrugged out of his jacket, then tugged off his tie. She watched in reluctant fascination as he unbuttoned the top two buttons of his shirt.

When his eyes met hers—his very angry eyes—the fascination died.

"Don't kid yourself into thinking you're some

kind of martyr. Except when you're being a mother, you don't do sacrificial very well.

"Steve, what's going on?"

"Think back. I want an honest answer. Was the only reason you were ready to hump me in the limousine because you wanted to service your President?"

Ginny's mouth dropped open. "I was ready to do what?"

"You heard me. And the stables. You got on Thunder for me, but when you pulled down those jeans, you were hot to trot and I don't mean on a horse."

He scared her; she'd never seen him like this. She ran her fingers through her hair, making a final disaster of the hairdresser's fancy coiffure. "I can't believe this." She tried to laugh, tried to turn it all into a joke. "You sound like me mouthing off."

"The way you used to." For just a moment his expression softened. "I'm trying to get at the real you, Ginny. I have ever since we met."

"And talking dirty does it?"

"Talking straight. Whether you realize it or not, sweetheart, you've been stiff and cold since the moment I asked you to marry me, laying down rules, holding yourself apart."

The truth of his words stung. "Except for the closet."

Heat flared in his eyes. "Yeah, except for the closet. You told me to get down and dirty. That's what I'm doing. And it begins with facing a few truths. You like sex as much as I do."

"What kind of a thing is that for a bridegroom to say?"

"It's what most of them would like to say. What part are you protesting? Where do you think I lied?"

Ginny wanted above all else to throw something sharp and clever back at him, but her mind froze. He was, after all, a politician and, worse, a lawyer as well. In a war of words, she didn't have a chance.

But words weren't the ultimate battleground. She needed a level playing field. Like a bed. Or even the floor. He was right. She did like sex. But she liked it only with him.

"So tell me what you want of me."

"I want my Ginny. The generous, funny woman I asked to be my wife. I want to bring you pleasure, and I want you to bring pleasure to me."

"So what are we fighting about?"

He shrugged. He did shrugging very well.

"I knew what it was when I started. Damned if I can remember now."

They stood there a few feet apart, not talking, the President and his First Lady, husband and wife, and though Ginny wasn't so blindly enamored with him as she usually was, she made up for it with heat. Whatever else his purpose had been, he'd managed to loosen her up.

"Down and dirty, you said."

"Right." He came close to a grin.

"Sounds like a plan to me."

He got her out of the blouse in record time, and the front-hook bra, while she was working at his shirt, pulling it open and then rubbing her bare skin against his. He backed her up to a wall and ran his hands over her breasts, licking her lips, dancing his tongue against hers, pretty much driving her crazy with his mouth and his fingers. And he hadn't yet gone below the waist.

Shoving him away, she slipped out of her skirt, showing a pair of bikini panties she had picked out herself, along with the white hose and white garter belt. She hadn't worn anything blue. This was not, after all, a traditional wedding, and she would never be a traditional wife.

While he was looking, she ran her hand down his chest and the front of his trousers, cupping his genitals, watching the expression in his eyes.

"You like my tool?" he asked.

He didn't surprise her; nothing could surprise her now.

"I didn't realize you watched the late shows."

"Edward Seale gave me a review."

She let go of him, embarrassed, as if the adviser were here in the room with them. It was bad enough thinking of strangers listening to all the innuendo. It was a disaster imagining someone she knew.

"You don't like it," he said.

He looked so cursed cute, pretending to pout, his hair a mess from her fingers, his bare chest and upper arms looking more sculpted than formed from hot flesh.

"I assume you mean your tool," she said. "I don't like it covered up like that."

He changed the situation fast, stripping and getting her down on the rug in front of the cold fireplace, the two of them putting out enough heat to boil oil.

A rascally finger eased inside her panties. "Thinking of the limo?" he asked.

"It's what got me here now."

"Then I'll have it dipped in brass."

"Not the finger, I hope."

He grinned all the way. "And not the tool."

She was right back to loving him as much as ever, knowing the awkwardness between them would return but not caring when they could have moments like this in which the outside world did not exist.

"You're my wife, Ginny. I'm glad. I want you to be, too."

"I was scared, Steve, that was all. Make me not so scared."

This time he was the one to roll down her hose, kissing his way along her bared legs, even licking her toes, an act she found to be just about the height of eroticism.

When he kissed his way back up, he paused to give her a far more intimate kiss, one with a lot of tongue, and she realized she had been wrong about that height.

Spreading her legs, he lay on top of her. "It's time, Mrs. Marshall."

"Sure is, Mr. Pres . . . Mr. Marshall," she said, teasing him, smiling with purely feline pleasure as he consummated the marriage in a fashion that left no doubt both husband and wife very much enjoyed sex.

Eventually they made it to the bed, where they spent an hour working up an appetite. Supper awaited them in the mammoth kitchen's mammoth refrigerator, along with instructions for heating the food. There was also a bottle of champagne, perfectly chilled. Naturally.

They were ravenous and thirsty and later, during an everything-bared midnight swim in the heated pool, they slaked another kind of hunger and thirst. Along with all his other prime characteristics, Steve had a buoyant body and an inventive way of showing Ginny his version of a synchronized swim.

Over the next two days they were in and out of bed, the pool, and the surrounding woods, but in the latter Ginny insisted they do nothing but tease each other with kisses. There was no telling where the Secret Service agents might be, and while she was up—or down—to just about anything in private, she hadn't fallen all the way to exhibitionism.

While they were walking and holding hands, they didn't talk much, certainly nothing personal outside of sex, just comments about how smoothly the wedding had gone, all things considered, and how supportive the people at the reception had been.

"The Grays are in California," Steve said, and Ginny wondered if he had somehow maneuvered to get them there.

They didn't talk about what life would be like for them now that they were married, or how they felt about one another. They just walked and looked around and then he would be kissing her and she would be telling him to cool it or else she would make him pay when they got back in bed.

Each time they returned to the house to find food waiting and fresh sheets on the bed—they went through a lot of sheets—and fresh towels hanging in the master bath and waiting by the pool.

Occasionally Steve had to take a telephone call, or work for a short while in his office; she always made herself scarce, keeping separate from the main part of his existence the way he clearly wanted. It was at those times that she felt out of her element, but by the time he was hers again, she was smiling and talking dirty—as dirty as she knew how, though sometimes he laughed at her and said her slut talk needed a lot of work.

They were supposed to stay another day, but a Wednesday evening phone call, this one to her, put an end to that. It was Professor Carl with bad news.

"I didn't want to interrupt you, Ginny. I know everything's all right, but the agents insisted either I call you or they would call the President."

"What's wrong with Jake?"

"He's disappeared."

She looked at Steve over the phone. Her expression brought him to her side.

"How could that happen? He's surrounded by Secret Service agents."

"He calls them the SS."

"You don't think anyone has . . . has done anything to him, do you?"

"No. Get that out of your mind. He slipped away at baseball practice. He's found himself a hiding place."

"Why?"

The professor didn't answer. He didn't have to.

His mother had left, and so had he.

Feeling faint, she lowered herself to the sofa while Steve took the phone. He talked a minute, and then he was making other calls, and before an hour had passed she heard the whir of the helicopter overhead.

They were already packed for the return ride to the White House. The honeymoon, short and sometimes very, very sweet, was over.

Chapter Seventeen

By the time Carl located Jake at midday on Thursday, sitting beside a pretty girl on a comfortable sofa in a comfortable Arlington home, eating pizza and watching a big-screen TV, he was ready to strangle him.

Here the kid was, enjoying life, while his mom was in torment and much of the federal government in the throes of a fruitless search. It was little consolation that the news media had not yet been tipped to the disappearance.

"How'd you find me?" Jake asked when he walked in.

The girl, small and blond and nervous, separated herself a couple of inches from him, but like Jake, she kept her eyes on the TV. Carl recognized the old sci-fi movie they were watching, *Invasion of the Body Snatchers*.

"A pod opened up in my backyard and told me," he said.

The girl began a laugh, then caught herself and stared at the piece of pizza in her hand.

The truth was, Carl had found out about Alexandra Lawrence from Jake's American History teacher and his American Legion coach, but he wasn't about to give them away.

"There's been a flock of girls following him ever since the news about his mother and the President broke," Cordelia Witherspoon had told him when he tracked her down in her summer school classroom. "He's quite the celebrity."

The coach had narrowed the search to Allie. "He's been talking to the same girl at the past two games. The reason I recognized her is, my wife and I are friends of the Lawrences."

"Does his mother know about the girl?"

"I doubt it. She could easily have missed her, what with all that's been going on in the stands lately. Besides, with Jake, a conversation is more like a nod and a quick hello than an out-and-out talk. I've been working with kids a long time, Professor Morris, some more lost than Jake. Trust me. The boy's interested in Alexandra Lawrence and she's interested in him."

Cherchez la femme. Jake the Loner had discovered the opposite sex.

The two young people were dressed like twins, in faded jeans and white T-shirts. Their chaperon, Allie's grandmother, came up to Carl and started explaining how she was here from her home in

Norfolk while her son and daughter-in-law were on a cruise.

"I hope nothing's wrong," Mrs. Lawrence said. "Jake came over the past two days to visit my granddaughter, and then he was back early this morning. They've not been out of my sight, I promise you."

"Nothing is wrong," Carl assured her; then, thinking of the pictures in all the papers in the past two weeks and on all the news broadcasts, he couldn't keep from asking, "He didn't look familiar?"

"Should he? Oh, dear, I told my son I shouldn't be doing this. My vision's not what it used to be, and sometimes I forget things. But Allie insisted I would work out just fine."

"I'm sure she did."

Jake didn't stir from the sofa, just kept chewing on the pizza and staring at the screen.

"Let's go," Carl said to him.

"Where?" he asked, still keeping his attention straight ahead, his long legs stretched out in front of him. "To the SS? I figured they would be the ones to catch me."

Carl hadn't lost his temper in a long while. Today he snapped.

"Now!"

That got the boy's attention. His head jerked around, and he stared at his friend the professor as if the man had lost his mind.

"Maybe you'd better go, Jake," Allie said. "Call me when you can."

"Is something wrong?" the grandmother asked. "I just know something is wrong."

"I'll explain later," the girl said, then turned to Jake, touching his hand. "You'll be fine. And I'll be here. Remember to call."

When Jake looked at her, the resentment and surliness were momentarily gone. He nodded once and pulled his lanky frame off the sofa.

"May he use your telephone before we leave?" Carl asked.

Jake didn't have to ask whom he was supposed to call, although he did request the number at the White House. The conversation was brief; Carl didn't listen in. Neither he nor the boy spoke again until they were riding in the Impala, headed home.

"Where have you been the last two days?" Carl asked.

"Allie let me sleep in her garage."

"Why?"

"Because I asked her."

Carl pulled across two lanes and stopped at the side of the road, ignoring the blare of horns around him. "I'll ask again. Why?"

Jake shrugged, looking straight ahead at the passing traffic. "I got tired of being treated like a criminal."

"The agents, you mean."

"Yeah, the SS. They're part of the oppressive, interfering government I've tried to tell Mom about. And now she's—"

He blinked and turned his head toward the window, away from Carl.

"She's gone over to the enemy, is that what you mean?"

Jake didn't reply.

Carl sat for a moment, thinking. He'd been listening to the boy's naive political spoutings for months now. If Jake was as smart as he seemed, he would eventually grow out of most of them. But too much had happened lately. Eventually wasn't good enough.

There was one place in Washington Carl hadn't been to in months; with the work he'd been doing over the past few weeks, it was time for him to return.

And it was way past time for Jonas Jackson Baxter to expand his narrow world.

"I've got something I want to show you," he said as he pulled the car back into the flow of traffic. "When we're done, you can go where you want to go."

After a couple of turns and a short ride, he parked the car near the Rosslyn Metro stop. "Let's go."

"Into DC? Not the White House. You heard me call Mom. She's cool."

"Don't be a fool, Jake. Of course she's not cool. And neither am I."

He got no further protest, and they rode into the capital in silence, getting off at the stop nearest the Smithsonian. The older museums weren't Carl's destination. He had a newer one in mind, this one

365

stark and almost brutal in its architecture, close to the shadow cast by the Washington Monument, in view of the Tidal Basin.

The setting was natural for a tribute to the artistic and creative accomplishments of humankind. But this particular monument had other kinds of accomplishments in mind. The words carved across the entrance were the boy's first hint of what awaited him: UNITED STATES HOLOCAUST MEMORIAL MUSEUM.

The exhibit began on the fourth floor. Carl made it all the way up and off the elevator before the tears came. Sometimes when he visited he tried to stop them; he didn't try to stop them today. He didn't care what he and Jake must look like—a weepy, white-haired old man and a foot-dragging, bored-to-the-bone youth. Besides, his weren't the only tears in the crowd.

The first display they came to was a mural of the concentration camps, the barbed wire, the American soldiers who first came across the bodies and the skeletal survivors from the camps. These were battle-hardened soldiers, but no battle could prepare them for the horror that they found.

Understanding that horror as well and cruelly as he did, Carl could still scarcely believe it himself.

"I've read about this," Jake said. "I don't need to see it."

"I do."

Carl walked slowly past the text and photographs detailing the history of the Nazi regime and the be-

ginnings of what Adolf Hitler called the Final Solution of the Jewish Question and what the world
would come to label the Holocaust.

When they came to a photograph of handsomely
uniformed German officers standing with their legs
apart, their arms behind their backs, Carl stopped.
As always, it was their smiles that got him.

"*Schutzstaffel*. The real SS. They ran the camps.
Come, let us begin the descent into hell and see
what they did."

They moved slowly, one horror following upon
another, some stark in the ordinary pictures they
presented: glassed-in displays of human hair cut
from the prisoners, and of shoes and clothing
tossed into an abandoned pile. And then came the
high-ceilinged hallway with its walls of family photographs, framed like ordinary family pictures, col-
lected in villages where families had been hauled
off and killed.

Ordinary people living ordinary lives.

Carl stopped before a photograph of a young,
smiling couple and their two sons. He stared a long
time, until he sensed Jake stirring beside him.

"I look upon them as my family, though I know
they're not. But they're here somewhere. I feel their
presence each time I walk this hall."

"Your family?"

"Part of it. I know only that my parents and older
brother, my aunts and uncles and grandparents, all
were taken to Dachau in 1938. It was a camp near
Munich. The first to be built. They were thrown on

a train that had stopped in our village to collect the Jews. Or so I was told. I was young. I can't remember them. Not even my brother, whom I supposedly idolized."

By now the tears had stopped and the emptiness had taken control, as it did when he looked at the photographs.

"I was playing in the fields and was overlooked. A cousin smuggled me out of Germany, to Switzerland and then the United States. I've asked them all, especially my brother, to forgive me for escaping. And for not remembering."

It was the cousin who had salvaged documents and journals of the family's history and passed them on to Carl. He had never been able to look closely at the records, not until the Baxters came into his life—brave, hopeful Ginny and her pessimistic son. They had eaten his poor cooking without complaint, and they had shared their lives with him, needing his presence as much as he needed theirs.

The time had come for him to put aside his guilt, and it was also time for Jake to accept the past for what it was and turn to the future, to explore all that it could give. Baseball, yes—he had been given a very special talent—but there was more awaiting him, much more.

Life. It was God's most precious gift.

He had no idea whether he had reached the boy until they came to the film that showed in grim detail what the soldiers had found when they walked into the camps.

Jake turned away, unable to view the scenes to the end. It was a reaction Carl shared, and others around them as well. They walked in silence into the bright sunlight and then from the Mall to the White House, circling around it to get a good view, going along the edge of Lafayette Park without Jake's being recognized.

Not once did he argue, or indicate in any way that this was not the direction in which he wanted to go. Instead he looked around him at the people who had come to the capital to see firsthand the heart of their government without fear of arrest, or worse.

He looked, too, at the protestors in the park, at the placards and the posters advocating a dozen causes, from animal rights to zero population growth.

What he didn't see were stormtroopers come to route them, or anyone paying much more attention than a casual glance, a nod or a frown.

Lastly, he looked across the blocked-off section of Pennsylvania Avenue to the White House. Behind the high iron fence, the North Lawn stretched in its manicured beauty to the stately Executive Mansion that was Ginny Baxter Marshall's new home. More than a hundred tourists alongside him shared the same view.

Carl guided him to one of the front gates and said to one of the two uniformed guards standing watch,

"Please put in a call to the President and tell him we're here."

"Move on, sir, please. I'm not authorized to call the President."

Carl could read the guard's mind. *Why do I always get the kooks?*

He looked at Jake. "Can you give him the authorization?"

Jake shrugged. "I don't know. I've never been important before."

A group of teenage girls broke the stoic, no-nonsense expression on the face of the guard.

"Look," one of them squealed. "It's Jake Baxter. Let's get his autograph."

In an instant they were on him. Additional guards materialized to hustle the First Stepson and Carl onto the driveway inside the gate, where they could safely watch as the crowd began to grow.

"You're important now," Carl said. He nodded through the fence at the half dozen girls who had made it to the fence first. "They asked for autographs. It wouldn't hurt to give them one or two."

Jake tried to look nonchalant, as though he didn't know if he could be bothered and the whole thing was foolish anyway. But the squeals of the girls and the smiles on their glowing young faces were heady tonics for a young man who had only recently discovered the opposite sex.

Carl leaned closer. "Just look at it as preparing for your pitching career."

The boy came close to grinning, looking very much like his mom.

More squeals. At a signal from Carl, the guards helped pass the brochures, scraps of paper and even a couple of T-shirts through the fence to Jake, who continued to scrawl *J-Bax* onto everything handed him until the Secret Service agents came running down from the White House.

"You go on," Carl said. "I need to get back to my writing."

Jake looked uneasily from the agents to Carl.

"Remember the German SS," Carl said. "These men are not the same. Neither are they forever."

"I'm not making any promises about getting along."

"Just remember today, that's all I ask. And one other thing you ought to take into consideration. These men who bother you so much will, if it becomes necessary, lay down their lives for you."

The boy had no reply, not even a shrug.

Carl stepped through the gate and watched it close. The last thing he heard was Jake, surrounded by agents, walking in the long-legged, bouncy way he had and saying, "Okay, guys, it's about time you showed up. I wondered where you got to."

By the time Jake made it upstairs to the family sitting room, Steve was ready to strangle him. But he didn't figure doing away with his bride's only child was the best way to begin married life.

He wanted a good marriage. He wanted a great

marriage. He wanted the best damned marriage in the western world. And how had he started it out? By arguing with his bride over motivation and humping and being hot to trot. And on their honeymoon, for God's sake.

And now he wanted to strangle her son.

When the boy walked in, Ginny spent about sixty seconds throwing "How could you do this?" and different versions of "Why?" at him, and then she was hugging and kissing him and in general acting like the besotted mother she was.

And here he was, the President of the United States, standing to the side feeling angry and helpless and most of all jealous. He had never been the recipient of such total parental devotion as Ginny was showing. He hadn't realized her love for Jake bothered him until now.

He wasn't proud of the jealousy, but he understood it. He wanted at least that much devotion from his wife. And he didn't mean parental. He was head over heels in love with her, another old expression, but it fit. He had no idea when it had happened, but he suspected the beginnings came when she looked up at him from the Oval Office rug.

And there had been a pretty powerful tug of emotion when she'd gone over Thunder's head. He couldn't remember ever feeling so afraid.

He should have declared how he felt about her when he was proposing marriage, that being the typical time for such an announcement. But with all her talk about prenuptial agreements and what she wanted and didn't want, he hadn't felt it would be much of an argument.

Watching her with Jake, he didn't know whether it would sound good to her now.

"You owe Steve an apology," Ginny said when she finally managed to break away from her son.

"No, he doesn't," Steve said. He might as well say it, even if he didn't believe it. Jake was about as ready to apologize as he was to give up baseball for knitting.

For a moment the three of them stood around looking uncomfortable. Steve broke the silence.

"Ginny says you were with a girl."

He knew right away that line of talk was a mistake.

"I didn't say anything about what you did with her," he added hurriedly. *Like fooling around*.

"She's a nice girl," Jake said.

"And so is your mom."

If he stayed a second longer in the room, he would say a hell of a lot more, the new stepfather taking control. And so he excused himself and left the two of them alone, going out to talk with William Alcorn and the agents assigned to the boy, to learn in detail just how he had given them the slip.

"One minute he was practicing ball," an agent said, "and then these girls were all around him, and the next thing we knew he was gone."

"I can see how that could happen," Steve said. "You're used to dealing with terrorists and would-be assassins and crackpots. Those teenage girls can be tough."

He let the reprimand go at that and went to take a hot shower and change from his Camp David jeans to his White House suit and tie, having given up on the honeymoon during the flight back to DC.

He didn't see Ginny again until dinner. It was just the two of them, Jake having gone back to the apartment in Ballston, along with enough agents to guard the Chinese premier.

"He wants to bring the girl and her grandmother to the White House," Ginny said as the butler put a salad in front of her.

"How do you feel about that?" Steve asked.

"Old."

"You're what, thirty-four?"

"Thirty-five next month."

"That's right. I remember the date now. It was in the FBI report."

She put down her fork and shoved the salad aside. "We must be the strangest couple on the face of the earth."

"Yeah. All we want to do is make love."

She looked down at the table, her straight brown hair curtaining her face.

"Okay, I'll amend that," he said. "All I want to do is make love. I got a call this afternoon from General Cartright, who started talking about Army pay, and I thought he said Army lay, and so I asked what category of government issue condoms and IUDs fell under."

She glanced slyly up at him. "You didn't."

He grinned, mostly because he thought she liked his grin. "So I didn't. But I could have."

Something worked—the grin or the stupid talk, or maybe the relief from the tension she'd been under since last night. Anyway, she threw down her napkin and said it was time to go to bed.

Holding her hand, he directed her to their room.

"I didn't even unpack," she said. When he didn't respond, she added, "I guess that was done for me."

"About the only thing that won't be done for you, sweetheart, is taking care of me. That's a hands-on, First Lady job."

The bed had been turned down, and the lights turned low. Both of them were stripped by the time they were crawling under the covers. While she was taking care of him, he was taking care of her. When he tried to tell her a few things, she shushed him. Tonight, she said, was not a time for talk.

Two days later Jake brought Allie Lawrence and her grandmother for dinner, upstairs in the family wing, and Steve assured the girl that she must return, the next time with her parents.

Flexing a little independent muscle, the boy asked to continue staying at the apartment, under the supervision of the professor and the watchful eye of his clan of Secret Service agents, whom he referred to as his "buds," especially his baseball-loving driver, who swore he was a Cincinnati Reds fan.

Ginny offered only token opposition. She wanted to say no, but she sensed that Steve would like a little longer to get used to having a wife. And it was probably best that Jake get used to their new life by working into it gradually.

Life in the White House wasn't easy, no matter how many servants and secretaries and advisers she had. Steve kept trying to get her alone for a talk, but she wasn't ready to hear what he had to say, didn't even want to guess what it might be, so she just loved him and kept to her separate ways.

And then Doris returned. Ginny would have liked to send her out to Ballston, too. Instead, she decided to take advantage of what the woman had learned in her time as White House hostess.

She put it to her straight. "I need help."

"With what?"

"With everything. I know I'm not what you expected as your nephew's wife. And I'm certainly not what the country expected, either. I've made some mistakes. I don't want to make them again."

Doris had been practically giddy, and the buying, the lecturing, the studying began. The First Aunt decided where she would go, the guests she would entertain, and the topics of conversation while she was entertaining. There wasn't a single controversy in anything or anyone, which was just as well. Ginny had gone through enough controversy to last a lifetime.

Sass was out, and so was dressing off the discount rack. Doris went first class, insisting that she wear her hair in a sophisticated upsweep, her clothes black or white or beige, always dressy, always uncomfortably severe, and her jewelry simple, tasteful, and expensive—"Steve's rich, he can afford it, my dear, and you certainly don't want to embarrass him." She couldn't resist adding, "Not again."

It was not a declaration that invited argument.

Ginny learned her speeches by heart and she gave them smoothly, although without a great deal of emotion, and somehow gained favor with most of the press. The public liked her, at least those members she was allowed to come in contact with, and so did the politicians, who must sense she was new and not yet fair game.

She even made a sweep through three southern states with her husband, smiling, waving, never saying or doing anything that anyone would want to recall an hour after she left.

In her mind, she was a mealymouthed twit who looked great, albeit a shade too much like a certain senator's daughter. But Doris dictated, and Doris knew best.

Except with the sex. There, Ginny reigned supreme. Steve admitted that he got her alone as much as the world would allow—in bed, usually, but once on the trampoline in the third-floor recreation room and another time, for nostalgia's sake, in the closet where he'd almost scored the night before the wedding.

Ever the politician, he set out to win her son, who

was down because his team had lost in the regional finals and would not be going on to the nationals in Oklahoma. When Edward Seale reported that Toronto would be playing Baltimore on a Sunday afternoon, he asked Cal Ripken and Roger Clemens to dinner, along with Jake, his coach, and the rest of the baseball team from American Legion Post 139.

Ginny stayed away, but from the reports she got the evening was a success. Jake knew how to play hardball; but then, so did Steve.

Later, when everyone was gone, Ginny proclaimed it was Appreciation Night.

"That was a wonderful thing you did," she said as she curled up on the sofa in the sitting room. "Goodness gets its rewards. Name the place."

He chose the trampoline.

The sex was great, tremendous, world-class. If only every aspect of her life could be like this—natural, honest, free.

Unfortunately, when they were lying naked on the undulating canvas, Steve ruined it all by telling her of an upcoming event.

"It's a diplomatic reception at the Department of State. Albert Brookings, the ambassador from Great Britain, will be there. And so will Senator Gray and his daughter."

"How nice." She tried to smile. "How long have I got?"

"A couple of weeks."

Two weeks to memorize her lines, to read up on

the guests, to practice her smile. Two weeks of being a Veronica clone, to get everything just right so that even Veronica would approve.

Something inside of Ginny snapped, right then, right there on the trampoline. She had some thinking to do. And she couldn't do it with Steve's hand cupping her breast.

With something less than complete grace, she managed to roll to the edge of the trampoline and drop to the ground, groping in the dim light for her clothes.

"What are you doing?" he asked.

"You gave me two weeks. That's not much time."

"Ginny, it's just a reception. You've had dozens of them."

"Cowboy, it's not just the reception I'm thinking of. Hold on to your boots. You've got a wild ride ahead."

Chapter Eighteen

Two weeks! Two weeks to quit playing Ginny the Robot, two weeks to shed her image of Ginny the Sophisticated Fraud.

She didn't blame Doris. The woman had been helping in the only ways she knew how. And Ginny had learned a great deal from her, for which she would always be grateful. But somewhere in the learning she'd lost her sense of self. If she stood a chance of living a long and happy life with the man of her dreams, she must shed the nightmare she had become.

For his sake as well as hers. He cared for her—he showed it in too many ways for her not to know—but she wanted a wild, crazy unconventional love, and she wanted tenderness and cuddling, too. And sharing. Oh yes, she wanted sharing more than anything. Steve could give all these things if the right woman came alone.

Regina Baxter had come along, and she was as

right for him as any woman could be. Once she learned how, in this strange new world of hers, to be herself.

And so she turned for advice to a person most others would consider a most inappropriate source: Edward Seale.

She caught him in the Green Room after a reception for the executives and on-air personalities of National Public Radio.

"I need help. Hair, clothes, the works."

She could tell he wanted to protest her need, then decided to be honest.

"I'll get my girlfriend on the phone."

"You have a girlfriend?"

He looked offended.

"Not that I didn't think you could or would, but you never mentioned her."

"It's okay. As I said, I'll get Julie on the phone. You can talk and set up plans. I have a feeling you two are going to get along fine."

Edward was right. The two women did get along just fine, so much so that when Ginny started spelling out the sort of things she wanted, Julie was able to come up with specific names of people and labels to do the jobs. Not once did she use the word *couturier*.

"This is like playing grown-up Barbie," Julie said at one session, "only this time the doll has money and brains." They were in Ginny's office at the time and were wearing cutoffs and T-shirts and feeling like a couple of kids.

Gathering information was all well and good, but she needed to get Doris out of the way. For that she called on the professor.

When she put the matter to him, he responded with a very fast yes. He had been needing some help redecorating his place. It needed a woman's touch. Doris not only had excellent taste, she was also generous with her advice.

The time came when Doris approached her with worries about being gone so much.

Ginny couldn't lie.

"I will always appreciate what you have done for me. And for Steve. You raised him. You did a great job. As for helping me now, it's time I took over for myself."

Doris took the news well.

But that didn't mean Ginny wanted her around for the reception. Again, she called Professor Carl.

"I've been collecting tapes of biker movies. *The Wild Angels*, *Easy Rider*, and of course the classic *The Wild One*. We'll have a film festival that night. It ought to last for a while."

"Whatever works," Ginny said, thinking that maybe she didn't know either Carl or Doris quite so well as she had thought.

The work went fast and furious. Sometimes Ginny went out to the stores; sometimes, when she flexed some First Lady muscle, the stores came to her. She refused to blink at the prices. Doris had taught her how to spend money. It was a lesson she had learned well.

She hoarded new clothes the way a squirrel hoarded nuts, packing them away for the time when they would be needed the most. She planned the reception as the place for her unveiling. Afterwards, when they were alone in their White House bedroom, she would confess that she loved her husband, and if he didn't have the sense to love her, he didn't deserve to be reelected.

That ought to get him.

As often as she could, she stole away for a few hours to work on a very special surprise, one that had nothing to do with clothes or hair or talk. No one knew—not Julie or Edward, not anyone except her and the few men involved.

She didn't call in the manicurist/pedicurist and the hairdresser until the afternoon of the Big Night. Julie was there to serve as dresser. She chose the Queens' Room as headquarters. Steve was to keep away until she came down to the sitting room to get him. She promised to be punctual.

She wasn't. She was five minutes late.

When she finally walked in, he didn't seem to care about the time.

She'd expected a *wow*, maybe up to a *triple wow*, but he just stood there in silence and watched her walk in, watched her walk around the room, looked at her as she smiled at him, and then at last he smiled at her.

She closed her eyes, knowing she would take the memory of that smile to her grave.

The stylist had cut her hair short against the back

of her neck, leaving the top and sides longer so that every time she turned her head, her hair sort of rippled and bounced. It was funny how cutting hair made a woman's neck look longer and her face thinner and better defined, and her eyes big, big, big.

They didn't look like ordinary brown eyes anymore. They looked like pools of rich chocolate fudge, or so Julie had said, and Julie wouldn't lie.

Ginny's dress was a shimmering green silk shot with gold threads, bare on one shoulder, slit to the knee. From the clasp on the shoulder a cascade of brilliantly colored diaphanous scarves descended to the hem, waving in a come-get-a-look-at-me manner as she walked.

Roni Gray would probably call it garish, but it was all-the-way gorgeous to Ginny.

She wore gold high-heeled thong sandals, two-inch gold drop earrings, and passion-fruit polish on her nails.

She had a closet full of clothes just as startling— dresses, suits, pants suits, shorts, crop tops, tunic tops, flat sandals, high-heeled sandals, walking shoes, running shoes, and even a pair of snakeskin western boots.

Most of the clothes were in vivid primary colors, but she didn't neglect pastels. She already had enough clothes in black and white. Nothing was skin-tight, except for some bike shorts and a pair of jeans, but the garments hung right and they moved with her and they let her husband know she had a great body underneath all that expensive cotton and linen and silk.

This was the way she had always wanted to look, casual and elegant at the same time, but she'd never had the money or the nerve. She had them both now.

And she had more, something indefinable, something the previous First Ladies would understand. Finally she had an understanding and appreciation for her position and her power. Okay, she didn't know exactly what causes she would espouse, what areas of public service she would concentrate on, though she leaned toward something involving the education of children. But she would not leave Washington until she could rightfully take her place on the Smithsonian wall.

She suspected it was the confidence that made her look good, as much as the clothes.

When Steve started for her, she backed away. "Don't you dare," and then over her shoulder called out, "Julie. I think I passed."

At the reception, she stood alongside her husband in front of the yellow chairs in the John Quincy Adams Room and greeted their guests. Barbara Davidson's mother was ill, necessitating a trip to Maine, but Edward and Julie were there in case she needed support.

"Your Excellency," she said when the British ambassador, Albert Brookings, took her hand.

"Lovely, my dear, lovely," he said. "Should I be

fortunate enough to steal a portion of your time, Mrs. Marshall, I would like to talk to you about the 1957 Chevrolet you mentioned before. I've done some research since last we spoke, and I'd be very much interested in learning to whom you sold it."

"I promise, Your Excellency, we will talk."

A few minutes later Roger Gray, the distinguished senator from California, and his daughter Veronica came through at the end of the receiving line.

Ginny had thought she would be nervous, not having laid eyes on the woman since the disaster of the blue dress. But too much had happened that night, and afterwards, for any resurgence of distress.

Besides, she had power now, and it didn't come from her position of authority, not entirely. Her real power came from within.

So she smiled and held out her hand to the senator and then to his lovely daughter, watching the narrowing of green eyes, hearing a slight hiss from between a pair of brightly painted red lips.

When Veronica cast those green covetous eyes in the direction of the President, Ginny wasn't distressed or worried or jealous. She wasn't even angry. She was pissed.

"Darling," she said to Steve. He looked at her in mild surprise since she'd never called him that before. "Excuse me for a minute. I'll be right back."

Taking Veronica by the elbow, she led her to the side of the room. If anyone was watching—and she imagined everyone was watching—she didn't care. They couldn't hear.

"You are a beautiful, educated woman, Roni," Ginny said, smiling, glancing around the room as if they were discussing the beautiful evening. "Unfortunately, you have the morals of a cat in heat. Stay away from Steve. He's mine."

"You don't fool me," Veronica said. "I know things aren't all that cozy between you two."

"And how could you possibly know that?"

"I have my sources."

"A spy?" Ginny ran through the possibilities and picked the one person on the White House staff she truly didn't like. "The butler."

"Isn't it always?"

"Then he's history. He wasn't a very good butler anyway. And he couldn't have been a very good spy, not if he told you there was trouble between me and Steve." She crossed her mental fingers, smiled brilliantly, stretching the truth. "We're madly in love. If you go near my husband again, I'll give you two black eyes and a few kicks to the stomach as a reminder that he's a married man. Now go out and find someone else, dear. Stephen Marshall is taken."

She had to give Roni credit. Not once did she blink or lose her own somewhat less brilliant smile. And not once during the evening did she go near Steve again.

Flushed with victory, Ginny was ready to take on Senator Williamson, another tormentor from the disaster night. But the woman wouldn't go near her, not after the very, very, very gracious greeting Ginny had given her when she first came in.

So she talked to others and she laughed at the jokes, some of them funny, and when she thought she could get away with it, she gave them sass. Nothing crude or rude, which would not have been in the fashion of Dolley or Martha or any of her other friends, just a little more down to earth than the guests were expecting, babbling at times about baseball and single parenting and dealing with the public from the perspective of an auto repair clerk.

After the evening was done, when she and Steve were alone in the limousine, he said she'd wowed them and he planned to wow her as soon as they got back home.

She thought of two things: one, she had some wowing to do of her own, in the tell-all category; and two, no matter how she dressed and presented herself, and no matter how comfortable she got in her role, she doubted she would ever truly call the White House home.

They were getting out of the limo when one of his associates hurried out to meet them. Ginny recognized him as Steve's national security adviser.

"We've got trouble, Mr. President."

"The Middle East?" Steve said.

"Where else?"

Steve glanced at her. She squeezed his hand and brushed her lips against his cheek.

"I'll be here if you need me, darling. I want to help in any way I can."

Over the next twenty-four hours it became obvious that the best way she could help was to stay out of the way. Steve had his hands full enough, what with the Israelis threatening the Saudis and the Saudis threatening the Israelis and the Iranians and the Iraqis and everyone else from Africa to the Indian Ocean urging them on.

He talked to her some, and she listened, but mostly when he found his way upstairs it was to grab a few hours' sleep.

The worst of the crisis passed without major incident, most world leaders giving credit to the strong stance taken by the President of the United States and his diplomatic corps. But she knew he would be sequestered with his advisers for days, and she stole out to Maryland, where she worked to conquer her last major fear.

Riding Thunder.

She had been practicing ever since she embarked on her makeover. It was supposed to be her big secret surprise. Now it became her consolation. She and the horse had come to an understanding early on: She wouldn't hassle him if he wouldn't hassle her.

Besides, he liked the way she smelled, and after a while she learned to return the compliment.

She was loping across a meadow, no longer under the watch of the riding instructor she had hired, when she saw a white horse galloping toward her. The rider didn't have on armor, just a denim shirt and jeans, brown leather gloves and boots, but he was the answer to the prayers of any maiden in need.

She reined Thunder to a halt and let Steve ride up to her.

"Hi," she said, surprisingly shy.

"Hi."

"How did you know I was here?"

"I always know where you are, Ginny."

"This isn't a surprise?"

"It was when I first learned about it. Believe me, sweetheart, it was tough to stay away."

"I'm not very good."

"Don't give me that. I've been watching you awhile. When I get you back in Oklahoma, you'll probably take up barrel racing."

"People race barrels?"

"I'll explain later. Right now I have a surprise for you. Back at the stables."

"Will I like it?"

"You'd better. I've got some guys snickering back there over it. A man doesn't like to be snickered at."

"I love you."

She hadn't meant to say it like that, not from so far away, not outdoors, not without any kind of buildup, like kissing or out-and-out sex.

"I was hoping you would say that. I love you, too."

She closed her eyes for a moment, and when she opened them he was still sitting there, still watching her with his warm summer-blue eyes, looking more golden than the sun.

"You really mean it, don't you?" she said.

"Oh, yeah. I really do. Now if we can get back to the stables, I can show you exactly how much."

Ginny forgot about the no-hassle pact with Thunder. Slapping reins, she took off at a gallop toward the stables, taking Steve by surprise. Naturally he recovered right away and kept pace. They dismounted fast, and if workers or agents or anyone else watching was snickering, she didn't see or hear it.

She took off her gloves and tucked them into the back pocket of her jeans. "I'm ready."

He looked her over, said, "Nice boots," and led her to a familiar door.

"Isn't this where we—"

"I'm glad you remember. I've labeled it the Regina Baxter Marshall Memorial Stall. No horses allowed."

Inside it looked much as she remembered it, hay scattered on the hard-packed dirt floor, riding tack on the walls, two gated stalls at the back.

It looked the same, but it smelled different. There wasn't a hint of horse droppings that she could detect.

He led her back to what she considered Their Stall. A lantern hung from the nail on the wall, sending out a warm, flickering light. The hay was thick on the floor, but it wasn't the hay that got her attention. The satin sheets and the pillows with the satin covers seemed far more interesting.

"I promised the sheets to you a long time ago."

"You brought them in yourself? No wonder you got a few snickers."

"And from you?"

"No way." She turned to face him. "I don't suppose you have kickboxing in mind."

"We could probably work out some variations. But later. Right now I have something to say and you are absolutely forbidden to interrupt. You're my love and my salvation, Ginny. Black Bart gave me what he could, but he was a hard man making his way in a hard world, and that's what kept his attention. The only time I pleased him was when I ran for Congress. He thought he would have inside help in Washington. But I told him no, and we were never able to talk much after that."

"Because you're honorable."

"I thought that was enough. I was wrong."

"So does all that still bother you?" she asked.

"Not anymore. What about you? How about your past?"

"My past brought me to my present. And there's not a single thing I would change about that."

"Good," he said. "Great. Tell me again that you love me."

They stared at each other for a moment, and then they smiled. Ginny heard the swell of imaginary music, sweeter than anything she'd ever experienced, and her heart filled with happiness. Whatever happened today or any of their tomorrows, she and Steve would be together. Together was where they belonged.

For all its citizens, the United States was indeed the land of opportunity.

"I love you." She gave him her best saucy look. "Now let's get undressed, Mr. President. I want to find out if those sheets are all they're supposed to be."

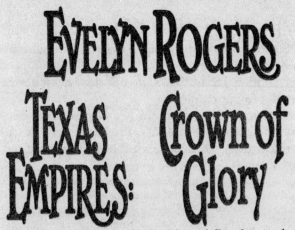

EVELYN ROGERS

TEXAS EMPIRES: Crown of Glory

It is nothing but a dog-run cabin and five thousand acres of prime grassland when Eleanor Chase first set eyes on it. But someone killed her father to get the deed to the place, and Ellie swears she will not leave Texas until she has her revenge and her ranch. There is just one man standing in her way—a blue-eyed devil named Cal Hardin. Is he the scoundrel who has stolen her birthright, or the lover whose oh-so-right touch can steal her very breath away?

___4403-X $5.99 US/$6.99 CAN

BETRAYAL Evelyn Rogers

By the Bestselling Author of
The Forever Bride

If there is anything that gets Conn O'Brien's Irish up, it is a lady in trouble–especially one he has fallen in love with at first sight. So after the Texas horseman saves Crystal Braden from an overly amorous lout, he doesn't waste a second declaring his intentions to make an honest woman of her. But they have barely been declared man and wife before Conn learns that his new bride is hiding a devastating secret that can destroy him.

The plan is simple: To ensure the safety of her mother and young brother, Crystal agrees to play the damsel in distress. The innocent beauty has no idea how dangerously charming the virile stranger can be–nor how much she longs to surrender to the tender passion in his kiss. And when Conn discovers her ruse, she vows to blaze a trail of desire that will convince him that her deception has been an error of the heart and not a ruthless betrayal.

___4262-2 $5.99 US/$6.99 CAN

"Evelyn Rogers delivers great entertainment!"
—*Romantic Times*

It is only a fairy tale, but to Megan Butler *The Forever Bride* is the most beautiful story she's ever read. That is why she insists on going to Scotland to get married in the very church where the heroine of the legend was wed to her true love. The violet-eyed advertising executive never expects the words of the story to transport her over two hundred years into the past, exchanging vows not with her fiancé, but with strapping Robert Cameron, laird of Thistledown Castle. After convincing Robert that she is not the unknown woman he's been contracted to marry, Meagan sets off with the charming brute in search of the real bride and her dowry. But the longer they pursue the elusive girl, the less Meagan wants to find her. For with the slightest touch Robert awakens her deepest desires, and she discovers the true meaning of passion. But is it all a passing fancy—or has she truly become the forever bride?

_4177-4 $5.50 US/$6.50 CAN

WICKED
Evelyn Rogers
An Angel's Touch

"Evelyn Rogers delivers great entertainment!"
—Romantic Times

Gunned down after a bank robbery, Cad Rankin meets a heavenly being who makes him an offer he can't refuse. To save his soul, he has to bring peace to the most lawless town in the West. With a mission like that, the outlaw almost resigns himself to spending eternity in a place much hotter than Texas—until he comes across Amy Lattimer, a feisty beauty who rouses his goodness and a whole lot more.

Although she's been educated in a convent school, Amy Lattimer is determined to do anything to locate her missing father, including posing as a fancy lady. Then she finds an ally in virile Cad Rankin, who isn't about to let her become a fallen angel. But even as Amy longs to surrender to paradise in Cad's arms, she begins to suspect that he has a secret that stands between them and unending bliss....

_52082-6 $5.99 US/$7.99 CAN

DELANEY'S CROSSING

JEAN BARRETT

Virile, womanizing Cooper J. Delaney is Agatha Pennington's only hope to help lead a group of destitute women to Oregon, where the promise of a new life awaits them. He is a man as harsh and hostile as the vast wilderness—but Agatha senses a gentleness behind his hard-muscled exterior, a tenderness lurking beneath his gruff facade. Though the group battles rainstorms, renegade Indians, and raging rivers, the tall beauty's tenacity never wavers. And with each passing mile, Cooper realizes he is struggling against a maddening attraction for her and that he would journey to the ends of the earth if only to claim her untouched heart.

_4200-2 $5.50 US/$6.50 CAN